BLEAK TIMES AT ORCHARD COTTAGE HOSPITAL

LIZZIE LANE

B

Boldwood

First published in Great Britain in 2025 by Boldwood Books Ltd.

Copyright © Lizzie Lane, 2025

Cover Design by Colin Thomas

Cover Images: Colin Thomas and Alamy

The moral right of Lizzie Lane to be identified as the author of this work has been asserted in accordance with the Copyright, Designs and Patents Act 1988.

All rights reserved. No part of this book may be reproduced in any form or by any electronic or mechanical means, including information storage and retrieval systems, without written permission from the author, except for the use of brief quotations in a book review. This book is a work of fiction and, except in the case of historical fact, any resemblance to actual persons, living or dead, is purely coincidental.

Every effort has been made to obtain the necessary permissions with reference to copyright material, both illustrative and quoted. We apologise for any omissions in this respect and will be pleased to make the appropriate acknowledgements in any future edition.

A CIP catalogue record for this book is available from the British Library.

Paperback ISBN 978-1-83656-406-5

Large Print ISBN 978-1-83656-407-2

Hardback ISBN 978-1-83656-405-8

Ebook ISBN 978-1-83656-408-9

Kindle ISBN 978-1-83656-409-6

Audio CD ISBN 978-1-83656-400-3

MP3 CD ISBN 978-1-83656-401-0

Digital audio download ISBN 978-1-83656-403-4

This book is printed on certified sustainable paper. Boldwood Books is dedicated to putting sustainability at the heart of our business. For more information please visit https://www.boldwoodbooks.com/about-us/sustainability/

Boldwood Books Ltd, 23 Bowerdean Street, London, SW6 3TN

www.boldwoodbooks.com

1

8 DECEMBER 1932

Ice that had lasted all day had refrozen to gossamer slickness beneath a sky full of stars. Icicles hanging from the bare branches of deciduous trees and caped around tiers of conifers tinkled like Christmas bells in the bitter cold easterly wind.

Inside terraced cottages, frost etched patterns on the inside of windowpanes and snow lay frozen along ledges and nooks, added to by further flurries.

The few gas street lights not blown out by the icy wind sent a series of golden pools dancing over the sheets of silver ice frozen to the ground.

The streets and alleys of Norton Dene, a market town set in the mining and quarrying areas of Somerset, ran off the main square like spokes in a wheel. At its heart was the triangular-shaped green and in its heart was the war memorial.

It was midnight and the world was empty, except for two figures, a man and a woman, bent into the wind, slipping and sliding along the frozen ground on the road that led to the hospital. On closer inspection, it could be interpreted that one was carrying the other, or at least partly. The bigger figure was a man. The slighter one a woman.

Their clothes sparkled with snow that was slowly covering the ground. Their breath steamed white on the chill air. Even the man's beard, his eyebrows and the ends of his hair were tinged with crystals. His hair might have been dark so that his age could be put at thirty. The addition of frost and ice made him look older.

Clamped together, their form was hardly human, but a black mass, shoes skimming along the thick carpet of ice, his occasionally sliding, hers dragging, knees bent and arms flopping in front of her.

The thicker arms of the man were wound beneath her arms and around her back in a bid to hold her upright.

If it had been daylight and there had been someone to see, they might have noticed the pink trail left by the woman staining the ice. The trail had begun red as blood, the ice diffusing it from a strong colour to pale and, because of the cold, it too turned to ice before being covered by a layer of newly fallen snow.

The man stopped suddenly, his breathing loud as his strength ebbed with the effort of holding up the woman. He'd carried her for some way, but his strength was draining fast. He fought for more air. Lungs inflated, he blinked the crystals from his narrowed eyes and peered into the darkness. Weary now, he desperately sought some kind of light so he could better see where they were going.

'Nearly there,' he said, bending his head to the woman so that his chapped lips were a fraction from her ear.

She muttered something. Perhaps it was a prayer. He couldn't tell.

Away from the town, there were few lights from friendly windows, most respectable people having taken to their beds.

The gas mantles on the street lights danced uncertainly, flickering with each gasp of wind.

The light he was looking for had to be some way ahead, though not far. They'd struggled here, her more than him and he could tell she was getting weaker.

'Hold on,' he breathed, his breath steamy white as it hit the cold air. 'We'll be there soon.'

He hoped he was speaking the truth.

A light. A light to guide their way. His narrowed eyes searched the night for something large and bright enough to pierce the unrelenting darkness and confirm that he was going in the right direction.

The woman's body grew heavier as the toes of her shoes dragged beneath her, over the frost-coated flags, cobblestones and the scummy black puddles that hadn't yet turned to ice.

He paused for another breath and spit a mouthful of phlegm onto a patch of unblemished snow gathering on the fringe of the uneven road and shook his head. 'Why did you do it? Why?'

If it hadn't been for what she'd done, he would be snoring the night away by now with a good few pints of beer inside him.

Bloody women. Why couldn't they accept the cards they'd been dealt with? They'd have managed – somehow. He would have helped her all he could. But no. She'd paid good money – half a crown, in fact – to some backstreet pedlar, who he didn't know, for a concoction to alleviate her of the baby she'd been carrying. That was what she'd told him. Enough to pay for a night's beer. And what good had it done?

The bile rose from his stomach and his right hand itched to fetch her a good clout. If it was anyone else but her, he would have done. But here, Ellen, caused a tickle under his heart that he just could not scratch.

And now she was bleeding. He presumed this was due to the

pills she'd taken, but now he wasn't so sure. His grim thoughts and clenched jaw slackened when he finally espied a light ahead. It seemed as though they'd been struggling to get here for hours. It was cold and he was tired.

Spurred on that he might at last have found the only place that he could leave her, a new strength came to his aching legs.

Darkness and light alternated some way ahead of him as the creaking branches and dark boughs of fir trees danced in the wind. It had to be the hospital.

His spirits rose when he saw twin orbs of amber-coloured light flickering through the gathering frost and the bare branches of trees shivering in the strong wind.

Sensing his task was coming to an end, his steps quickened when he finally saw what he was seeking. Up ahead of him, two glass-encased lanterns pierced the gloom. He likened them to small lighthouses, two of them fixed on the top of stone pillars. Lighthouses at sea kept sailors from going onto the rocks, their steady beam guiding them to safety. That's what these two were doing, though he had to get closer to confirm.

To the side of the right-hand light, he read a sign saying, 'Orchard Cottage Hospital'. His relief caused him to pause.

The twin lights had a welcoming beam and picked out the fact that the icy ground had been cleared. Somebody had been out with a shovel. Not that it would do much good. By the morning, the cleared ground would once again be covered in a layer of ice.

The woman he was hanging onto groaned and sank against him, her head dropping forward, her height diminishing as her knees gave way.

'Keep going. For your sake. For my sake too. Please, or I'll 'ave to drop you 'ere.'

Whether she heard the exasperation in his pleading, he could not tell. The truth was that he was desperate to get help, to leave her in safe hands. Their journey was coming to an end. His ordeal was finally over, though he hated having to do this.

The solid shape of the Orchard Cottage Hospital loomed ahead of them in the darkness. A porch light hung at the entrance. Few other lights showed, but that was hardly surprising. It was late. He assumed the patients were asleep and there would only be a night nurse on duty, two at the most.

Determinedly and as gentle as he could be under the circumstances, he dragged his charge towards the three marble steps leading up to the porch. Once standing on the clay red tiles of the covered portico which had been cleared of ice, he let her sink to the ground. She did so almost gratefully, her head falling sidelong so that she was laid out full stretch, her cheek resting on the cool tiles, small chunks of ice clinging to her hair.

Rubbing the wetness of his hands onto his trousers, he looked nervously around. The last thing he wanted was to be recognised, but at this time of night and in this appalling weather, anyone with any sense was staying inside. He didn't want to have to explain who she was and what she had done. Let them sort it out.

Leaving her lying there at the top of the steps, he retraced his route then stopped. What next? There was nobody around, but to his credit he did consider how best to get her presence noticed. He didn't want her to die.

He bit the skin around his fingernails, a bad habit for a grown man, but he wasn't a cruel man. At least he didn't think he was. He liked being thought well of. *I have a bit of a conscience*, he thought to himself and reconsidered what he should do. What if they didn't see her until daylight? Her clothes, her face and her hands were cold to the touch, and she was bleeding from her private parts. His mother had told him the pills were responsible for that. She was a woman. She knew all about that kind of thing.

Despite his fear of being seen, he made the decision to summon help.

As he stepped over her, he tried not to look at the pinkish puddle seeping out from her clothes, though the colour wasn't so obvious against the black and red of the terrazzo tiles.

The door knocker was big, black and made of iron. He reached out for it, but at the last moment his cowardice returned and his big, blunt, bitten fingers curled into his palm. He wanted help for her. Any good Christian man would, but staying would mean having to explain, being implicated and that would mean the police – and possibly prison.

He spotted a light some way to his right, shining through a small square window. No doubt that was where a night nurse or caretaker would be holed up – waiting on the patients' nocturnal needs – waiting also for new arrivals – emergencies that hadn't been able to make it that day.

Drawing his gaze back from the window and onto the locked double doors of the hospital building, he spotted a printed black and white notice secreted like a bashful bride behind a bell pull.

PULL FOR ATTENTION.

The bell pull seemed a better option than the knocker.

He hesitated, both sides of his nature fighting for supremacy. At last, his better side won the battle. His blunt fingers curled around the bell pull and its notes clanged out – loud enough to wake the bloody dead, he thought.

Job done, he ran, slipping and sliding over the thick ice. He was halfway towards the broad open gateway when he heard one half of the door behind him open and was vaguely aware of light falling out into the arctic night, golden and warm. He thought that if he turned round and saw that amber glow he'd be tempted to run towards it just so he could feel its warm embrace.

A voice almost as raucous as the bell he'd pulled rang out into the night. 'Who's there?'

Then a pause before she shouted again.

'You can't leave this woman here like this.'

Oh yes, he could. He had to. It was a hospital, wasn't it?

The raucous voice shouted out for assistance, the light from a lantern flitting into the night.

He didn't stop. He'd done his bit. Told himself that it wasn't his problem. Her predicament had been of her own doing, her and her lover, a man of wealth who believed that everything had a price – including women. Anyway, he had other things to deal with. London beckoned and the sooner he was there, the better.

* * *

Back at the hospital, Sister Edith Harrison engaged the help of the caretaker to bring the woman inside. When asked whether she would get Doctor Brakespeare in, she shook her head sadly.

'No. This poor woman's beyond anyone's help.'

2

The following morning, a milky sun had the nerve to send its feeble rays over the frozen land. Bereft of leaves, the spidery twigs on the bare upper branches of trees scratched the sombre sky.

Doctor Frances Brakespeare wasn't paying attention to the weather but was wrapped in a blanket by the fireside, head bent, eyes scanning the letter she'd received the day before.

The words had not changed since yesterday, yet she still found it hard to believe and thus felt a need to read it for the fourth – or was it the fifth time?

A prestigious London hospital of modern thinking had opened its own family planning facility and wanted an experienced and forward-thinking person to lead it. She was being offered the job at an eye-watering salary.

Seeing as Christmas intervened, the offer had given her until the new year to meet up and take a tour around facilities they assured her were the last word in modern medical practices.

> We are able to give you a month after that to accept, plus two more months to facilitate notice in your present position.

Biting her lower lip, she stared into the fire's rosy glow as she considered the implications.

London was the place of prestige and who knew how high she might climb, what prominence she might gain? And surely, she would be going home. London was where she had come from. She'd grown up there.

Fleeing London had been her only choice when Izzy, her guardian, had died. The house they had shared had been snatched by Izzy's sister, who had no time for an orphan taken from the workhouse and raised by the unmarried Izzy as a daughter.

Not only that but she had been fired from her job in London when she'd challenged the arrogance of a male, senior doctor.

At first, she'd had no idea what to do next, until a fairy godmother, in the guise of Lady Araminta Compton-Dixon, had worked her magic behind the scenes.

The position had called for a general-purpose doctor to take charge of the Orchard Cottage Hospital. The hospital committee had jumped at the chance of employing a doctor from London. Assuming she was male and called Francis, they didn't hesitate to offer her the position but were a bit put off on finding out that she was female and Frances. The vote to take her on was directed by the chair of the committee, Lady Araminta Compton-Dixon – Minty to her friends. Friends were what they became.

The hospital, which had been a bit run-down, was now thriving thanks to Doctor Brakespeare's innovations, the most modern of which was her setting up a family planning clinic.

As with all new ideas, there were detractors, but things had settled down.

So, could she really abandon all she'd achieved here in exchange for moving higher up the medical innovation ladder?

Deciding to think on it, she folded the letter back into its envelope.

Despite the cold weather, she was headed for the hospital. Thick coat, hat and sturdy boots were the order of the day. She looked out of the window, where dawn was attempting to throw some light. The path outside was glassy and crisp ribbons of snow clung to bare branches.

Her musings were interrupted by Ma Skittings, her bulky frame filling the doorway, icy specks flying from her coat as she shook herself.

'If the devil cared to make hell cold instead of 'ot, that's it out there,' she proclaimed as she took off her coat and hat, stamped the snow from her boots and rubbed her hands together. 'Is yer mother awake yet?'

'Not when I looked in on her.'

Ma Skittings nodded as though she'd expected nothing else.

Her mother's health was swiftly deteriorating. Ma Skittings came in every day to see to her and take charge of the housework, which Mary was no longer capable of.

Frances was grateful. Her natural mother had appeared only a short time ago and her health had been suspect right from the start. Now it seemed her mother's health was swiftly deteriorating.

'I'll give her a bowl of porridge with a good dollop of my honey on it. That'll get her going.'

'I'm sure it will.'

Comfort, thought Frances. That's all the honey would be.

'Let me know if you need me. You know... if anything...'

'Nothing's going to happen today. I'm 'ere to take care of 'er. You get on, Doctor. There're people waiting for you.'

As satisfied as she could be that her mother was being well looked after, Frances closed the coach house door behind her and tramped off down the path.

Mrs Cross, the vicar's housekeeper, gave her a cursory wave as she climbed the steps to the vicarage where she cleaned and cooked for the vicar.

The Reverend Gregory Sampson was standing in the bay window at the front of the vicarage, cup and saucer in hand. He raised the cup in salute as she marched past. She waved in return and wondered what his response would be when she told him she was considering heading back to London.

'A bridge to be crossed,' she muttered.

* * *

At Waterloo Terrace, Nurse Lucy Daniels was up and dressed. *Have I put on enough layers?* she asked herself as she peered out of the landing window of the cottage she shared with her Aunt Rose. Frost crisped the winter grass and snow stacked branches of trees and shrubs. The path to the front gate looked unblemished by human footsteps. The light falling from the cottage windows picked out small paw marks and the trident tread of birds.

Before she left the landing and headed downstairs, the smell of overheated fat wafted up to meet her. On gaining the kitchen where the hot coals of the range heated the frying pan, there was Aunt Rose, enveloped in a fog of bluish smoke. Bacon rashers sizzled angrily in the frying pan, sounding for all the world as though they would dearly love to escape.

Lucy sighed. 'Aunt Rose, you don't need to do that. I can do it.'

As was usual, the bacon would be overdone if she didn't step in.

'I want to give my girl a good breakfast inside 'er on a morning like this,' said her aunt. 'It's perishing out there! Even the cat wouldn't go out last night, though can't say I blame 'er.'

'Neither do I, but unlike her I've no choice. Now leave it to me,' she said as she gently nudged her aunt aside. 'Let me do that whilst you drink your tea and rest your legs.'

Her aunt readily accepted, her plump fingers enfolding a delicate china teacup and matching saucer. Not that she sipped tea in a ladylike manner but poured the contents of the cup into the saucer and slurped it back from that.

On coming up for air, she said, 'I could do with a sit-down. Me old legs ain't what they used to be.'

Lucy grimaced at the bacon before parting it from the pan base with the aid of a metal spatula. She disliked crisply fried bacon, especially when it was beginning to blacken around the edges. The fat needed to be changed before she added eggs, or they'd be much the same. However, she didn't have time. Instead, she forked the bacon from the pan and pressed it between two slices of bread – fortunately not quite the doorstep sizes her aunt usually favoured, but thick all the same.

One bite was all she took. Too much fat and that smell... No wonder she couldn't manage any more.

The scene beyond the window had not changed by the time she'd eaten breakfast and drowned the slightly burnt taste with two cups of tea. Roll on warmer weather, she thought to herself as she wrapped her cloak tightly around her.

'I'm off,' she called out.

Aunt Rose grumbled a response, busy as she was scrubbing at the burnt frying pan. A blast of cold air came in and helped clear the smoke that pervaded the entire room.

Closing the door on overcooked food, Lucy picked her way down the narrow flagstone path and out onto the lane. From there, she headed through the heart of town and out onto the road leading to the Orchard Cottage Hospital. The cold air pinched her cheeks, but she was cheered by the sight of shop windows, their light easing the gloom, shopkeepers scraping the ice and snow from pavements, carrying on regardless even though it was not yet light.

By the time she got to the hospital, the first hint of daylight appeared. Wally the caretaker was raking leaves and twigs brought down by the wind into manageable piles ready to be added to the bonfire, where a thin wisp of white smoke rose disconsolately from the damp mound. She was no expert but suspected the fire wouldn't amount to much. Nevertheless, the smell of wood smoke was welcome on the frozen air. Such a contrast after that of burning bacon, thought Lucy and briefly wondered why Wally was there so early.

On seeing her, the gardener/odd job man, his bushy eyebrows white with frost, doffed his cap. 'Morning, Nurse Daniels.'

'You look frozen. Time for a cup of tea, do you think,' she said with a smile.

'I could do with one and that's a fact. I didn't get a wink of sleep last night. Or not much anyway.'

'That's a shame. A man like you working outside needs a good sleep.'

'Couldn't be 'elped,' he said, shaking his head in a forlorn manner that was unusual for him.

Presuming he was referring to the weather, she slowed her steps to accommodate the slower pace of his bowed legs as he fell into step beside her. Wally seemed to have a natural yardstick for the weather; when it would rain, when it would be fine and all seemingly done by studying the birds and bees. He had often informed her that the arrival of spring could be ascertained by how early – or late – the birds would build their nest.

Pale eyes regarded her from beneath shaggy grey brows and bags beneath his eyes that were almost pouches. 'What a night, eh?'

'Very cold,' she said. 'There was ice on the inside of my bedroom window this morning and the water in the washbasin was frozen. I shouldn't have poured it last night but didn't expect it would be so cold.'

'I ain't talking about the weather,' he exclaimed.

His face was alive with the excitement experienced by those who suddenly realise they are party to a piece of news not known by everyone. Lucy had hoped that he was going to declare an imminent thaw. It turned out to be something entirely different.

'The woman that got dumped out front last night. Blood everywhere. Dead of course.' He went on to tell her how he and Sister Harrison had lifted the body onto a trolley and taken it to the room at the back of the hospital. The room faced north so was always icy cold, which had led to rumours that it was haunted.

'Last night? Goodness. Who was she?'

He shook his head. 'Don't know.'

'Poor woman.' Lucy placed one foot on the first step up to the hospital entrance.

'Now you be careful,' he added. 'After I've had a cup of strong, sweet tea indoors, I'm going to clear this ice away before anybody slips and breaks something.'

'I'll leave you to it.'

She left him to his mug of tea. Her cheeks made pink by the nip in the air, she went bowling along to the cloakroom, blaming the cold weather for needing to pee again – the third time that morning.

Once acclimatised, she took off her cloak, hung it up and headed to where Sister Harrison would be waiting to brief her.

Hopefully none of their patients – eight only at present – had deteriorated overnight. No doubt she would hear more about the woman Wally had referred to.

She knocked on the door of the small room that served as office and staffroom. Sister Harrison looked up from the pile of medical records she was shuffling from side to side, seemingly without any definite purpose. She looked tired, eyes red rimmed and an uncharacteristic sag to her middle-aged features.

'Ah. Good morning, Nurse Daniels,' she said in her usual formal manner. Even though they had worked together for some time now, it was not Sister Harrison's habit to be overfamiliar.

'Good morning, Sister Harrison. How are you this morning?'

'Tired. Very tired,' she replied somewhat dolefully.

'Wally was telling me it was quite an eventful night.'

'Oh, did he now! And what did he tell you?' There was a hard look in her eyes, as though Wally had no business mentioning it.

Lucy carried on regardless. 'He meant no harm. He looked tired and I asked him why.' It wasn't true but she thought it as good an opening gambit as any to find out what had gone on. 'He told me about the dead woman that arrived last night.'

Sister Harrison snorted derisively. 'He didn't tell you how she died, I hope. He's an odd job man, not a doctor!' Her manner was sniffy.

Lucy controlled the surprise she felt at Sister Harrison's surliness. The woman had an abrupt manner at times, but this was the first time Lucy had seen her face flushed with anger and spitting words like bullets.

In for a penny, in for a pound, she said to herself and dared ask what had caused the woman's death.

Sister Harrison eyed her for a minute, as though she was taking her time to moderate her response. At long last, a stiff nod told Lucy she had come to a decision.

'Close the door,' she ordered, jerking her chin at the door Lucy was holding open. Her tone was still brusque, but Lucy did as requested.

Once it was closed, she leaned against it, using it to support herself as Sister Harrison related the horrific details of the woman's death, the fact that she had undergone a physical intervention to end a pregnancy. She'd come across suspected abortions before, mostly of those who had been lucky enough to seek medical advice before such action killed them.

'She also had a bottle of pink pills.' She gave Lucy a knowing look from beneath a creased forehead. 'I can guess what they are, but seemingly they weren't enough to do the trick. Something sharp was used by someone with only the most basic knowledge.'

Lucy thought of how it would have been. It made her feel sick, but perhaps her greasy breakfast might also have had something to do with it. The smell of grease lingered in her nostrils.

Sister Harrison interrupted her thoughts. 'I've made out a report for Doctor Brakespeare, but of course, as she is the doctor, it's for her to examine the woman and concur.'

'Of course, Sister.'

A cup of tea was poured and a biscuit offered.

Lucy accepted the cup of tea but declined the biscuit.

'The poor woman,' she said weakly as she imagined the scene from the night before, more so the events that might have led up to it. 'Do we know who she is?'

Sister Harrison shook her head. 'It's nobody that I know. Look,' she said, raising her pen, 'I want to finish this report before I go home. You're a local. You know everybody in this town. Go along and see if you recognise her.' She held up a warning finger. 'But refrain from discussing the case until Doctor Brakespeare has examined the body. Is that clear?'

Lucy eased herself away from the door and said, 'Yes, of course.'

In fact, she was already having reservations about the task handed to her. What if she recognised this woman? Sister Harrison was right; she knew many of the townsfolk. Some of them she'd known all her life. In a strange way, she felt almost guilty that the woman had not come to her to share their troubles – as if that was likely. Of course it wasn't. Both she and Sister Harrison knew from experience that women who sought to rid themselves of an unwanted pregnancy kept the secret to themselves.

After taking her leave of Sister Harrison, Lucy retrieved her cloak from the clothes peg where she'd left it, wrapping it closely around herself.

The task itself was enough to make anyone, even an experienced nurse shiver, but entering the rear of the hospital in such cold weather was like entering a tomb. The cold would be intensified by what awaited her there.

3

On her way past the main ward, Lucy came across Iris Manning taking breakfast around to those patients who were hungry. Iris was a general dogsbody who did the more menial tasks, including the cleaning of the wards and other more lowly duties, sometimes with one of the nurses, sometimes, such as now, when the hospital was not busy, by herself.

Catching sight of her, Iris came bowling out of the ward, smiled a toothy smile and asked how she was.

'I'm fine but could be better if it was a bit warmer,' said Lucy, adopting a breezy manner.

'We all would,' said Iris, eyeing the warm cloak Lucy was wearing. 'Going back out into the cold, are you?'

'On my way to the sluice room.'

'The morgue?'

Lucy blanched. The room she was headed for was dual purpose: sluice in one half, morgue the other. In her opinion, cleaning bedpans and suchlike was preferable to examining a dead body.

'Yes.'

Iris followed her for a few steps, arms folded in a matter-of-fact manner as though she knew something that Lucy did not know.

'Mind you, it's always cold back where you're going. And not just because of what it is,' she whispered, a secretive, furtive look on her bony face, an elbow digging into Lucy's ribs. The rumour of haunting again. That was one thing Lucy did not believe.

'I just wanted to take a look at the woman left on the doorstep last night, just in case I can identify her. Now, if you'll excuse me...'

Lucy was about to walk off until it came to her that Iris was a local of long standing. She was bound to know if the woman was from Norton Dene.

'Have you seen her?'

'Sister Harrison asked me to.' Iris shrugged. 'I obliged, but it wasn't anyone that I know.'

It was a small town and she knew the same people that Lucy knew. If she didn't recognise the woman, then it was likely Lucy wouldn't either. She was somewhat relieved. To gaze on a stranger wouldn't be quite so heart-wrenching as someone she knew.

The room at the back of the hospital was served by a narrow corridor that dipped down into what had been cellars in times gone by. Stone slabs ran in a straight line between white unplastered walls. Because it dated from an earlier building before the modern frontage had come to be, the ceiling was markedly lower than in the rest of the hospital.

The sinks and shelves where bedpans and other metal receptacles were washed and stored occupied the area to either side of the door. There were no coals burning in the empty grate, no fat radiator sitting on staunch legs, no form of heating at all, except for a grey geyser next to a cold-water tap above a deep sink, its pilot light glowing blue but giving no heat whatsoever.

The gurneys where bodies were laid out were set in a row at the far end of the room. There were only three. Two were bare. A hump of white sheet occupied the third one, the body covered in a more casual manner than the neat trickery used on the live patients lying in their beds.

Lucy's breath misted the air, great clouds of white dissipating into the cold, bare room. The silence was palpable, as though it were a living thing just waiting to be heard but biding its time. She stood like a statue, hearing only her own breathing, which seemed to reverberate upwards into her skull. In a bid to halt the sensation, she held her breath. To her great surprise, she could still hear it and found herself searching the far corners for some other entity that was in here with her.

'Blimey, it's as cold as the devil's ass in here...'

The voice made her jump.

'Just me,' said Iris. 'I thought I might take a second look. Just in case.' She gave a thin little smile. 'And thought you might want a bit of company.'

Lucy patted her chest, the spot where her heart was galloping like a steeplechaser determined to win the race. She gathered her senses and said, 'In case you were mistaken?'

'In case you might be frightened by a ghost.'

Lucy laughed without a trace of nervousness. 'I might do if I believed in ghosts. But I don't.'

Iris's small, sharp eyes swept the room. If they'd been fingers, they would have been poking into corners. Her voice dropped to a whisper. 'They come out when you least expect it,' she said, her eyes flickering from one corner, one wall to another. 'First one, then the other.'

Lucy had always considered Iris an ordinary person who

carried out the tasks set her with due diligence. She'd never met someone who believed in anything except the here and now.

'You mean there's more than one?'

'Could be.' Iris let the words out one at a time – and low – very low. 'I've heard stories of a woman in white who only puts in an appearance when there's snow on the ground. And there's monks. This part of the building is very old. An abbey or monastery or suchlike. Some people have heard the monks singing.'

'But only in winter?' Lucy tried to keep her amusement from her voice.

'Oh no. Any time.'

Lucy shook herself. This was all nonsense, and she'd come here for a purpose. 'Never mind all that nonsense. Let's see what we've come here to see, then go and get ourselves cups of tea.'

Taking on a more businesslike manner, she marched to the mound of white sheet and peeled it back from the lifeless woman, exposing her face. The woman, who she judged to be around thirty years of age, had a peaceful expression and for that Lucy was grateful. Finding tortured features would have upset her and probably lingered in her mind far into the night.

Her face was round, not a classic beauty, but she was handsome. In life she might have had a more tired countenance – so many women did, but this woman didn't look like one worn out with poverty and exhausted by pregnancy. There was a serenity in the woman's features, so much so that Lucy found herself smoothing the pale hair back from her brow. The eyebrows were arched and dark, the brow not overly furrowed, except, as she smoothed back the hair, she noticed an angry purple bruise on the left temple.

Iris had noticed it too, peered over Lucy's shoulder. 'Oow. That's a bit of a whack.'

Before Iris offered conjecture that Lucy did not wish to hear, she said, 'Perhaps she hit her head when she fell to the ground.'

Or was flung to the ground. The alternative possibility came and stayed in her mind. She couldn't tell for sure, but a third possibility was that it was the result of a blow from a fist or hard object. That too she kept to herself, although guessed Iris might be thinking the same. Best, she decided, not to encourage her.

'I believe it happened when she fell.'

That should put any gossip on Iris's part to rest.

After smoothing the hair back down onto the forehead so the bruise was hidden, Lucy pulled the sheet down a little further. The woman had quite a plump, strong neck that included a fold about half the way down, enough of a fold to hide what at first looked like a lump. Lucy prodded it with her finger.

'What's that then?' queried Iris whose sharp little eyes closed in lower on the dead woman.

Lucy's long white fingers probed the object and gently pulled. 'Looks like a shell.'

At first, it seemed the shell had merely been placed there. On closer scrutiny, she could see that it hung from what looked like a leather frond. She discovered decorative gold bands at regular intervals.

'Pretty little thing. On a string, is it?'

'Something like that.'

'A keepsake? A gift from her husband, sweetheart or whatever?'

'It's a possibility,' said Lucy, holding the shell between finger and thumb. 'If we could find out who gave it to her, then we would find out who she is.'

Her curiosity aroused; Lucy brought the sheet up over the woman's face, but before inspecting the woman's lower body suggested that Iris must have other things to do.

'I don't mind assisting. Honest I don't. And I'd be company. Just in case...' There was pleading in the small, sharp eyes, a slackening of the mouth as though Iris was getting herself ready to taste an ambrosia long denied. 'If I may,' she entreated. 'I want to be a nurse. I could be if I applied meself. Trouble is my reading and writing aren't so good. Only wish they were. But it isn't all about reading and writing, is it? Taking care of people, making them comfortable and all that matters just as much – doesn't it?'

Iris's plump little hands, almost childlike in their shape and size, were clasped tightly in front of her bosom.

Lucy didn't want to admit it, but she preferred her to stay. The feeble northern light coming into the room was at the very least disconcerting, at the most threatening. She had no wish to be alone in this cold-stone room that smelled of dead flesh and damp mould.

She nodded. 'You can stay. But don't touch – not unless I say so.'

'Anything you say.'

It was settled.

Lucy took her prying fingers to the hem of the woman's skirt. The fabric was of good quality, a mix of English wool and soft, silky cashmere from India.

A woman of some worth, she thought to herself. The clothes examined and evaluated; she prepared herself for the next task. To some extent, she knew what she would find.

Dried blood caked the hem of her skirt and felt brittle beneath her touch. There were clots in places, blood that had not dried but stuck there in iron red globules. The woman's underwear was rank with blood. As a mere nurse, it wasn't really for her to examine the woman further, but she felt a kind of duty. Whoever had done this had not been qualified. Not all backstreet abortionists were unqualified but carried out by those trained –

or partially trained – in medicine. There were various reasons they'd taken on the profession, but ultimately it was about money.

She sucked in her breath, horrified at the bloodstained inner thighs and abdomen. A lump came to her throat on realising that Sister Harrison had already removed the partially formed foetus and afterbirth. She averted her eyes from the rack of bedpans, already washed and cleaned – except for one. The coroner would want to see everything.

'I don't suppose Doctor has had a look at her yet?' It was a question she could easily answer herself. Doctor Brakespeare wouldn't be here until around eight o'clock, perhaps a little later thanks to the inclement weather.

Iris shook her head.

Lucy took extra care replacing the woman's clothes before covering her with the heavy cotton sheet. It was from compassion that she tucked it in all around the body until it resembled a cocoon enclosing a chrysalis waiting to be reborn as a butterfly. Only nothing would be born. There was only death and the smell of it blended with the ice-cold air.

'I hope we can track down whoever did this.'

'An abortionist,' suggested Iris.

'A murderer,' muttered Lucy, hardly able to control her anger.

4

The door to Doctor Brakespeare's office was open. She had made a house call on the way in so had not as yet removed her coat and was standing at the side of her desk, hands tensed over her medical bag as she listened to what Sister Harrison was telling her.

'I'm sure I saw someone run away.'

'A man?'

'Very likely.'

'But you didn't recognise him.'

Sister Harrison shivered and shook her head, brown eyes like pools of river mud in what was usually a ruddy face but was now quite pale. 'No. It was too dark, and he ran quickly.' The corners of her pink lips turned downwards as though once again running the scene through her mind. 'I did what I could for her.'

Doctor Frances Brakespeare clenched her jaw. At the same time, her hands tightened over the handle of her medicine bag. Facing the weather had been bad enough, but she would have preferred to have Mabel, her trusty little car, swerve all over the place and end up in a ditch rather than come in to this. All the same, she nodded in understanding and said, 'I'm sure you did. You now deserve to get home. You must be tired out.'

'I thought I should stay on until you got here. Perhaps you'd like me to accompany you when you examine the corpse. She'd lost a lot of blood even before she'd got here, walked all the way I shouldn't wonder, and then the baby and afterbirth...' Whereas others would have shuddered or sighed in exasperation, the shoulders of the senior nurse stiffened like someone steeling themselves prior to a confrontation – or riding into battle.

'Has Nurse Daniels arrived?'

'Yes. She went to look at the woman just in case she was local, and she knew her.'

'And did she?'

'No. She did not.'

Frances nodded. 'You get on home. Your bed awaits you.'

Sister Harrison got as far as the door but stopped suddenly as a thought seemed to grab her. It turned out to be an expression of her feelings, a rare occurrence for the most experienced nurse in the hospital. Sister Harrison had initially been sceptical about Doctor Brakespeare's ability. Since then, Frances had earned her spurs and there was mutual respect between them. 'I feel so angry about this. I know there are several who would carry out something like this.'

'But we need evidence before we can accuse anyone out of hand. Anyway, you did everything that was required of you. It's down to the authorities to track down the guilty. Speaking of which, what did the police say?'

Sister Harrison puffed up with exasperation. 'They said they'd be out as soon as they could, couldn't give a time but just gave the excuse that because of the weather they were extremely busy. Such rubbish! A woman has died. Someone is responsible and should be tracked down before the trail goes cold.'

Frances admired her forthright indignation and sense of purpose. When Sister Edith Harrison wanted something done, she liked it done there and then. Her attitude was brusque and impatient. Frances understood her consternation.

Iris Manning came breezing through the open door with a cup of tea.

'Thought you might be needing this, Doctor.'

Sister Harrison threw her a disapproving look – not because she had brought in tea without knocking but because she had interrupted a serious dialogue between two medical professionals.

For her part, Frances was more than ready to drink the cup of tea Sister Harrison had placed on the pink blotting pad.

'Thank you, Iris.'

'Not a problem, Doctor.'

Iris backed out of the office, then paused.

'Do you want the door closed?' she humbly asked. Although she was only in her late twenties, her manner resembled that of an aged servant willing to do all she could to ingratiate herself for years to come.

Frances responded, forestalling the likelihood of Sister Harrison biting her head off. 'Thank you, Mrs Manning.' Another thought occurring to her, she turned back to Sister Harrison. 'Did she speak at all?'

'No. I think she died within minutes of being dumped on the doorstep.'

Frances rubbed her knitted brow.

'No identification on her?'

'No. Nothing.'

'And we don't know the identity of the man who brought her to our door?'

'We do not. The moment I came out, he was off like a rat up a drainpipe – and that is indeed what he is. A rat. No human being would act so irresponsibly, leaving the poor woman in such circumstances.'

Thanks to her dealings with humanity both on the Great War battlefield and since, Frances thought otherwise.

'Are you sure it was a man?'

'It was dark, but it had to be a man. Only a man would have been strong enough to bring her here. They had to have walked. I didn't hear horses' hooves, cartwheels or a motor car. The state of her!'

Frances noted Sister Harrison's bottom lip curling with deep-seated contempt.

She knew very well that Edith Harrison had a low regard for men who had not treated her well in the past. No wonder she preferred the fictionalised men in the romantic novels she read, heroes who fell at the heroine's feet, pledging their undying love.

Unfortunately for Sister Harrison, life isn't like that, thought Frances.

'No belongings at all?'

'Only these.'

Nurse Harrison passed her a phial of small, pinkish tablets.

Frances frowned as she held them up to the light. 'Where did you find these?'

'In the inside pocket of her coat.'

'No handbag?'

'No.'

'No jewellery?'

'Only a necklace. Nurse Daniels found it around her neck.'

The pills rattled in the bottle as Frances examined it. The tablets were both familiar and alien. Familiar because she could guess what they had been used for, alien because she knew they were beyond the law, bought only from sources whose aim was purely to make money, not to help women in dire need.

It was easy to feel rage, also to feel pity. The rage was directed at whoever it was who'd supplied the pills. The pity was for the circumstances relating to the poor woman who had been so desperate she'd sought and bought the pills, possibly at an extortionate price. On finding they didn't work, she'd taken a more desperate measure. Whoever it was that had carried out the medical procedure was guilty of killing the poor woman.

Face grim, Frances held up the tablets and shook the bottle again, the pills rattling within – like a child's rattle but made to prevent a child being born. 'It's only half full and has no label and does not name the contents. Neither does it give directions or their source.'

'Do you wish me to wait until the police have put in an appearance?'

'No.' She took hold of Sister Harrison's elbow. 'You, my dear Sister Harrison, are going home to bed. I'll take over from now on.'

'But the police...?'

'No doubt they'll head for your door should they wish to speak to you – which of course they will if they've an ounce of common sense. Now come on. I'll walk you to the door.'

It seemed almost comical to see the senior nursing sister off the premises, but Frances recognised it had to be done. Sister Harrison was nothing if not dutiful. In the absence of a man and now that her domineering mother was dead, the Orchard Cottage Hospital was the centre of her world.

Frances waylaid the caretaker, who was scraping around the edges of the space he'd cleared of ice, and asked if he would escort Sister Harrison off the premises.

'In case she slips,' she added, though that was only one of the reasons for getting her home.

Now it's my turn to inspect the body, she thought, standing outside her office door and wishing she could go in, sit down and drink another cup of tea, although that would have to wait. First things first.

'Doctor?'

'Lucy.'

They had taken to using first names when no other member of staff was around. Lucy had been a friend from the very first day Frances had arrived at the hospital.

They stood outside the closed door.

'I heard from Sister Harrison that you've already seen the dead woman.'

Lucy said that she had and frowned as she did so. 'I took an initial look, with Mrs Manning hanging over my shoulder. Once she was gone, I took another look just in case I'd missed something. Such a shame and yet she looks so peaceful, as though at last there is nothing to worry about.'

'I'd like to judge that for myself,' Frances said somewhat grimly.

She had considered fetching her medicine bag from the office but decided against it.

'You might as well come with me. If you don't mind.'

Together they retraced Lucy's route from the morgue.

The room was as coldly clinical as when Lucy had left it. Steel shelving and enamel receptacles only added to the unyielding silence and coldness.

They stood on either side of the woman as Lucy uncovered the woman's face just as she had earlier.

Frances shook her head at the sight of the pale, stony features as she contemplated what this woman had gone through.

At last, she sighed and said, 'I think we both know that this woman has experienced a miscarriage – with the assistance of a purveyor of illegal medicine.'

In her haste to see Sister Harrison off home, she had slipped the bottle of pills into her pocket. She now took them out and wrapped her fingers tightly around them, almost as though she wanted to lock them in so they wouldn't escape and do to someone else what they'd done to the woman lying dead in the morgue.

'It's hardly anything new,' declared Lucy, who was beginning to shiver uncontrollably. One visit to the morgue was enough. Two was unbearable, but she squared her shoulders and straightened her spine.

Lucy pointed out the adornment around the woman's neck.

Frances leaned forward and peered at it. 'A seashell.'

'It was hard to see at first. The string it hangs from is very fine. It looks like a bootlace.'

Frances frowned, her eyes appraising the item Lucy referred to. 'I don't think it is a bootlace. It's far too fine.' She bent her head so close, the metallic smell of blood stung her nostrils. She stroked the item with the tip of her finger. 'It's a silken thread, the kind used in embroidery.'

'A black thread?'

'Or dark green or blue. It's hard to tell.'

She deftly undid the thread from around the woman's neck.

'We'll put this in my drawer for safekeeping but mention it to the police. Perhaps they can use it to identify her.'

'Could she have been a seamstress perhaps?'

Frances agreed that it was possible. 'With a seafaring husband? The shell from him, the silk thread from her.'

Lucy shivered, which made Frances remark that she looked pinched with cold.

'It's icier than usual.'

'We could do with a cup of tea. On the way back to the wards, we'll get Mrs Manning to make us one. Come on. Let's get out of here.'

'Don't you want to look at the other end of her,' asked Lucy as she pulled the sheet back over the woman's face – a face that resembled a marble angel in St Michael's churchyard.

'Let's leave the woman with some dignity – and to His Majesty's Coroner.'

Lucy eyed the gloomy corners of the room that Iris had fixed on. 'I heard tell that this room was haunted,' she said somewhat nervously.

'So it should be,' said Frances as she turned towards the door. 'A place shared by corpses and empty bedpans.' She grinned. 'Neither of them is welcome company.'

They found Mrs Manning whilst touring the wards. She looked to be in the process of smoothing the pillows of the rough-faced man who had opened a garage in town and had been injured when a car battery had blown up in his face.

'Now don't you worry about anything,' she was saying, which was exactly the kind of thing any of the nurses would say.

She jumped back from the vicinity of the bed on realising that Frances and Lucy had arrived.

'Mrs Manning. When we've finished our morning inspection of patients, we'd like a cup of tea. Can I rely on you to bring us some – when you've got time of course.'

Iris was quick to respond. 'Yes. I'll do that. Pleased to be of assistance.' Her face shone with enthusiasm.

Recalling Lucy expressing Iris's yearning to become a nurse, Frances invited her to accompany them on their tour of inpatients.

Iris's sallow face lit up. 'Yes, Doctor. Of course, Doctor. It would be an honour,' she gushed and looked hardly able to believe her luck.

Being situated in a mining and quarrying area, the Orchard Cottage Hospital saw its fair share of industrial injuries.

There were six men in the male general ward. Mr Greendale, the man who had sustained acid burns to the face on account of the car battery exploding, was to be released this morning. He looked over the moon when he was told this.

Three of the other men had injuries resulting from their work in the mines or quarries. All of them were recovering well. The other two were both suffering from chest infections. Frances was more worried about these. Neither was responding well to treatment and although she expected that his youth would pull one through, she was more concerned about the other. His skin was yellow, and his belly distended, the latter a sign that his abdomen was filled with fluid.

She'd read a paper about draining the fluid by the insertion of a tube directly into the stomach. However, although she was confident it could relieve discomfort – if only momentarily – the man refused to contemplate such bodily invasion.

'Three score years and ten,' he'd said when it was first suggested that he might die if the procedure wasn't carried out. 'That's all the good Lord meant us to 'ave.'

She'd tried to persuade him again, but he was having none of it. Her only recourse, she'd decided, was to have the Reverend Gregory Sampson come in and reassure him that the Lord God Almighty would willingly let him live longer than that if it pleased him. That evening, Gregory had promised to get in when he could.

'But, like Saint Nicholas, I tend to be a bit busy at this time of year,' he'd informed.

'Though not climbing down chimneys,' she'd returned with a merriment that dimpled her cheeks.

'No, though I have managed to rustle up some fiery heat for the Christmas services.'

The braziers he'd referred to were usually lit for the church in winter, though he needed the blacksmith's attention before they were wheeled in to provide extra and very welcome heat.

'Otherwise, we'll have ash and glowing coals all over the nave.'

'Come when you can.'

His congregation and the celebration of Christmas was as important to him as her patients were to her.

There were no expectant mothers on the women's ward, which was slightly disappointing seeing as it was getting close to Christmas. What greater joy could there be at this time of year than a baby being born close to, or even on, Christmas Day.

Lucy echoed her thoughts. 'I wouldn't have minded coming in over Christmas if a birth was imminent.'

Frances's mind went back to the dead woman in the morgue. Could the distribution of those pink tablets have something to do with the absence of pregnant women in the maternity ward?

Once everyone had been seen, they made their way back to Doctor Brakespeare's office, brown files containing patient records clasped against their bosoms.

They settled themselves with the bundles still on their laps about five minutes or so before Iris entered with their cups of tea.

'Much appreciated, Mrs Manning,' said Frances with a beaming smile.

'Very much. Thank you, Iris,' added Lucy.

The drinking of tea accompanied the inspection of the patient records. Comments were made, prognosis agreed before returning to the dead woman.

Lucy placed her cup and saucer back on the tray. 'Poor thing. We don't even know her name. Have the police phoned back?'

Frances sighed. 'They said they'd made enquiries, but to no avail.'

'But they haven't come here to see if she's known to them.'

Frances drained the last drop of tea and replaced the cup back in the saucer before shaking her head. 'No.'

'It makes you wonder at her circumstances. Wife, mother, single? Women are so vulnerable.'

'And no wedding ring.'

Frances was thinking the same thing. Details of her office blurred around her. She was no longer here but lost in the past. Some of that past was not lived by her but had affected her life. Isabelle, her adoptive mother, and Mary, her natural mother. Both had been seduced and made pregnant by an older man – the same man. It was a cruel history that haunted her to this day.

Dismissing her thoughts, she noticed a concerned look on Lucy's face. 'It's troubling you.'

Lucy nodded. Her thoughts were meandering. She knew what rumours might take hold. She leaned forward with fear in her eyes. 'You know who's likely to get the blame, don't you?'

Frances pursed her lips, interlocked her fingers and looked at Lucy. The same thought had sprang to mind. Sister Harrison had mentioned unqualified people brewing up magic potions in their backyards.

'Not necessarily...'

'She's pointing the finger at Ma Skittings.' Lucy shook her head. 'She wouldn't do that.'

Frances had already considered whether there was a possibility that Ma Skittings was involved. She did brew herbal remedies, but charged little for her concoctions, most of which were based on honey harvested from the bees in her garden. A few herbs too. But a linctus that could bring on a miscarriage?

Frances thought about the pink pills. The fact that they were pills and presented in a glass bottle was not Ma Skittings' style. Pills went through a production process more efficiently done by someone with a background in chemistry. Ma Skittings had none. All she had was knowledge learned from antecedents. Another consideration was that her herbal remedies were in liquid form, added to that she recycled old bottles, and it was easy to see they had held something else before she'd reused them.

Frances slammed her hands down on the desk in a decisive manner that was meant to reassure. 'I'm inclined to agree with you. Whoever is peddling these pills is very professional. I would guess that this person – or persons – has some knowledge of making medicine – possibly possessing a background in chemistry. To which end...' She frowned as she thought it through. Amass the chemicals and equipment to make the pills in vast numbers and, in order to make a profit, advertise. 'Producing such pills in quantity could make a good deal of money. But producing them isn't enough.' She sighed. 'Somewhere,' she suggested slowly, 'there's a newspaper advertisement for these pills which might in turn lead us to the woman's identity. My gut instinct tells me it has to be a national newspaper. Either that or more than one. Which may give us a clue to where she got the pills. Also who she approached next when the pills failed to work. The person who carried out the operation.' She shuddered. 'I dread to think what she used.'

5

The police finally arrived at the hospital late morning on the tenth of December: one uniformed sergeant, one pimply faced young constable and another man who was grappling with a camera, three legs hanging from its square body, like the Martian spaceship from *The War of the Worlds*. They explained that they'd already interviewed Sister Harrison.

Frances expressed her surprise that they hadn't come the day before.

Judging by the sergeant's expression, they didn't see a problem. 'Well, seeing as she was already dead, and what with the weather and that...'

'A crime has been committed. Abortion is a crime, or didn't you know that?'

'There's no need to take that attitude, madam. Of course we know that.'

'*Doctor*. Doctor Brakespeare,' she responded somewhat indignantly. 'May I remind you, Sergeant...?'

'Carver.'

'That the sooner the coroner has taken charge, the better. Even in this weather, a body can decompose quite quickly.'

The embarrassed shuffling of feet followed. Then a clearing of throat before introducing the cameraman as Mr Mayler.

Frances queried why he was there.

Looking put out that he had to bother explaining anything, the sergeant responded in a gruff and offhanded manner. 'Whether she's known to us or not, Mr Mayler will take photographs. Either way, they'll be distributed to the newspapers. We need to know who she is. Somebody might know whoever dumped her on your doorstep.'

'I understand, Sergeant. Just try not to disrupt my hospital too much. And quickly if you could. One of my nurses will show you the way.'

'Certainly, Doctor.'

'Please also note that neither I nor any other nurse was on duty the night before last. Just Sister Harrison and you've already interviewed her.'

'That is true, Doctor, though there may be a little something that you might have noticed without really noticing – if you know what I mean, Doctor.'

'Like what?' Frances could barely refrain from snapping.

'Well,' said the police sergeant, priming the end of his pencil with a flick of his tongue. 'If I might ask a couple of questions...'

'Go ahead. Ask away.'

'Right.'

'What sort of woman do you think she was?'

Having an idea of where this question might be going, Frances felt her jaw tighten.

'Explain what you mean by that, Sergeant,' she stated, making no effort to hide her indignation.

'Well...' Made uncomfortable by her forthright glare and

authoritative tone, the heftily built man shifted from one foot to the other. 'Well... did she look like a respectable woman?'

Frances drew in her chin. Her glare intensified. 'What would make her look respectable, Sergeant? How would I tell?'

'Well... her clothing, rouged face and lips – the things that a woman of low morals—'

'Sergeant,' Frances pronounced sharply. 'It is not for me to judge a person by how they present themselves. I presume you asked Sister Harrison the same question. Am I right?'

'Well... yes, but—'

'Then whatever she said, I say also. The poor wretch, whoever she is, came here seeking help. I am a doctor and thus a signatory to the Hippocratic Oath. It is my job to heal and save lives if I can. I do not judge or categorise, but seeing as you've asked, she wore good-quality clothes and no rouge. Now, do you have any other more pertinent questions that might help this situation? If not, I wish you good day.'

Suitably chastised, the sergeant's naturally ruddy face turned the colour of a ripe plum. Discretion the better part of valour, he turned as if to leave, then turned abruptly back.

'Sister Harrison inferred that the woman died from... from... interruptions to the birth cycle... caused by pills. Illegal pills... or similar means... Did you...'

'At first sight it would seem that Sister Harrison is right.'

'These pills are evidence, so I need—'

'The pills will be handed over to the coroner.'

'Ah. Yes,' he said, his tone placatory, his manner humble. 'That would be correct procedure.'

'No matter who this person was, she is dead because she trusted a cure for her troubles from an illegal source. I trust that in time you will make enquiries as to where they came from. To my mind, it is more important than her background.'

Her statement was delivered with a professional air that commanded respect.

Without giving him time to respond, she put him on the spot. 'And what enquiries will you be making, Sergeant?'

His handlebar moustache went up and down as if it had a life of its own before he regained his composure.

'Once the chief constable gives permission, we're circulating an article and accompanying photograph nationwide in the hope of giving the woman a name. As for the supplier of the pills, we'll be making enquiries of the women round 'ere known to peddle home-made tinctures and suchlike. Herbal remedies, as they call them. Danger to society, they are.'

Frances eyed him as she might pus running from a burst boil. The comment rankled. Why would he think of that, unless...

'I take it you had everything you needed from Sister Harrison?'

'Yes,' he said, his jowls settling in fatty layers on his stiff collar. 'It was her who suggested that the abortive medication came from somebody local who dabbled in selling to women in need.' He gave a stiff little chuckle. 'And there was I thinking that we burnt the last witch years ago!'

Frances refrained from glancing in Lucy's direction, though sensed an alarmed look had come into being on her pretty face. Ma Skittings, who was Lucy's sister's mother-in-law, was well known for brewing herbal cures.

' I have patients to see. Good day, Sergeant,' she said in a tone that left him in no doubt that the interview was at an end.

There was a stiffness to his face that made her think there were other questions he wanted to ask; or was it something to do with the pointed way he looked at the empty teacups anticipating a brew before he left?

Whatever it was, she wanted him gone.

They were there another hour or so. They heard from Iris – who had an aptitude for finding things out – that the photographer was freelance, worked for the police when needed and for the local *Norton Dene Gazette* on a more regular basis. The photograph would appear on police posters and in the newspaper.

* * *

'I can't believe they asked that,' said Lucy when she and the doctor were making ready to go home for the evening. She shook her head.

'I take it you mean his insinuation that the woman was a prostitute.'

'Yes. What about the man who brought her here? Not a word about who he might be.'

Her tone of voice was indignant, and she kept her head turned, eyes away from the teacups and plate of digestive biscuits sitting on the desk.

Frances had thought the same thing, but voiced her opinion that seeing as he'd scarpered, there was no chance of circulating a photo of him, hence she was inclined to agree with the plan to circulate a photograph of the woman.

'Hopefully someone will recognise her.'

They'd learned later that before leaving, the police sergeant had insisted on speaking to Wally, who had a natural aversion to policemen – perhaps stemming from his poaching days – and he had given them short shrift.

Her cheeks dimpled and laughter barely submerged, Gwen Peebles, district nurse, had reported the conversation.

'He said, "I've got a cantankerous boiler on the boil so don't have the time for idle chit chat. I've told you what I know and that's it."'

Knowing Wally was a man who used as few words as possible, delivered with rat-a-tat speed, they all knew he would have said everything pertinent to the subject matter and no more. After that he shut down.

'Wally doesn't suffer fools gladly,' mused Frances. 'I don't think he likes policemen.'

'I don't think he likes people very much,' offered Lucy. 'But only those who ask him questions he doesn't want to answer.'

* * *

A crisp, misty evening following a stressful day of digesting the happenings of the eighth and the visit from the police earlier.

There were lesser events that irritated rather than shocked. The coal-burning boiler at the hospital began clunking, perhaps in protest at having to work harder than usual to keep the old building warm.

Before heading home, more blankets were placed onto beds to keep patients warm just in case the boiler fizzled out.

Ice filled ruts in the road and a skim of snow on the flatter surfaces that morning had led to Frances leaving her beloved car, who she'd nicknamed Mabel, in the garage between the vicarage and the coach house. Frances and Lucy walked down the icy drive together from the hospital. A faint smattering of snow speckled their shoulders and blew into their faces. Their complexions glowed.

Now the dead woman had been taken away, a feeling of relief accompanied them.

'Gregory is making supper for me tonight.' It was something to say, something to make conversation and stop Frances thinking of her freezing-cold toes.

'That's nice for you.'

'He's a good cook.'

'That's more than I can say for Aunt Rose,' said Lucy, her tone laced with amusement. She told Frances about the dreadful breakfasts she presented.

Frances eyed her sidelong. 'Did you have lunch today? Even if you go without breakfast, you should eat something at lunchtime.'

Lucy shrugged. 'I can't remember. I got so absorbed with bandaging Mrs Carter's sore leg whilst she wittered on about the goings-on in her family. She repeated herself several times regarding her son, Henry William, and the fact that he's been accepted for the grammar school. Can't blame her, I suppose. She must be very proud, the first in her family to gain a place at the grammar school. It is something of an achievement.'

'Very much so. She told me he was quite a clever little boy.'

'She's told everyone,' said Lucy, laughter threaded through her voice.

'Isabelle, my guardian, was very proud when I gained entry into medical school. She always felt that women had to be that much better than men in order to make their mark in the world. She insisted that a woman's only worth should not be confined to being a wife and bringing up a family. And she hated housework. Her philosophy was that when the dust reached a certain height it wouldn't grow much further.'

Their amusement was shared in light, introverted laughter. Frances had told Lucy quite a bit about the woman who had brought her up, a woman she had respected and loved.

'Still,' added Frances, 'for the most part, women are contented with their lot.'

'True.' Lucy fell into thought before piping up, 'I wonder if she had a family, the dead woman?'

'She might have. Wife, mother or woman of loose morals – it

doesn't really matter, does it. She was known to someone, loved by someone.'

Frances thought of what awaited her at home. Ma Skittings made sure she popped in at least three times a day to check on Frances's mother. Frances was grateful to the bluff, powerfully built and very capable woman who also made tinctures and gave people advice about their health. She recalled the police sergeant referring to such women as witches. She also knew that his comment had worried Lucy.

Although she was a woman of science, she was loath to condemn Ma Skittings and her remedies out of hand. Homespun logic handed down through the centuries had been relied on when there was nothing else to hand. Some of them worked. Some of them did not.

Frances decided to change the subject, to lighten the conversation.

'I presume you're looking forward to better weather for your wedding in June.'

'I am.'

Although she'd answered in the affirmative, Frances detected a slight reluctance.

Frances slowed her steps. 'You don't sound too sure.'

Lucy laughed the comment aside. 'I think Devlin and I are a little nervous. Most of the guests are strangers to me.'

'But not to Devlin.'

'No. But I'm not sure he likes crowds. You know how it is.'

Frances got the picture – or thought she did. One half of the couple worried about being out of her depth, and blindness sapped the confidence of the other.

Devlin Compton Dixon was Lady Araminta's son and had been injured at the end of the Great War. Lucy had made his acquaintance when invited up to Orchard Manor to take care of him. That was when they had fallen in love.

As they neared the rectory and its neighbouring coach house where Frances lived, Lucy asked the question that she had been expecting her to ask.

'Will you tell Ma Skittings about what's happened?' she asked a little worriedly.

'You're worried about what the police sergeant said.'

'Yes,' Lucy said softly, her nose tucked into the scarf that encircled her neck. 'I can't believe she would have had anything to do with it.'

'I think you're worrying unnecessarily.' Frances laughed. 'Lucy, this is Norton Dene. Do you really think I need to let her know what's happened?'

Lucy heard her tone of voice, detected the meaning and laughed. 'I don't suppose so. The news will be all over by now.'

'Lucy,' said Frances, coming to a stop and standing resolutely before her. 'I will stress here and now that I cannot believe that Ma Skittings was responsible for the woman's death.'

Lucy sighed and nodded.

'Now you get on home. And make sure you get some food inside you – even if you have to cook it yourself.'

'I will. Even if it's only bread and cheese,' she added with a grin. 'Aunt Rose can't spoil that.'

Lucy headed off in a homeward direction, persuading herself as she did that she would eat something. Dry bread would be best. Or ginger biscuits.

The ground was slippery, and each step was aided by gripping the stone wall running alongside the pavement. Beneath the fluttering glow of a gaslight, she stopped, took a breath and rested her hand on her stomach. Through the thickness of her rib knitted glove, she could feel that her belly was a little more rounded than it normally was.

Her breath steamed on the evening air. Her heart was racing. She didn't need anyone to tell her that she was in the family way.

The family way! The words resonated in her mind and flowed out on her white breath, her voice catching on each word, each syllable.

It was too early for this to happen. What about the wedding? It was still a long time until she was legally married. What would Devlin say? What would his mother say?

Lady Compton-Dixon was on the crest of a wave, sending out invitations to the wedding which was scheduled for June.

'It's the fashion to marry in June. All the best brides do it.'

That was what her ladyship had said.

Was she, Lucy Daniels, a best bride? She was of humble background. Would her ladyship be appalled when she found out that this wonderful wedding would have to be brought forward? And what about when posh people found out that she was in the family way? What then? Her ladyship had given her blessing to the marriage, but would she be of the same mind when she discovered the new circumstances?

An icicle crashed from a tree and momentarily distracted Lucy from her worrying thoughts, which now turned to Devlin. He'd been a bit distracted of late. She'd expected him to ring the hospital today and tell her he was missing her. The weather was partly to blame – at least that was what she told herself.

That was until she bumped into Roberts, one of the kitchen maids, shopping in the High Street. Somehow, she'd managed to get from the manor into town, possibly with her father, who farmed out there and had a tractor.

An oversized hat the shape of a tea cosy covered most of her head. Eyes, nose and mouth were all that was left showing.

'Have you heard? The master's former fiancée is visiting a relative and staying for a day or two at Orchard Manor. There's a thing!'

Roberts was one of those who took pleasure from passing on malicious gossip.

So why didn't I know? Lucy asked herself. She had a great urge to knock her stupid hat off but settled instead to say, with sharp disapproval, 'You could apply for the post of town crier with the foghorn voice that you've got.'

'I don't know what you mean,' said Roberts airily.

'Oh, I think you do,' Lucy hissed close to her ear. She hated being the subject of gossip.

Still seething, she stalked off, but try as she might, she couldn't help dwelling on the consequences of what might happen next. For a start, she wouldn't be continuing to work at the hospital if she was in the family way. How ironic was that? A hospital with modern ideas about family planning and it could be said that she'd failed to listen to sage advice. There was nothing she could do but face it head on; when the time came, which she would hold off as long as she could.

6

The cold weather persisted into the next day. Less snow now but some roads still had icy patches. Frances's car remained in the garage.

Wearing stout brown boots, a muffler and hat and scarf knitted by her mother, Frances turned into the drive that led to the rectory and then off onto the path leading to the coach house.

Icy fingers of cold air pinched her cheeks. She knew without needing to see that her cheeks were flushed and the tip of her nose was like a small cherry. Although it was only late afternoon, lights were on in houses, squares and oblongs of amber falling out on the crisply even covering of snow.

It was hard not to push aside the vision of the poor woman left to die on the hospital porch and train her thoughts on happier things.

Christmas both at the hospital and at home was an exciting prospect and like a child she had been looking forward to them very much. How quickly things could change, a hapless event at a time of year when all should be holy, jolly and focused on the birth of a child, not the loss of one.

And who was she? Perhaps she was a widow, unable to support even one child without a man to bring in a wage. A notice giving information and asking for relatives to come forward had yet to be successful. If no relatives were found, she would be interred in a pauper's grave – possibly at St Michael's. Gregory was of a generous disposition, bless him. He wouldn't hesitate to hold a service and say prayers for a woman, even though there would be no headstone and no name. Not until someone offered to pay for it.

All the way home, the grim thoughts stayed with her. Cold thoughts that wouldn't melt until she entered her darling little home, where a fire would be blazing in the range.

A blanket of warm air met her as she pushed open the coach house door. Standing in the middle of the room, Ma Skittings was just putting her hat and coat on. Both items of clothing looked as though they belonged to a man – a farmer of advanced years who had no further use for them. Nobody could describe them as attractive, even as feminine. But that was Ma Skittings. She spent as much time outside with her bees and planting as any farmer, so earthy colours and worthy clothing made sense.

Frances refrained from looking at the wall-mounted clock, its brass pendulum swinging backwards and forwards in perfect time. It amused her that Ma Skittings also kept perfect time and was always ready to go the moment Frances entered the door.

Her greeting was short. 'Good evening, Doctor.'

Frances returned the greeting, then listened as Ma Skittings ran through how the day had gone, mostly with reference to how her mother was doing.

'I've given her a bowl of hot soup and a nice bit of bread and butter.'

'Has she eaten any of it?' asked Frances, hoping the answer would be yes.

'I don't know for sure. I've left her alone to think about it. Don't want to force her.'

Frances sighed wearily, put down her medical bag and shrugged off her coat, which Ma Skittings took from her and hung up.

Commitment to the hospital was made more tense by her mother's illness. She'd moved her mother into the house from the lodgings where she'd lived when first coming to Norton Dene. Her mother had insisted that she take over the housekeeping of the pleasantly comfortable coach house. Frances had agreed that it was a splendid idea. She'd known from early on that her mother was not in the best of health so had asked Ma Skittings to keep an eye on her.

At first, her mother – Mary Baker as was, or Mrs Devonshire as she'd become – had been able and willing to do a bit around the house but had slowed thanks to the lump in her lung. The changing seasons had not helped. The dampness of autumn had replaced the dry summer. It was now the first month of winter, which seemed to have arrived early this year and had brought on frequent coughing and a tightness in her mother's chest. The return of warmer weather was a long way off. Frances wondered if she would last until then.

Ma Skittings bustled about the place, like a large angry cat looking for a mouse, her large coat open and flapping around her, hat pulled more firmly down over a head of unruly grey. 'Let me get you a cup of tea whilst you take them boots off.'

'I'd like that.'

The old leather chair creaked as she sat down and gratefully toed off each boot one at a time.

'I've left her up there with a bit of knitting for after she's 'ad her soup. She likes knitting. I thought it might keep her awake long enough to eat the soup and drink an elixir I made for her. No charge,' she added.

'An elixir?' Frances was sceptical but kept an open mind.

'Just a tonic. It'll make her sleep,' she said more softly, almost as though Frances's mother was close to hand and already half dozing.

After peeling off her gloves, Frances gratefully took the cup and saucer, placing the saucer onto the three-legged footstool. Wrapping both hands around the cup warmed her hands. The tea was hot and refreshing enough to make her close her eyes.

Her duties finally at an end, Ma Skittings buttoned up her coat and pulled her hat more firmly down on her head.

Frances had never ever been able to fully read the expression of the large woman. Her body was solid, her shoulders as straight and square as a sergeant major on an army parade ground. This afternoon, there was a more open look on her face than usual.

'Are you seeing the vicar tonight, me dear?'

Frances nodded. 'He has asked me to dinner again.' She laughed lightly. 'He's always cooking for me. I do believe he thinks I can't cook – either that or I'm wasting away.' A telling look came to her face. 'I'm tired out and there's my mother to think of.'

A broad smile split her housekeeper's face in half. 'Thought 'e might 'ave. You go and enjoy yerself. Don't worry about yer ma. I'll pop in again later and make sure she's all right. Not that she's likely to notice. That tonic I gave 'er will make 'er sleep. And besides, you're only next door.'

Frances felt her eyelids grow heavy and the cup and saucer being taken from her, for a moment feeling it was floating away rather than being taken by human hand.

'Now you go and 'ave a nice nap before you go. Nice bath too if you can.'

Frances eyed her quizzically, sensing that something else was going on here. 'I feel I'm imposing.'

'Nonsense.'

'Thank you, Mrs Skittings.'

Her housekeeper tossed her head in an amenable manner. 'You've got time to pop up and see her before you goes out.'

'I will. Thank you for looking after her.'

Ma Skittings nodded her head, then held it to one side, as though she was listening to something Frances could not hear.

She presumed she could hear her mother wandering around upstairs – using the chamber pot perhaps. She'd check later. In a bid to refresh her heavy eyelids, she referred to a happier subject.

'Roll on June and Lucy's wedding. I take it you're invited.'

'Of course, I am. Nancy's her sister and my daughter-in-law. Wouldn't miss it for the world. It's a family affair for us as well as for the nobs up at the big house.'

A wicked-looking smile coupled with a sparkle in eyes of speedwell blue came to her face. 'I thought you and the vicar would be making marriage plans yerself by now.'

Frances refused to blush and kept her voice even. 'We both have careers that we love.'

A work-worn hand reached for the door latch. The twinkle was still there. 'Loving what you do don't mean you can't love people too. And both of you do that in your jobs, don't you?'

As she tugged back the pine plank door, a blast of cold air from outside prised flames of all colours from the coals piled high in the range.

'Have a good night.'

'You too, Mrs Skittings, and please, you don't need to pop in later. After all, I will only be in the vicarage.'

Mrs Skittings nodded. 'We'll see.' Then she was gone.

Frances rested her elbow on the arm of the chair, chin in

hand, eyes watching the colourful flames – fading now that the door was closed.

Not that she was really appreciating the spectrum of colour. She was seeing through them, thinking about Gregory and herself. Ma Skittings had hit a nerve. For ages now, she'd suppressed her feelings, immersing herself in the work she loved. Helping married women in their lives had taken over her own. But what about her future? What about Gregory? Could they really go on as they were for the rest of their lives?

At the heart of the matter was the aching truth that she loved him and knew he loved her. They also loved their work. Would their commitment to each other be as strong as their commitment to medicine on her part or religion on his? What did she really want?

The offer of the job in London nagged at her nerves.

Picking up the poker, she gave the coals a prod. At the same time, she opened and shut the device that gave and took oxygen from the ever-burning fire.

She went over what Ma Skittings had said whilst she prodded and poked, not just the coals but with reference to their conversation. One thing – one rather important thing – had not been mentioned. Ma Skittings had made no reference to a dead woman being left on the front porch of the hospital. Either the news hadn't travelled around the town just yet, or Ma Skittings was being polite – waiting for her to mention it first – holding back her fascination and curiosity out of respect.

Leave it, she said to herself with a toss of her head. Out loud she said, 'A bath. A change of clothes...'

But first she tiptoed upstairs.

The previous vicar, a man with a taste for modern architecture and personal comfort, had had the foresight to install plumbing in the coach house. He'd done this at the same time as replacing the original Victorian porcelain fitments and claw-footed bath in the vicarage. Hot water was on tap, syphoned from pipes heated by the kitchen range. Modern luxury few had access to in the rows of terraced miners' cottages, where a privy huddled in the back garden and a tin bath hung on the wall.

On reaching the landing, Frances listened intently until she heard movement and the faint sound of laboured breathing.

She chided herself for being so foolish as to think her mother might have faded away in the last few minutes.

She made the final steps to her mother's bedroom and peered around the door. The bedroom was at the front of the house, a pretty room of mauve flowered wallpaper, white and green curtains, a lacy coverlet covered by a satin eiderdown in pale lime.

Her mother was asleep. Frances had time for a bath, to relax and think, grateful to close her eyes and sink into the hot water.

If later she found her mother awake, she would put on a brave face and try to convince both of them that death was still some time away – not much time but enough.

Life, she thought, *is so unfair*. After all these years, her mother had found her, but their time together would be short-lived, and despite all her medical skills, there was precious little she could do about it.

7

The bath was greatly welcome, the steam thick as a fog in winter, warm as mist rising from the heated land of August after a thunderstorm.

It was hard to drag her thoughts away from the day's occurrences, but Frances needed to check on her mother, tell her she was off out, and perhaps dare to ask her what she'd done today – though wasn't likely to get much of an answer.

Once dressed in a bluish grey woollen dress that complemented her eyes, she paused outside her mother's door, took hold of the white ivory doorknob. Keeping very quiet, she listened for the sound of regular breathing, not the gurgling rasp that sometimes accompanied her mother's living and sleeping hours. One, two, three. She counted each breath. All were even. Normal breathing, a little shallow but not laboured.

Relieved, Frances took a deep breath, turned the handle and stepped into the room. The air was close, thanks to the fire burning in the cast-iron fireplace.

With soft footfall, she took three further steps into the room.

Her mother's fragile frame made only a small mound beneath the green satin eiderdown. Like a child.

A white heart-shaped face framed by tousled hair turned to face her.

'Goodness, Mother. I thought you were asleep.' She said it both breezily and gladly.

'I was eating my soup. Mrs Skittings left it warming over there on the hob.' She inhaled a rush of breath as she nodded towards the fireplace. Although it was small, it boasted cast-iron hobs to either side of the coal-filled grate, ideal for leaving something to keep warm. 'Anyway, I wanted to see you before I fell asleep for the night.'

The sentiment was touching. Knowing that her mother's health was deteriorating, Frances was touched to hear that she'd stayed awake just to see her.

In response, she adopted a happy and reassuring expression, the kind she mostly reserved for her favourite patients or those who had overcome serious illness or trauma. 'That's quite wonderful. I'm flattered.'

An urgent rasp of breath before speaking.

'And I've got supper to eat.'

'Then you'd better eat it up. I want my mother to have a good night's sleep.' Her widening smile reflected her relief. Simple words, she thought as she considered what she'd said. Caring words. The only word that felt slightly alien was that of 'mother'. Most of her life, she'd had no mother. She'd been an orphan, though could not recall her earliest years when she'd been abandoned in the workhouse. She'd known nothing about her mother, not until about a year ago. Her mother had been absent, an unknown in her life. There might have been an empty space, no mother at all, but things hadn't turned out like that.

Izzy, her benefactress, had filled that position, though

insisted, even at a young age, that Frances called her Izzy – as though they were sisters – which turned out to be true.

The soup looked untouched, though the dish was warm.

'Shall I feed you?'

'No. I can manage.'

An arm bereft of flesh reached for the spoon. Barely half a spoonful went into her mother's mouth and the spoon trembled as it did so. A few more spoonfuls followed. Her mother, who had been in service, a common housemaid when she'd been taken advantage of by an older man, began trailing the spoon through the soup. The level had hardly reduced.

Her hand stopped twirling the spoon when Frances sat on the bed close to her. She eyed her mother, then the soup.

'It's going to get cold before long if you keep playing with it instead of eating it.'

There was command and gentleness in her tone, making her sound as though she was the mother, telling her child something for its own good.

If it did sound at all brusque, her mother seemed blithely unaware.

'Are you off to the vicarage tonight?' she asked, her eyes, paled by sickness, suddenly keener.

A change of subject, ignoring entirely what Frances had just said. That in itself told Frances that she was unlikely to eat much more.

Feeling slightly defeated, she answered, 'Yes. I'm only popping into the vicarage. Mrs Skittings has promised to drop in just to make sure you're all right. Do you mind...?'

'Of course not.' The sudden expression of interest lifted the tired, pale face and for one moment it seemed to Frances that she was getting a glimpse of the younger Mary.

Since reuniting after all these years, she often caught her

mother eyeing her with pride. The daughter she'd been forced to give away. The little girl who had grown up without her had done extremely well in the world of medicine. That was the look she was getting now.

The expression in her eyes turned mischievous. 'I already knew you were going round there tonight. He called in this afternoon.'

'Did he now,' returned Frances and pretended to be abashed, as though she had been found out for something far worse than having dinner with a gentleman friend.

The pale eyes took on a hint of China blue sparkling in an impish face, almost childish, although fine lines ran around the eyes and lips like skeins of silk thread.

A sudden realisation arose that her mother must indeed have been beautiful when she was a young girl. Sad that her fragile beauty had tempted a man old enough to be her father – even her grandfather.

In a bid to banish the past, she forced herself to bring Gregory to mind, a smile curving her lips. Her eyes downcast, she went on, 'Gregory is a good man. Genuine too. Many of his parishioners say that he's the best vicar they'd ever had.'

'And you like him?'

'He listens when I unload all the problems of the day…' She frowned, wondered whether to mention the woman who had died. She began telling her. 'She's in the police morgue now. The coroner needs to examine her before he issues a death certificate.' She shook her head. 'Poor woman. We cannot know what happened to bring her to such a tragic end.'

The spoon fell into the soup with an air of finality. A faraway look came to her mother's eyes as though her thoughts had gone back over time to when she'd been young and in a similar situation.

Frances wished she hadn't mentioned the incident.

Enough of gloom. She turned the conversation back to Gregory. 'Gregory is a good man,' she said again.

Her mother nodded in a slow methodical manner. 'Yes. I can believe that. Despite all the mistakes in my life, I know a good man when I see one.'

'I'm sure you do,' Frances said softly.

Her mother closed her eyes and laid her head back upon the pillow.

Frances assumed that she was going to fall asleep, but her assumption proved wrong.

Her mother's eyes flashed open again. 'Did you not tell me that he's asked you to marry him, or is my memory failing along with my body?'

'Yes.'

'But you haven't said yes or no.' Her look was direct and unblinking. Almost accusing.

'We both have a lot to think about,' she said quickly, unwilling to comment further on the matter which had been on the backburner for some time. Pressure of work was her excuse for keeping it there. A swift smile was all she had to hide the uncertainty behind the excuse. 'I'll come back later for the dishes. Now eat that soup.'

* * *

The dark outside the window was total. After wrapping her ash blonde hair around a wad of felt, Frances eyed her reflection. The woollen dress had a cape neckline. A thin yellow belt defined her waist.

Look at me, she thought to herself. *I'm thirty-three years old. Do I wish to become an old maid or a stay as a doctor?*

The question had an obvious answer. Her inclination was to be both.

It was a matter of duty to take one last look at her mother. Perhaps it was guilt. She noticed the soup congealing in the bowl, a few crusts and one slice of bread curling round the edges left on the plate.

'Before you say anything, I've had enough. My appetite is very small nowadays,' her mother said before Frances had chance at reprimand.

'Not enough to keep a bird alive,' Frances responded.

The truth was obvious, but her mother retained a defensive attitude.

'Nothing's wrong with me.'

There's nothing for you to worry about. That's what those few words really meant.

Frances put a brave face on it. 'Goodness. I wondered for a moment whether you'd gone off Ma Skittings' cooking. She'd be mortified if you had.' There was a brittleness to Frances's humour which she hoped had gone unnoticed. Dealing with sick people could drain the soul; doubly so if that person was a close relative. The humour was a veneer, a way that helped her to cope and the sick person to live in hope.

Overwhelmed for a moment that despite all her medical skills, she was unable to do more for her mother, she pretended to look out of the window.

'She made me some herbal tea,' her mother added.

Frances turned from the window. Her attention went to the empty cup sat a little wonky on the saucer. 'Did it taste good?'

Her mother's eyes closed in a languid manner. 'Yes, but it didn't leave much room for the bread and soup.' An excuse for having left so much.

Frances played along. 'Good. At least you've had something.'

But hardly enough.

The words remained unsaid.

It was suddenly as though her mother, small, frail and fading away, seemed to become as white and at one with the pillow. 'I'm tired. I need to get some sleep.'

Frances cupped the nape of her mother's neck with one hand as she raised her up, her free hand pummelling the pillows with the other. Carefully she lay her mother's head back into the plush softness of the eider feathers contained therein.

'Comfortable?'

'Yes.'

The single word was no more than a hushing sound, like a hairbrush through silky tresses.

Frances felt a little tightness in her chest. Her mother looked so thin. Her eyes were sunken.

There was no word in response, just a soft moan that could have been a word but perhaps not.

Frances stacked the crockery for taking downstairs. Plate first, then soup bowl, being careful not to let the thickening liquid slop over the edge. Lastly the cup and saucer. The cup was empty, the only item that was.

Curious as to what it might have been, she brought it up to her nose and sniffed. She smelled nothing. Whatever it was, her mother's fast falling asleep made her wonder. Something to soothe. Something to blank out the pain and smooth the unending path to the end of life.

Dishes taken care of, she headed back upstairs.

'Now I'm going round to Gregory's for dinner. You do remember that?' she asked softly.

Perhaps she'd asked too softly. There was no response and for a moment her heart skipped a beat. She sucked in her breath and leaned closer. To her great relief, her mother's breathing was steady.

It was her experience that she wouldn't stir until the morning. There was nothing to worry about.

Frances smoothed the fluffy, white hair back from her mother's face, a mother's way of soothing her darling child.

All will be well, she told herself, at least for tonight. Ma Skittings popping in later was reassuring. She'd let herself in. Everybody did. The locking of closed doors in Norton Dene was unheard of. Crime was minimal and popping in and out of neighbours' houses was an accepted pastime.

Her mother's lack of appetite was worrying. The way her slender body was becoming ever more fragile. Some of her hair had fallen out and what little was left was wispy. It reminded her of the feathery seeds of the plant her and school friends had called Old Man's Beard. As though a breath of wind could take it flying.

Deep in thought, Frances stared at the blackness beyond the window. One thought above all others was uppermost in her mind; how long it would be. That was the problem in being a doctor. She knew the signs and although she couldn't accurately predict the exact day, the hour, or minute, she knew that the inevitable was on the horizon, death like a shadow sitting in the corner, ready to reach out and take the last breath from a dying body.

There was no doubting her mother was dying. Accepting it was hard. And unfair. It would always be unfair.

Frances had been happy growing up in the zany household of Izzy Brakespeare, where intellectual women had put forth opinions that men would prefer they didn't have.

Her natural mother had never been mentioned. It had been as though she'd never existed.

Just a few months ago, her mother had sought her out. No longer Mary Baker, she'd returned from Australia, where she'd married a man named Devonshire.

Her sudden appearance in Frances's life had been surprising enough, though not as much as finding out that he had also fathered a child on his own daughter. The child had died, but cold revenge had lingered in Izzy's soul. She, Frances, was that revenge, a child indulged in by Izzy to make up in some part for the death of her own child.

The only other member of the family who knew the appalling truth was Izzy's sister Beatrice, a child embittered by the fact that she had been lesser loved by their father.

Beatrice's attempt to destroy Frances had ended in failure. The possibility that hatred still raged in her mean chest could not be discounted. Frances hoped that the woman who was both her sister and her aunt – monstrous as it was – had mellowed and would never trouble her again.

8

Nurse Lucy Daniels was doing what she did every day, buzzing around the hospital in Norton Dene unaware that something happening in London would be of consequence to her.

Lady Grace Leinster-Parry had recently gone to her doctor to spell out her fears regarding the prospect that infection had passed to her from her husband.

'I know it's confidential, but my husband's had many...' She'd paused for the right word or words. 'Female sexual partners,' she finally exclaimed in as calm a voice as possible.

She was frightened by the rash from which she was suffering. No doctor would normally betray what was written in a husband's medical records, but Doctor Joseph Eastman was an old friend of her father. She trusted him to do the right thing.

'You know I should not divulge this,' he pronounced as he eyed her over the top of the crescent-shaped lenses of his spectacles. He was entranced by her beauty and saddened by her choice of husband.

Grace had married and suffered her husband's bad behaviour for some time – fourteen years, in fact. If asked why she had not started this particular ball rolling, she would have said that it would have broken her father's heart. He had died four months ago. That's the excuse she would have given, but in all honesty there was another reason. Like any married woman, she was afraid of scandal. She was also afraid of being destitute, both her and her son and daughter thrown out onto the street.

Doctor Eastman sat back in his chair and rested his clasped hands over his paunch. That look from his pale blue eyes was incisive, like a steel needle, designed to prick strong fabric.

He'd known Grace since she was a child. He'd known her father for longer. They'd been good friends and had both served in long-ago wars that had taken them abroad. Both had played a part in saving the other's life. Theirs had been a reciprocal friendship of deep bonding.

He was a man of principle, but his love for his old friend and his promise to look after Grace held sway. She would receive his advice, though in a roundabout way, as a warning rather than a blow-by-blow excerpt from her husband's medical records.

'Let me put it this way, my dear Grace. It might be best if you sleep in separate beds. I would advise you cease having marital relations with you husband.'

Grace swallowed. 'And the rash?'

The doctor shook his head. 'In this instance, nothing to worry about. Just a female thing.'

'Thank you, Doctor.'

'But please,' he said, leaning closer to her. 'I have not divulged what your husband is suffering from. I have merely advised you not to have relations with him and sleep in separate beds. Do you understand?'

She nodded that she did, paid her bill there and then – for she didn't want the bill to go to her husband. If that happened, it might lead to him finding out what else she was up to and she didn't want that.

There was no guilt. That's what surprised her. She had coldly and efficiently worked out what she could do to end this marriage. The plan had begun when she'd been talking to powerful men at a reception her husband had held. Funny, she thought, how those men had homed in on her good looks, surprised when she'd asked them about investments, of women who had made it in a world of men. Not many. Barely any, as it turned out.

'Don't worry your pretty little head about things like that. Leave such matters to your husband. It's for a man to bring home the bacon.'

My God, she'd wanted to smack their faces, to tell them that she had a brain inside her 'pretty little head'. They just didn't see beneath the surface to the woman planning to kick over the apple cart and leave her husband as soon as she could.

Gerald didn't know that she was planning a life away from him. To some, it might appear that she was a harpy and evil for even thinking about leaving her marriage. But they didn't live with her behind closed doors. Most of her money but not all was governed by him. Her father's elder brother had passed away and left her a tidy sum. It was a lucky stroke that she'd kept hidden from her husband and enough to put down the foundation of a different life. That was besides the pretty sum she'd inherited from her father and the subject of a trust fund that her husband could not access. Only she could do that. 'Money is a facilitator,' her old uncle had told her. 'Used wisely it will snowball and serve you well. Give you freedom in fact.' She'd thought hard about it and decided she would take a leaf out of her husband's book and invest in property. Even for a married woman, property and wealth could lead to a greater independence. Not that this would lead to immense fortune straightaway. That would take time.

Feeling both nervous and excited, she prepared herself for viewing the property she had in mind. Finding it had been pure chance. She was a great one for walking the streets to sort out her thoughts, as well as to escape the cloying atmosphere of the matrimonial home in Mayfair. Most of her wandering took her out of the grand gentility that was Mayfair, Kensington and Chelsea and into the more crowded areas where women sold items from barrows in the street. Most of the men she'd met in her wanderings were working men with dirty but interesting faces; and they were courteous, tapping their hats in deference as she passed. They got quite used to seeing her around.

'Nice to see you again.'

She'd smiled as she'd returned the greeting. In time, she got talking to them and found herself surprised by what they had to say. And that was why she was viewing this building today.

Although a weak sun was shining, she had need to wear a fur jacket. Suitably dressed and with her heart beating like a metronome keeping time, she asked a servant to hail a taxi. She was off to the West End, not the area of theatres and upmarket department stores but the area where terraced houses huddled in symmetrical rows and the sound of the underground rattled the doors and windows. The underground would form the foundation for her future life.

Late afternoon in London, she alighted from the taxi. Buildings of five storeys or more and past their best loomed over her. Faces were glimpsed at windows, the curious wondering what a refined lady was doing here.

She was dressed in a businesslike manner in a white blouse beneath her jacket which went well with her black and white skirt. Her hat was maroon, perched on her head at a jaunty angle.

In each ear, she wore a clip-on earring of black jet and a cameo brooch at her throat. She was here on business and determined to look the part. Hopefully first impressions would get her what she wanted.

Mr Yardley, her bank manager at the Fakenham Mutual, arrived to show her around the property. In fact, it was him who had suggested she might be interested. She hadn't been sure at first, not until a conversation she'd had with one of those who'd got used to seeing her around – a navvy working on a sewage pipe. She'd remarked on the filthiness of his job. He'd told her it wouldn't be for much longer. He would be moving on soon. The underground was being extended.

She hadn't known that at the time and neither, it seemed, had anyone else. And that was when her plan had formed.

'I understand this building is fully tenanted.'

'It is.'

'You are sure about that?'

'Indeed, dear lady. That's why, following our conversation of a few weeks ago, when the owner of this property mentioned their wish to sell, I immediately thought of you. Not only that, but I'm sure I know of someone who could manage the building for you in exchange for a suite of rooms. He's quite keen on living in the basement at the front of the property. The rear is the kitchen and laundry area.'

'I see. So, the price you told me, the rents I can expect plus someone to look after it free of charge.'

She could have told him then and there that she would no longer rent out tawdry rooms for a paltry price. Following her conversation with the navvy, she had other plans but would keep them to herself.

Mr Yardley, who also maintained her husband's account, had been sworn to secrecy over this visit.

'It's a surprise for my husband,' she'd explained.

'Of course, madam.'

He was the type of man who thought it amusing to indulge a woman out to surprise her husband. In time, the husband would take charge of the venture. He was sure of that.

Grace had other plans. She determined to endeavour to make him believe that she would indeed be continuing to keep the building tenanted. He would believe that because it was what her husband did.

'You say a manager would require living in the basement?'

'That is correct, your ladyship. A basement is never very sought after, especially by those with children. They can be damp, you see. But that's the working class. If they didn't have so many children and worked a bit harder, they could seek out something better.'

Grace gritted her teeth and made a non-committal sound that neither agreed nor disagreed with what he had said. It seemed to her ears that Mr Yardley's train of thought varied little from that of her husband. Humanity didn't count for much to them. Only money and power.

Misinterpreting her silence as acquiescence, the bank manager carried on. 'A worthwhile return on your investment, I think?'

Grace narrowed her eyes as she scrutinised the crumbling façade. This place needed demolishing and it wouldn't be long before it was, but only she was privy to that information, not her dyed-in-the-wool bank manager.

Calculations of how much money she needed to pay for this place whizzed round her head. She hoped and prayed that her plan would work out and she wouldn't need to rent out this appalling place to anyone. Not if the navvy was right.

It was still something of a gamble, or had been up until she'd asked the advice of Vincent Kennedy, a financier and old friend of her father who had once been sweet on her. She'd sworn him to secrecy when she'd asked him about the likely extension of the underground system.

He'd looked fascinated by her question – or was it merely her face?

'I had heard a rumour.' A quizzical look had followed. 'No one is quite sure where they're going to be extending.'

'But some properties on that route are likely to be demolished.'

'Obviously. It's just knowing where. Whoever knows that will make a fortune.'

Grace had positively glowed. 'That's all I wanted to know.'

Her husband had categorically forbidden her to invest the money left to her on the occasion of their marrying.

'Your father should have given that to me to handle for you.'

'So that you could gamble it away or spend it on your whores!'

The comment had got her a hard slap. Her vision had spun with the violence of the blow. But she'd hung onto it tenaciously despite the harsh language and occasional blows. She'd not conveyed the fact that her uncle had also left her some money.

She often wondered how it might have been if she'd married Devlin Compton-Dixon regardless of his affliction. Looking back, she recalled it had been his decision rather than hers. She'd tried to maintain some correspondence between them, her letters addressed to his mother for her to read to him. Lady Araminta had written back, a strong woman for whom it must have been hard to say how he had turned inwards and would see nobody.

Before retiring at night, she would enter the hallowed silence of the drawing room, bereft of anyone else at that time and whisper into the night, 'I will escape this prison. I will be a woman of means. A wealthy woman. Men passing me by on the pavement will recognise me and wish me good day. Men of greater importance – their wives too – will ask me to dine with them at their elegant houses in Chelsea or Kensington. I will be exalted among my peers. I will be... a thoroughly modern woman. Independent and answerable only to my conscience – just like the friend Araminta told me about. Isabelle.'

Burning with fire to succeed and her own private thoughts, she wasn't aware of the bank manager peering at her questioningly. Neither did she hear him saying that he didn't want to press her, but there were other interested parties...

'I'll take it.' She didn't care whether there were or not. The information she'd received made it exactly what she wanted.

In years long gone, it had been a gentleman's house, lived in by a respectable family who had made their money in shipping. That was back when this part of London had been more salubrious than it was now. Once the area had deteriorated, the residents – families for the most part – had moved out to detached houses of black and white timber, a nod to Tudor times. They had developed a yearning for bigger gardens and the new underground system had meant the heart of the city was never far away.

As was the way of most town houses in areas that were becoming more populous, the property had been split up and the rooms rented out to diverse families many years ago. And now it had reached the end of the line. Her only remaining concern was for the residents, though she had heard that the underground people had bought other properties that might not be as close to the line extension as originally thought. Perhaps she could persuade the company management to move the people from this run-down property into one of those.

Grace was still wary of letting the cat out of the bag to Mr

Yardley just in case he passed the information on to her husband. He'd said that he wouldn't, but she couldn't be sure. Best to play a game of smoke and mirrors, make him think that nothing much would change.

'If you could have the ledgers for this place sent round to me, I would like to study the debits and credits in greater depth.'

His surprised expression verged on contempt. 'But you are a lady. Do you really want to bother your pretty little head with such dull figures? I can recommend an accountant who is not long—'

'I am not a fool, Mr Yardley. Please do not treat me as such.' She also thought that if he referred to her 'pretty little head' one more time, she would scream.

On the contrary, he looked surprised, having never heard her snap before.

She tucked her fur coat more closely around her shoulders. 'I am quite capable of checking figures. I expect a good return for my money, but first I must satisfy myself that there are no hidden costs or things going on that might be distasteful and therefore likely to damage my family's reputation. I simply won't have it. Good working people – that's the kind of tenant I encourage. Ones capable of bringing in a regular wage.'

The pavement, a bit cracked in places and grass growing where it connected to the garden wall, was only a dozen steps from the taxi she had asked to wait for her. She stopped abruptly and with the air of a schoolmarm laying down the law to an incalcitrant schoolboy reaffirmed that she was intent on ensuring that nothing improper was going on.

'Do you understand what I mean, Mr Yardley? I want you to be honest.'

'Quite so, dear lady,' he said, raising his hat and flashing her a lesser smile than the kind he gave to many businessmen. Similar was in fact all it was and although Grace might think herself in the riding position, the person who would gain most from this venture, she couldn't be more wrong. He was getting a fat purse – a kickback for getting rid of this place with as little fuss as possible. Thank God for women who thought they knew more about business than men did. As if!

He couldn't believe his luck. Her knowledge of the place prior to the finalising of the legalities would remain at a minimum. It was a good buy, but it had problems that the present owner was not prepared to deal with, hence the low price.

'I will ensure the accounts are sent round to you within the next few days,' he said to her.

He helped her up into her taxi, which was an extravagance she'd hired purely so she could get to this house in the east of London as quickly as possible – and back again.

The goodbyes behind them, each of the participants in this meeting went off in their own direction, both pleased with themselves; Grace because she was banking on what a simple, lowly workman had told her. Mr Yardley was pleased because he'd offloaded what could in time become a problem for the present owner. Thus, he would receive a generous reward.

'A job well done,' he murmured to himself as he bounced along the pavement, his heels barely connecting with the ground and his smile wide enough to crack his face in half.

As far as Grace was concerned, this was the opening round in her plan to divorce her husband and become an independent woman. The buying and selling of the house in Sears Road was only one aspect. The other was compiling a dossier of her husband's philandering. But where to start?

Theatres. Gerald loved seeing showgirls kicking their legs into the air. Pure curiosity had her sending her driver to purchase an evening newspaper.

Once she'd seen the photograph and headline, read the first few paragraphs, a plan formed in her mind.

She read on, read again about a woman who had been dumped on the steps of a hospital in the Somerset town of Norton Dene. Anyone who knew her was being asked to come forward. The circumstances of her death were couched in a gentile manner, nothing terrible that might put respectable folk off their supper.

Grace, however, knew that face!

There, white and still as marble, was a woman she recognised as Ellen Grant, one of her husband's stable of loose women.

And Norton Dene!

Was it so very mercenary to use however she had died to help her get the better of her husband? The details in the article were obscure. She needed more information and to get that she needed to go there. If her instinct was right, Gerald had had a hand in her demise. Sad as it was for Ellen Grant, her misfortune could be her gain.

Back in the house she shared with her husband, she sat down at the small bureau in the bedroom, took out pen, paper and envelope and wrote a letter to Lady Araminta Compton-Dixon. It wasn't an easy job. She had no wish at this moment to divulge her real reason for the visit. Admitting her husband's infidelities was something she did not wish to do. An element of subterfuge was essential if she was to make this work. Secrecy was paramount – at least until everything had fallen into its rightful place.

'I'm visiting a relative who lives close by. That should work.'

She wrote that down. Perhaps reference to the past and to Devlin might also help. She'd read the engagement announcement. Perhaps they would assume she was coming down to inspect the woman who would become his bride, a position she had once filled. Or would they think she was trying to reignite something that had been discarded many years ago?

She smiled sadly. The romantic young girl was left far behind. Pragmatism had replaced romanticism. It would be quite touching to see Devlin again, but that was all. She had two children to protect and to that end would do everything she could – or had to do.

It might be considered a little underhand, but she couldn't help that. Finding out more about Ellen's demise would hopefully give more ammunition to cement her long-term plans and form part of the evidence to enable a divorce. All she needed was proof.

9

The view from the window of the manor house was just as wintry as everywhere else. The parkland bordering the main drive had been turned into a white wilderness. A doe foraged beneath a tree that had sheltered the feeble grass growth from the snow, nuzzling the ground, small hooves delicately pinching the dark earth.

'Is the snow very deep?'

Devlin Compton-Dixon stood in front of a large window that let in all the light of the whitewashed winter's day. The light from outside bathed his face and touched the dead corneas of his eyes, making them seem alive again.

He'd just finished breakfasting with his mother, Lady Araminta Compton-Dixon. Like him, she was gazing out of the window, its lofty length stretching from ceiling to floor. Unlike him, she could see the icy cold world that had come into being earlier than normal this winter.

'Yes. And it's very cold. It began last night, the snow falling onto an already frozen ground. I've asked for the fire in your room to be banked up. I trust it will have been done by now.'

Devlin nodded appreciatively. 'Billy is on the ball. He would have carried out your orders.'

Billy Noakes was an orphan rescued from a miserable life on a narrow boat where he'd received regular beatings, was ill fed and forced to work from dawn to dusk. Found hiding in the laundry room, starving and scared, he'd been taken in by the family. When the people who'd abused him showed up at Orchard Manor, they'd been given short shrift – and a blow from Devlin's walking stick and told never to darken their door again.

'Orders! I don't give orders. I say please and thank you.'

He managed to raise a knowing smile because he knew that she was trying to inveigle his thoughts. His mother had always had an ability to disarm him.

'It's a dreary day. An empty day.'

He knew the heavy sigh and hint of melancholy in his voice would unsettle her, but he couldn't help that. He was missing Lucy. The weather had prevented her from visiting, though he firmly believed she would appear eventually.

'I take it there was no post this morning.'

'No.'

'But there was yesterday, wasn't there? I thought I heard him wobble up the drive on that bicycle of his. No post for me?'

'No. Not for you.'

'Mother, I discern from your tone of voice that you received something of interest. Please tell.'

His mother drew in her bottom lip. She'd been waiting for the right moment to tell him – but then only if she had to. This looked as good a time as any.

'Yes.'

A purposeful abruptness entered his mother's voice. 'I received a letter from Grace. She's visiting sometime before Christmas.'

Devlin stiffened. 'Why?'

'Visiting an old friend in Bath. She asked if she could come and stay.'

'And you said yes? Are you sure you didn't invite her?'

'Absolutely not,' responded his mother with a defiant toss of her head.

She too had been surprised by the request. Grace was Devlin's ex-sweetheart dating back from the time of the Great War.

'But why now?'

'I suppose she saw the announcement of your engagement in *The Times* and was curious to see who had supplanted her.'

'You just said she was visiting an old friend in Bath.'

'Killing two birds with one stone!'

Devlin gritted his teeth. 'I suspect that she wants to give Lucy the once-over, as she might a new horse she's considering buying.' Grace was a keen horsewoman and regularly rode to hounds. Devlin had not been so keen.

'I think you're being a little unfair. Anyway, she's married.'

'But her husband isn't coming.'

'No.'

'She belongs in my past.' He frowned. 'I do wish she wasn't coming.'

His mother lay a gentle hand on his arm. 'Why are you so afraid of an old friend's visit? As you said yourself, she's part of the past.'

'All the more reason to be suspicious of her visit.'

'Don't be silly.'

'Her being the daughter of an earl, I expect she found the news of my marrying my nurse quite amusing.'

His mother tapped his arm reprovingly. 'Devlin, I believe you are overreacting. She's only coming for two days.'

'I'm surprised you invited her. And suspicious. What were you hoping to achieve?' He couldn't help the tone of his voice. Why invite her now? Although his mother had always insisted that she was in favour of his marriage to Lucy, in fact had instigated the alliance, he could never be quite sure.

'I didn't see any harm in doing so. Lucy is your soulmate. You have nothing to fear from Grace.'

Devlin sighed heavily. 'I don't know what I would do without Lucy and that's a fact. As you've just said, she's my soulmate. I only wish she was here now. I'm missing her dreadfully. Bloody weather!'

'You can't expect Lucy to visit any time soon. Not only is the drive icy but so too is the main road. Plus, the sky has that odd yellowish grey colour. I shouldn't be surprised if we don't have more snow. It's certainly cold enough. Very pretty outside and reminiscent of one of those Christmas cards depicting an old inn, horses sweating outside and sheets of unblemished snow on roof and roads...'

Her voice trailed away once she realised that he wasn't going to share his thoughts with her. He could be very enclosed at times.

A picture of absolute silence, he turned back to the window, tracing his fingernails down over a cold pane.

'I might put on boots, a hat and a muffler and go for a stroll.'

It wasn't quite true but intended to placate her curiosity – at least for now.

The truth was that in the absence of Lucy, he was thinking of what had happened between them. He told himself that he hadn't meant it to happen, which was a lie. In his mind, the tingle of their lovemaking remained, like the last notes of a particularly moving concerto. The silky feel of her skin, the smell of her hair and the softness of her lips were conjoined with the movement of their bodies.

Lack of eyesight, the most intense of senses, meant the others he possessed had intensified. Touch was the main one, of course, closely followed by smell, taste and finally hearing. Nothing could compare to touch. Without seeing her with his eyes, his fingertips had conveyed to him the curve of her hip, the compelling rise of each buttock, the pressure of her breasts against his chest. It seemed to him that no woman he'd ever known compared to the feel of her. It was a sensation he wanted to enjoy forever.

Any man would be proud to marry her. And that was the problem. She was perfect. Long before he'd lost his eyesight, he'd seen her as a child with her friends, where she'd seemed to be the centre of attention. The years had rolled on. He was older than her and maimed by a cruel war. The wedding would happen next June. His mother was already writing out a guest list and speaking to caterers. It would be quite an event. Everyone who was anyone would be invited – friends, family and business acquaintances. Everyone would be happy for them, so why did he feel he didn't deserve her, that something would happen to part them? That, in fact, she was only marrying him out of pity.

He blamed that Brontë woman. Both Lucy and his mother had been reading *Jane Eyre* to him, a story he'd seen vividly in his mind's eye, to which he couldn't help making comparisons. Jane, the governess of humble background, Mr Rochester, a brusque man of experience. He hoped he wasn't brusque, but there was no getting away from the fact that he was of a different life experience to his wife.

He heard his mother come close; knew she would ask what he was ruminating about.

'Is there something you want to tell me?'

There was an element of control in her voice that made him think she was holding her breath, dreading what his response might be.

He didn't answer.

She didn't leave it for long before trying again.

'You're not having second thoughts about your marriage to Lucy, are you?'

He bit back a sour response, instead saying, 'What makes you think that?'

The breath she took was almost a sigh, but hesitant. He imagined the piercing look in her eyes, the slight pursing of her lips. There was something that needed saying. If he waited long enough, she would speak her mind before he spoke his. So, he waited, willing her to speak.

The long-awaited full sigh finally came.

'Lucy is right for you. I've never doubted it, so please don't let the issue of class obstruct your happiness. You're not, are you?'

Genuine concern sounded in her voice.

He realised he was holding his breath. What he felt could no longer be held back. It needed to be shared.

'I love Lucy with all my heart and with all my soul. I want to spend my life with her. Eternity too. Forever and ever.'

He heard her emit a deep sigh of relief. 'Good. I'm glad to hear it, but you see...'

She paused a beat. He imagined her long delicate fingers had been interlaced tightly over her middle and were now loosening.

'It's just that I wonder if you're having second thoughts when I see you daydream...'

'Staring out of the window at a scene I cannot see – which means of course that I'm not staring – I'm turning inwards, thinking deep thoughts.'

'I am chastised and apologise unreservedly.' Another deep

sigh before she gave a nervous laugh. 'It feels as though I've invited the whole world to your wedding. My inkpot would be empty and my writing hand limp with exhaustion if I had to inform them it was cancelled. Silly me!'

She patted his hand, hers warm upon his cold one. Always cold. Like the hand of a man who had just come in from an arctic blizzard.

His smile was accompanied by a soft sound that was almost a chuckle. 'I would hate to put you through such a trial. A lot of work for nothing...'

'Very thoughtful of you.' She ignored the hint of sarcasm and paused again in the fashion she often adopted when she was planning a speech. She was good at speeches, good at organising people with a volley of words. A set piece.

'*Jane Eyre* is one of my favourite books, though you already know that I think.'

He visualised the confused expression. Their conversation had gone from his wedding to a work of fiction. He began to outline the story, specifically the bit that was plaguing him.

'If you recall, Jane is the disadvantaged orphan girl, the governess who at that time was looked upon with something close to contempt. It almost feels as though Rochester is doing her a favour, raising her up to become his wife and thus mistress of a big house. Following the fire, everything changes. He's the one who is disadvantaged. Rather than the little wife who depends on him, he ends up depending on her; an older man in ill health dependent on the health and support of his younger wife.'

'Yes. Happy ever after,' said his mother with great exuberance.

'You don't think he was being selfish?'

'No.' His mother sounded puzzled. 'They loved each other.'

'But then he's not me.'

She felt his hand tremble beneath hers.

'Devlin. What do you mean?'

'Like Rochester, I'm a decrepit wreck of a man. And older than Lucy. She's young. I feel that I must remind her that she could have her pick of the young men hereabouts – or anywhere for that matter. I don't want her to feel obliged to marry me, and most of all, I have no wish to be pitied.'

'Devlin!'

The smile on her son's face was sad and thin.

He fell to silence and when he opened his mouth, he'd changed the subject.

'Is this weather likely to last, do you think?'

'The gardeners say so.' She sounded puzzled, even afraid.

'I can't get into town – not even into the quarry office. Though, doubtless, they won't miss me. It's not as though I'm a big cog in that particular wheel.'

For some time, Devlin had contributed as best he could in the site office, listening and giving his opinions. But it wasn't work that was on his mind.

His thoughts kept going back to the beautiful moments when he and Lucy had made love and the world had melted away. Yet again he'd felt like lord of all he surveyed, a king among kings and the luckiest man in the world. He'd survived the war unscathed until just before the end so knew beyond doubt that luck was like breath steaming on cold air; it didn't last.

Lucy was always uppermost in his mind. Just a few days ago she'd fallen to silence, her thoughts seemingly far away as she'd cut his hair. It was a deeply intimate sensation. Every so often, she'd stroked his hair flat so she could evaluate where to cut next. Her hands were soft, her fingers sure in their movements. Comb and fingers had traced a path along the nape of his neck, not sexual but an innocent movement that had made him tingle. Such was the power of touch alone.

Moved to make comment, he'd stilled the travelling hand and kissed the tips of her fingers.

'You will still marry me?' he'd asked her.

'Of course.' She'd kissed the top of his head. 'Why do you ask?'

'Because I want you to cut my hair for the rest of my life.'

She'd laughed at that. He imagined her throwing her head back, her white throat, her neck swanlike.

'Unless you have other things to do, of course.'

'Like what?'

'Attending social events. You know that in time you'll take my mother's place as Lady of the Manor. Has that occurred to you?'

She'd fallen to silence. He hadn't thought much of it at the time, but on reflection he wished he'd enquired if anything was the matter.

After taking a deep breath, she'd responded.

'Just think of it, me, Lucy Daniels, brought up to serve, not to be waited on. I'm not sure I'll ever get used to being in such a position.'

'Of course you will.' He'd held her hand more tightly and told her he could never let her go, could not see his life without her in it.

She'd also said something about being committed to him, that she was his eyes.

It was only later in the depths of the night when the sound of guns had recurred in his mind, echoes of that terrible time when his sight had been taken. His face was wet with tears when he'd jerked himself awake, feeling helpless. He depended on others to see the world. He walked with a stick. At night, he was plagued by nightmares. What right did he have to impose all this pain and decrepitude on her.

'I wonder when Lucy will be able to get out here. I will send the car when the roads are a bit clearer.'

His mother's voice brought him back to the here and now.

Obviously, she'd guessed who he was thinking about.

'Absence doesn't just make the heart grow fonder,' he said somewhat glibly. 'It makes you think.'

'I trust they are good thoughts.'

Although she sounded forthright, he sensed concern hovering just beneath the surface.

He didn't answer. He couldn't admit to her this feeling of selfishness and a fear that Lucy was marrying him out of pity. The sooner the bad weather cleared, and she could get here, the sooner he could reassure himself that all was well.

10

Homefield Alley was a place where Victorian terraced houses nestled cheek by jowl behind gardens. Some of the gardens were choked with a forest of weeds. In others – the majority as it worked out – the dark earth had been prepared to take neat rows of carrots, onions, potatoes and cabbages. At this time of year, the cottages looked cosy enough when their windows showed a light. Otherwise, they looked lifeless, except for the pale unwashed faces of kids gazing round-eyed from doorways and the square windows which held back more light than they let in.

This alley and the other mean streets in that area were the province of District Nurse Gwen Peebles.

She had been called out in the early hours to attend a woman who had gone into labour late the previous evening but had waited to call her out until the morning. And why not? Everyone knew that babies favoured those grey hours just after midnight. For the most part, they were right. Luckily there'd been a thaw, her bicycle wheels splashing through surface water covering the road and racing past her down the gutters.

Task done, baby born, Sister Peebles lovingly wrapped the

newborn into the spotless pillowcase supplied by the mother before applying the torn-off half of a blanket. Cocooned in extra warmth, she handed the squirming bundle to its mother. 'There you are, Mrs Reakes. And a lovely little girl she is too.'

Anne Reakes, her face lined with exhaustion and her damp hair clinging around her sweating complexion, looked lovingly down into the little pink face. 'Well, she got here regardless, didn't she.' Exhaustion was in her words, but the divine joy of having something tangible at the end of her labours had brought graciousness to her eyes.

Gwen Peebles smiled broadly and didn't ask what the new mother meant by her comment, though could guess what the 'regardless' referred to. Best to concentrate on the positive and leave any negative thoughts to the past, and possibly the future.

'A little sister for your other children. I bet they're looking forward to seeing her.'

She knew from experience that the children had been looking forward to the arrival of the new baby more than her mother, who already had five children and wasn't much older than twenty-six. Another mouth to feed.

Same the world over, she thought.

Gwen had been a district nurse back in Wales's Rhondda Valley. The women there had been more outspoken about the 'frailties', as they put it, of their bodies. It was a polite way of mentioning pregnancy; in the pudding club; expecting; methods of making them regular, in other words they wanted to see their periods again, the monthly bleeding assuring them that they weren't carrying yet another addition to their already large families.

She found the women of Norton Dene less open about their bodily functions, though goodness knew why. They were miners' and quarrymen's wives just like the ones in Wales, but for some reason there was a difference.

Fastening the buckles on her all-purpose leather bag, she smiled down at the newborn and its mother. 'I'll call in again next week. Let me know if you have any problems,' she said cheerfully.

Mrs Reakes nodded and expressed her thanks, which Gwen accepted with a dismissive wave.

'All in a day's work. But I'm here whenever you need me.'

Yes, it was another mouth to feed, but Gwen Peebles knew that the sheer fatigue of giving birth was forgotten once a mother had sight of her newborn child. Gwen was pretty sure she wouldn't be called upon for help.

'I'm going to name her Gwen, after you, if that's all right?'

Gwen blushed involuntarily. 'I'm flattered.' She tickled the baby's cheek, curled against her mother's breast, rosebud lips sucking at a nipple on a breast enlarged with milk. 'Just look at her. Making herself at home.'

There was something Gwen couldn't quite read in the new mother's eyes. It could have been contemplation, perhaps regret.

'She didn't ask to come into the world, but now she's here...'

Gwen finished the sentence for her. 'She's cherished.'

After saying her goodbyes, Gwen collected her bicycle from where she'd left it leaning against the garden wall, fixed her saddlebag on the back and prepared to swing her leg over, ready for a cup of tea back at the hospital.

'Sister Peebles.'

The miners' cottages were linked in an unbroken terrace, roughly twelve or more. They had square front gardens, three windows and one front door. The rear of the houses butted against a green slope, at the top of which rumbled trains carrying aggregate and coal to London to the east or Bristol and other large cities to the west, north and south.

She recognised the woman who called out to her as Pearl Barnett who lived three doors along from the cottage she'd just come out of. She too was pregnant, though not much past four months.

Like a lot of the wives of working men, Mrs Barnett had a sallow complexion, though Gwen guessed that at one time she'd been a good-looking young woman. Like Mrs Reakes, she was worn down with too many pregnancies and too hard a life, but she had energy from a source Gwen couldn't quite put her finger on.

Pearl came rushing out of her front gate, her apron flapping against a dull brown dress and her hair in curlers. Most of her teeth were rotted away thanks to pregnancy, poor dental hygiene and an even poorer diet. Potatoes and bread were a mainstay. A slice of beef or chicken never tasted.

'I wanted a quiet word,' she said once she was standing in front of Gwen and able to speak without being overheard.

'I'm all ears,' said Gwen, lowering her voice to the same decibels as Pearl's. 'How are you?'

She glanced down at Pearl's belly, which bulged a bit though not too unduly.

'That's what I wanted to tell you. I'm fine. No need to book me in for a confinement with you or the midwife. My best friend's visited.'

The 'best friend' to these women was a monthly period. Pearl was telling her that she was no longer pregnant.

'Oh I'm sorry.'

'I'm not,' Pearl retorted.

Gwen nodded in understanding. 'I see. Would you like me to examine you just to make sure everything is in order?'

'No need. I'm feeling fine. Never been better.' She cackled in a nervous manner and looked truly joyful that she was no longer expecting, which came as no great surprise. Gwen had seen that same exultant look on the faces of other women who did not welcome another addition to their already large families.

'That's good.' Gwen leaned in closer. 'Look. If you don't want any more children, why don't you pop into the clinic and we can get you fitted with something that will stop you getting in the family way again?'

An oddly coy and youthful expression came to Pearl's mature face and her eyes flickered nervously, as though afraid someone might be about to leap onto her for saying the wrong thing. 'I don't know about that. If I'm seen and my old man finds out, he'll go at me something rotten. He don't believe in all that stuff. Says it should all be left to God and nature.'

Gwen felt an inner collapse of something close to faith and enlightenment.

'It's your body, not his,' she said briskly. 'Your choice. What if you get pregnant again? You might not miscarry next time. Please excuse me saying this, but you're not getting any younger.'

She'd expected Pearl to at least give it a second thought. Instead, she looked pleased with herself.

'Well, Sister Peebles. There are other ways and means.' She took a newspaper she'd had tucked beneath her arm and waved it meaningfully.

Was that a wink Gwen detected?

'Wait,' she said, meaning to explain further and even offer to have a word with Mr Barnett regarding the prospect of limiting their family. But Pearl was already through her garden gate and halfway to her front door.

Gwen surmised that it wouldn't be too long before she saw

Pearl again, but that wink had meant something. There are other ways, she'd said. Gwen frowned at what those ways might be.

Deciding there was nothing more she could do at present; she cocked her leg over her bike and cycled off in the direction of the hospital and the hot cup of tea she so badly needed.

* * *

The Orchard Cottage Hospital held not just a peaceful atmosphere but also one of hope. Gwen had noticed it the moment she'd arrived from Wales to fulfil the position of district nurse a while back. It was still evident now.

Doctor Frances Brakespeare had a lot to do with it. She'd come here from London, where she'd come up against the male establishment and was unafraid to change things and try the latest ideas. Gwen had liked her from the first. The door to her office was always open – as it was now.

Gwen tapped lightly on the door. Her intention was to report on the events of that morning. Frances liked to keep her finger on the pulse of what went on.

A leafy green plant stood on a ceramic stand in the corner, just to the right of the doctor's shoulder. There was a picture on the wall of a group of women, feisty-looking types, and from what she'd heard, one of them was the woman who had adopted Frances from the workhouse. That in itself impressed on Gwen what a formidable character Frances was, to have been born in such dire circumstances and worked her way to becoming a doctor.

Frances was dressed in a pale blue silk dress with a white collar and cuffs. To many, she had the look of a nurse, with her bearing that of a matron perhaps. Whether she chose her dress with that in mind was a strong possibility. Rather that perhaps than the tweedy jackets and waistcoats so beloved of doctors who had trained for their qualification in a different age. Her serene demeanour evoked trust in those who met her and the way she dressed gave her an air of confidence.

On this gloomy morning, when the ice seemed reluctant to melt and the first flurries of snow threatened to inflict more difficulties, the atmosphere in the doctor's office was, as always, like a warm oasis in a hostile world.

Frances had a look of welcome on her face, and kindness in her eyes when she invited Gwen to take a seat and share the pot of tea set for two on the tray on her desk.

She smiled. 'Lucy always brings two teacups. I think I have a reputation for entertaining – or keeping people here whilst I run through my unending plans for the future of the hospital. Looks like you're the one I'm going to bore to death this morning.'

The latter was added with humour. In Gwen's experience, Frances was never boring. She sat down gladly and waited as Frances poured the tea.

The town had been surprised when a female doctor had been appointed to run the cottage hospital. What did a woman know? Doctors were always men, weren't they?

Gwen banished the annoyances that peeved her and turned her thoughts to more serious matters.

Not being insensitive to what she could see before her, Frances asked her what it was she wanted to tell her.

'What is it, Sister Peebles? I can see from your expression that something is troubling you.'

'Yes. There is. I called at Homefield Alley this morning...'

Frances picked up her teacup and saucer, sipped lightly, her grey eyes calm as she waited for Gwen to begin.

Gwen took a big gulp of tea, wetting her whistle before she proceeded to put her worst fears into words.

'With regard to the woman who was brought in aborting, possibly due to some kind of medicine she had taken or...' She paused. 'Other methods.'

Frances frowned. 'Go on.'

Heavy frown lines appeared on her forehead as she considered what to say next. 'I don't know for sure, but I think you might find some answers in Homefield Alley. Mrs Barnett looked quite smug that she was no longer pregnant. Almost crowed it in my face, she did.'

'You think she might have got hold of some pills.'

Gwen nodded and took another sip of tea but still seemed reluctant.

'I believe the pills were made from tansy and turpentine but can't confirm,' Frances informed.

Sister Peebles' eyes fluttered and her lips shifted from side to side as she fought to spit out what she wanted to say. 'I think we have a wider problem – or it's connected.' Her eyes flickered. 'Or it might not be. I might be jumping to conclusions.'

She went on to tell Frances about Pearl Barnett. 'Now I know a few of these women concoct their own medicine – a bottle of gin and a hot bath – but I couldn't help feeling that she was inferring something else.'

Frances rested her chin on her hands, elbows resting on the desktop. Her eyes narrowed as she analysed what Sister Peebles had said. 'Are you suggesting that someone has set up shop and is dishing out solutions to women's problems under the counter, so to speak?'

'I think so,' said Sister Peebles. 'Not necessarily from around here, but she was waving a newspaper around when she was telling me this. I put two and two together. The only thing I failed to do was to note the name of the newspaper. I should have asked her for it.'

The realisation of what the dead woman had gone through was bad enough, but worse was the fact that someone had undoubtedly made money from her dire predicament. But who?

Frances got up from her chair. There was more tea in the pot, but she had no appetite for it. Her mind was fixed on finding out what was going on, but where to start?

'All we can do is keep our eyes open. Let me know if you hear anything.'

'About medicines for miscarrying?'

'Or by any other means.'

Sister Peebles knew by the serious tone that the doctor was referring to an abortionist. Everyone knew there were those who would take payment for 'getting rid of little problems'. It was an old practice going back over centuries and whilst the demand was there, it wasn't likely to go away.

* * *

All of this was mentioned in a conversation on the telephone that morning.

Lady Araminta was adamant that although the woman was dead and would shortly be buried, the matter was not.

'I've had a word with the chief constable and informed him that I am not pleased with the lack of progress. We were promised that the photograph and story would be circulated throughout the country and then someone who knows something might be able to help. Once that person comes forward we might get somewhere,' she said indignantly.

The case of the dead woman was not the only subject Araminta mentioned.

'Something is wrong with Devlin, but when I ask what it is,

he blanks me out. It's not physical, you understand. But he's musing on something. In his mind.'

Frances couldn't help the knowing smile that came to her face. Her ladyship liked to know what was going on. In lesser circles, she would have been termed a nosy parker, but she was more than that. It wasn't so much about being in control. It was more about ensuring that everyone in her orbit led a happy life and if she could make it happier and more content for them, she would.

'Perhaps it's Lucy that should be asking him,' Frances offered.

'No. I don't think that would be wise. You see, I'm worried that he's having second thoughts about marrying her.'

'Because she's of lowly background?'

'Partly, though I'm not sure. Do you recall me telling you about his former fiancée?'

'Yes.'

Frances recalled it very well. Devlin had been engaged to a very presentable young woman before the war ended. On his return, blinded in the last year of the war, he'd terminated the relationship.

'I've recently received a letter from her to say that she needs to visit the area and wondered if she could stay for two or three days.'

Frances suddenly had a worrying thought. 'Is she coming to see Devlin?'

'No. I believe their relationship is firmly in the past. Besides, she's married and has two children.' Araminta paused. 'I still can't help but think there must be a reason for this sudden visit. Though I'm intrigued, rather than suspicious.'

'Did she say why?'

'Something about visiting a close relative, but I wasn't convinced. It could be that she's heard about the forthcoming marriage. I believe she may still carry a torch for my son even though she is married and has two children. There. There it is! Will you have a word with him, Doctor?'

'Does he know that she's coming?'

'Yes.'

'And his response?'

'He's not keen. He said the same as you, why now.'

'And Lucy?'

'I've told her that Grace is an old friend. That's all.'

Frances got to her feet. 'I'll adopt my best bedside manner and say I'm just calling to see how he is. And to ask how the wedding invitations are proceeding.'

'Do that.'

* * *

Devlin was listening to the recording of yet another book on his gramophone. He called 'enter' in response to the knock on the door.

'Devlin.'

'Doctor. I wasn't expecting you.'

'What with the bad weather I haven't seen you for a few days. I do apologise.'

'You don't need to.' He reached out to the gramophone, picked up the needle arm and switched it off. 'I'm in fine fettle.'

'You do seem so,' Frances said, smiling as she took the chair opposite from him. 'I expect that, like the rest of us, you're looking forward to June.'

'Ah yes,' he said, somewhat sardonically. 'June.'

Frances frowned. 'I thought you'd be looking forward to your wedding. I know that Lucy is.'

At mention of Lucy, his expression altered. For a moment, he seemed to think on that before saying anything more.

'She's not nervous?'

'Why should she be? She quite often hums the Wedding March as she goes about her duties.'

'Does she?' He gave a little chuckle.

'Yes. Marches around the ward as though it's an orchestra playing, not just her humming under her breath.'

The truth was that she had indeed heard Lucy humming the Wedding March, though not so much of late.

'Is there anything troubling you? Medical or otherwise?'

He hesitated before saying that there was not.

Frances wasn't entirely convinced but felt reassured by the slight loosening of his jaw and relaxation in his shoulders.

Whatever might be troubling him, he was keeping it to himself. Coping with it.

11

The woman who stepped from the train at Norton Dene Junction carried herself as though a rod had been inserted down her back. Like a metal mannequin, designed to forever stand in a shop window wearing sumptuous garments that only the very rich could afford, a tailored suit beneath a three-quarter-length mink coat.

Alfred, the chauffeur, recognising her from Lady Araminta's description, tapped the brim of his cap in time-honoured fashion. 'Lady Leinster-Parry?'

An aloof countenance jerked in his direction and a pair of striking eyes fixed resolutely on his face. 'Yes.'

'My name is Alfred. Lady Compton-Dixon sent me to take you to Orchard Manor. Do you mind telling me the whereabouts of your luggage?'

He half turned towards the well-dressed man getting off the train behind her. He was carrying a pair of coffee-coloured leather cases trimmed with brown snakeskin which were obviously hers. They were far too glamorous to belong to a man. They had to be hers.

His assumption proved correct.

'Here you are, old man. Over to you.'

The two cases were placed on the platform beside the new arrival's silk-stockinged legs and shiny patent shoes.

'Good day to you, your ladyship.'

The man stalked off, which Alfred, having met all sorts from the upper class, took with a pinch of salt, though a real gentleman would have helped with the cases or found a porter to take them to the car. He might also have slipped him half a crown for his trouble. He didn't do that either. Still, that was as may be, he had a job to do.

'This way, your ladyship.'

He held the door open for her before strapping the cases on the back and covering them with a tarpaulin to prevent them getting covered in mud.

The bad weather had gone, although there was nostalgia for a white Christmas. Apart from that it was hoped by one and all that the New Year, once it had arrived, would show a more clement face, though nobody was banking on it.

Water was lying in the ruts dug out by the ice. The car ploughed through mud that was as thick as oxtail gravy, the tyres sending up spouts of the glutinous muck from the deepest puddles.

There was no conversation. Alfred was quite used to the upper crust being engaged with their own thoughts and lives far removed from ordinary folk. He was a man of the old school. With the exception of Lady Compton-Dixon who talked with him about the town or the weather, or how the harvest would do this year, or Nurse Daniels, a sweet girl who always asked about his arthritis, women tended to talk about fashion, families and social events – mostly to their own kind. He cared little for any of it. Fashion was something only the rich could afford, ditto the social events. As for families, he had none himself and had no regrets.

Throughout the journey, his passenger stared out at the passing scene, the sombre fields, the stalks of bare branches stark and black against the sky. Her face was pale, eyes deep-set pools of an indiscernible colour.

Every so often, a flock of crows dived onto the few remaining stalks left over from the harvest of late August, the ground now hard and almost as black as coal. Such was winter.

A silent journey ended in front of the Palladian pillars at the entrance of Orchard Manor.

Grace sucked in her breath on seeing the façade she had not sighted since her break-up with Devlin in that last dreadful year of the Great War. Logically, old memories would have resurfaced, sweet moments she still held dear. They didn't. Her mind was preoccupied with the true reason she was here, a seeking of a truth which would finally close the door on her marriage. Evidence gained from an unarguable source.

Lady Araminta awaited her in the drawing room, her kindly eyes echoing the warmth of her smile. 'My dear, Grace. It's so wonderful to see you.'

'I hope I'm not inconveniencing you in any way.'

Air kisses were exchanged, Lady Grace making sure that her pursed red lips did not land on Araminta's unblemished cheek.

'Of course you're not. You're looking well.'

Lady Araminta eyed the fur coat worn over a black and tan checked jacket and skirt. The outfit was completed with a black fur hat trimmed with speckled net that reached the middle of her nose. It was not the right kind of attire for a stay in the country, more Chelsea or Kensington. Grace had London and big city life stamped all over her.

'Thank you.'

'I'll ring for tea.'

'That's very kind of you.'

'Not at all.' She indicated a chair with a wave of her hand. 'Please. Take a seat and tell me the reason for your visit – the true reason,' she added. Her firm adjunct elicited a flickering of deep grey eyes that had tints of turquoise at their heart.

'Do you mind if I join you for tea after I've unpacked? I am a little tired after the journey.'

Araminta deduced that Grace had not wished any questions to be asked and not one iota of judgement to be made. However, she was nothing if not patient.

'Of course. Join me in the drawing room as soon as you've unpacked. I'll ring for tea then.'

'Thank you.'

Araminta's smile disappeared as she watched her leave the room. Whatever the reason, she was determined to find out why Grace was here and she didn't think it had anything to do with her son. If that had been so, Grace might have asked after Devlin's health, but she had not.

She recalled the letter she'd received and the phone conversation that had followed when she'd been tardy in answering. Although she had informed Devlin of the letter, she had not told him of the telephone conversation.

'I desperately need your help.'

'My dear, whatever is the matter?'

'I can't tell you by phone or in a letter. It's most personal. I'm sure that you can help me.'

Araminta knew that Grace was married, but other than that was unaware of the more minute details of her life. As for her reference to visiting a relative close by, she didn't recall her having one. She'd read in *The Times* of the passing of her parents and an uncle. Was she telling the truth, or was there something else? Whatever it was, she would know soon enough.

However, she'd always thought Grace straightforward and full of confidence. Now she wondered if she'd judged her correctly. There was something more distant about her now.

I will know soon, she told herself. *The truth will out.*

* * *

Grace had stayed at Orchard Manor before in the days when she'd been engaged to Devlin so knew the room she'd been placed in. The old manor house had changed little since those times.

This was the rose room. The walls were covered in a chintzy wallpaper, huge pink cabbage roses climbing up dark green trellis, the bed quilt in a paler pink with a dark red border.

Going to the window, she pulled aside the net curtains and looked out at the gardens surrounding the old manor house without really seeing it. She was trying to formulate her thoughts. Devlin's mother was canny, to say the least, and must be wondering exactly why she was here. Yes, she did have a close relative hereabouts, but that wasn't the true reason she was here.

Turning away from the window, she went to the suitcase lying on the floor after specifically telling a maid not to unpack.

'I'm quite capable of unpacking my own luggage,' she'd ordered when the maid had shown reluctance to leave the room. 'Please,' she'd added, aware that her tone had been a little sharp.

Taking a firm grip of the tan leather handle, she heaved the case from the floor and placed in on the bed. From within its confines, she brought out an article snipped from a newspaper along with a photograph – a death mask photograph of a young woman. The police were asking if anyone knew her. They were also making enquiries of the identity of the man who had left her outside the Orchard Cottage Hospital.

Grace felt the blood drain from her face and her bottom lip quiver on yet again seeing that familiar face. She needed to know how she died, some pointer that evidenced her husband's involvement, evidence of the woman's demise that she could use in divorce proceedings.

Even now, much as she hated her husband, she had to be sure. Only then could she get rid of him for good even if it meant using a substantial amount of the profit she would gain from the sale of the house to London Underground once all the details were finalised. The sooner the better as far as she was concerned.

12

Lucy breezed into Devlin's room, desperate to see how he was reacting to his ex-fiancée's visit.

'Your old flame has arrived. I must say that despite being married with two children, she's very glamorous.' She allowed brevity, a sure way of hiding her nervousness. Would she measure up well to the stunning woman she'd espied disappearing up the stairs and along the landing?

Well, she was going to give her a run for her money. She'd prepared herself to look gorgeous in her favourite dress, the one specially reserved for dinner at Orchard Manor. It was a very fine dress, clung to her figure, the silk undulating like a wave on the sea as she moved. Her very favourite, but on seeing Grace, a society beauty, she felt dowdy, the comparison between a brown mouse and a bird of paradise. It was hard to admit, but impressing Devlin's former fiancée mattered. Her heart fluttered at the prospect. She so didn't want to let him down.

To help raise her spirits, she twirled enough for the silk to sing so Devlin would hear and could guess which dress she was wearing. It was pale turquoise embroidered with silver thread in a deep 'V' at the waistline.

To her surprise, Devlin said nothing about her dress. Perhaps he hadn't heard.

She did it again.

'I'm wearing the turquoise. Your favourite. My favourite too.'

'That's nice.'

His lack of comment and enthusiasm caused the corners of her mouth to turn downwards. It wasn't unknown for him to occasionally turn inwards, and she easily forgave him when he did. After all, he'd been through a terrible time in the Great War, but she'd learned to deal with his darker moods.

He was sitting on the edge of the bed, the ends of his bow tie dangling black against the white of his shirt. A silky skein of dark blond hair fell over his forehead. She was tempted to take it between her fingers and smooth it away from his puckered frown.

He looked out of sorts, a saggy downwards pull to his face, a blankness of expression. Grace was the reason of course. He'd been angry with his mother for inviting her and had stressed that he didn't want to see her.

'Has she called on you, yet?' Lucy asked, steeling herself for whatever answer he might give.

'No.' He frowned. 'I really don't know what she's doing here.'

'Perhaps she wants to look me over,' she countered laughingly. 'Like a racehorse. To check if I have I any discernible quality.'

She desisted from mentioning breeding possibilities, but it was there at the front of her mind.

'I don't think it's anything to do with me. Our youthful intimacies were curtailed many years ago.'

She wore a pensive, slightly worried look. Devlin was looking boyishly forlorn. She only hoped he had not changed his mind about marrying her. She'd be ruined for life if that happened. Still, she held off telling him. Her natural exuberance had allayed misgivings about their differing backgrounds, up until now. Getting pregnant was sure to be frowned on. The situation might yet be saved by the arrival of her period. That was what she was holding on to.

For now, she would put a brave face on it, determined to look and sound as effervescent as she ever was.

'Would you like me to deal with your tie? I know how you hate this thing. An ordinary tie is bad enough, but this penguin suit, stiff collar and black tie must be torture.' She forced a jovial cheerfulness.

'If you could.'

He got to his feet. Her fingers tangled with the ends of the hanging tie.

His scent was clean, without a trace of tobacco that so many men wore about their person. He'd told her he'd given up smoking of any kind back in the war, hating the taste and smell of it because it reminded him of cordite.

She gritted her teeth as she wrestled with the bow tie, ensuring his detachable stiff collar wasn't likely to strangle him. Why did men wear such awkward clothes? Was it something to do with the fact that they no longer wore metal armour into battle, and this was the best they had come up with? She reminded herself that most women still wore corsets; nothing could be as uncomfortable as that.

Her thoughts returned to the reason Grace was here. Why now? Even Araminta was curious. If anyone could discern the reason, it would be her. As long as it was nothing to do with her past liaison with Devlin. Pray God it wasn't that.

'There. All done.'

She patted both of his shoulders and maintained her cheerful demeanour and a wide smile that he could not see. Unfortunately, his expression did not come even close to matching hers and made her wonder at just how resentful he felt towards his former sweetheart.

'You haven't decried my ex-fiancée's reason for being here. I sense there's a reason. I'm curious.'

She stroked his brow. 'It's all in the past, Devlin.'

'She invokes dark memories in me.'

When she studied his face, she sorely regretted not having known him years ago.

'Do you hate her?'

'I used to, though I don't really think it was about her. It was the time. I can't help linking her to what happened to me, to the deaths of old friends, carnage. Sheer carnage.'

Lucy found herself swallowing hard as she sought a way to placate his inner demons.

'And you think her visit might rekindle that hatred?'

His sightless eyes seemed to stare into the distance as he contemplated her question. A pair of tawny eyebrows met in a deep 'V' on his forehead.

'It's confusing me.'

Her heart went out to him. Never had she heard him sound so vulnerable – so hurt – and it brought a lump to her throat, and a feeling inside that undermined her confidence. She needed to be reassured. To that end, she asked, 'Your decision to part was by mutual agreement, wasn't it?'

'Yes. I didn't want to be a burden to anyone, and she didn't want to have to deal with a broken man when she could have a whole man, one without blemish.'

She detected bitterness in that last sentence. It begged the question why there had been such misgivings between him and his former intended but was not an issue between them? Or was it?

She decided to make light of it.

'I'm not jealous, Devlin, and I can cope with her being curious about me, if that's what's worrying you.'

At her words, he seemed to come out of himself, shaking his head and covering her hands with his. 'It's not that. Grace is a reminder of a time when my experiences in the war made my mind feel as though it might burst.' Head hanging forward, he sank back onto the bed and folded his hands between his knees.

Fearing too loud a voice, too quick a movement would break him in two, she joined him there, one arm around him, her free hand stroking that loose silken strand back into his hair.

'Darling. You can tell me anything. You should know that.'

She waited expectantly, unsure of where this might go.

Finally, it seemed just by his stance that he'd come to a decision.

'I've never told you of my experiences – not in any great detail.'

'You don't have to. They're over now.'

'Over but not forgotten.'

'Then tell me,' she said, her lips close to his ear. She stopped stroking his head and wound her arm tight around his body.

There was no response at first, just that calm sightless gaze fixed on the failing daylight beyond the window. But seeing more. Quite what, she could only guess at.

'My mate Bill went to set up targets for rifle practice. A mortar came in from out of nowhere. The Bosch weren't practising. They were still out to do damage.'

She saw him swallow and his jaw tighten. Fear that she might have done wrong made her unsure whether to encourage him to go on or to let sleeping dogs lie.

At first, a deep breath, holding it in, then letting it out along with some of the horrors he had held inside.

'I could see all his ribs. The flesh was ripped off him like when you see a butcher cleave the meat from the carcase of an animal.'

Lucy controlled her urge to gasp in horror, though what he'd said made her sick to her stomach.

His fingers tightened over hers almost to the point where it hurt.

She resisted crying out. She had to be there for him. 'It must have been awful.'

He nodded in an absent-minded way, almost as though he had retreated inside. Without him saying, she chose to believe that he could see his memories etched in vivid details behind his closed eyelids. 'It was.' His voice came out in a subdued monotone. He went on. 'But that was only one incident. I saw a lot more than that, equally horrific. I saw men become slabs of meat, piles of bones, features unrecognisable. Headless. Legless. Armless.' He shook his head. 'All manner of savagery. In my naivety, I welcomed losing my sight because it meant I could no longer see the horrors, but the memories remained behind my eyes and in my mind. I still close my eyes to blot them out. But I can't. They are there. Part of my soul.'

'Horrible.' She whispered the word, but it still seemed too loud.

'In the midst of death, I saw a priest administering a communion wafer to a dying man. Shells were exploding all around, sending fountains of mud into the air, clods of it coming down and sending the horses running. Men were screaming for their mothers, for relief from pain and for redemption in the world to come.' A sarcastic curling of his mouth, a breath tinged with humour before he said, 'I've never grasped how a single wafer might give comfort. But I suppose it did. Those who are about to die paving their way without pain to whatever might come after.'

There was nothing she could say to follow Devlin baring his soul. It was hard to deal with the visions he'd transferred from his mind to hers, but she had to be strong for his sake. She knew without asking that he'd imparted to her much that had never been heard by anyone else.

She kissed the top of his head, then gently raised him to his feet and brushed his shoulders as though they weren't already brushed and clean. 'I'm with you, Devlin. I'll always be with you. Shall we go downstairs for dinner now?'

He nodded. 'Yes.'

* * *

The dining room at Orchard Manor was comfortable rather than grand, though it might have been so at one time. Too much history had happened since then.

Three windows stretching from floor to ceiling were girdled by thick heavy curtains of green velvet edged with gold fringes. Night's darkness ruled outside, but inside gas-lit chandeliers shone down on the guests and candles flickered from silver candelabra.

If there was one thing Araminta loved, it was hosting a dinner party. Not that it was much of one, there being only six of them. Herself, of course, Lucy and Devlin, Grace, plus the Reverend Gregory Sampson and Doctor Frances Brakespeare. Perhaps she might have a chance to ask Frances if anything was troubling her. It might be something or nothing, but there were occasions when her mind seemed to be elsewhere.

In time she might find out what that was, but not this

evening. This evening was for warm conversation and the exchange of banter, views and news of their individual lives.

First, she wanted to know the true reason for Grace's visit. She took the decanter from the butler and began offering a drink to Grace before the others arrived.

'Sherry?'

'Yes. Thank you.'

The cut glass caught the light from the overhead chandelier as it was passed from one soft hand and manicured fingers to another.

Grace was dressed in a silver lurex dress, a cowl effect at the front and an open back. The sheath of fine material clung to her feminine curves.

'You're looking very well, Grace. Married life must agree with you.'

'I try to take care of myself,' she replied in a rather perfunctory manner.

Araminta was not one to beat about the bush. She believed in being honest. 'You don't sound too sure, my dear.'

There was a sympathetic tone to Araminta's voice, but on receiving Grace's letter her sharp mind had perceived that something was going on, so much so that she'd sent off a hasty telegram to her old friend Deborah in London to see what she might know. Rumours abounded within the London social scene, gossip about who was in love with whom – regardless of being married to another – or whose fortunes were in danger of crashing to earth. Many a wealthy family had found themselves in dire straits, mainly thanks to a male head of the house who was keener on gambling or women than on business.

Deborah had been best friend to Izzy Brakespeare, guardian and mentor of Doctor Frances Brakespeare. It was through her that Frances had learned of her parentage. She'd been Izzy's confidante and seemed to know everybody. Ear to the ground over many years, she gathered social gossip as some people did flowers. If anyone had heard gossip about Grace's marriage, it would be her.

Just as Araminta had hoped, the response had been swift. There were rumours. Sir Gerald had the reputation of being a serial adulterer. That was the general drift of Deborah's reply.

'Here's to the blessed estate of matrimony,' offered Araminta, a curdled smile on her face as she raised her glass.

'Thank you.'

'You look just as ravishing as when I last saw you – allowing for the passing of the years, of course.'

'I've put on a little weight since having the children,' Grace responded.

'Nonsense. In fact, I would say you're slimmer than when I last saw you.' A worried frown creased Araminta's brow. 'Are you sure you're eating properly, my dear?'

'Yes,' Grace answered laughingly. 'Running around after the children keeps me fit.'

'They're at school surely?'

The pale face flushed slightly. 'I try to have them with me as much as possible. And I play tennis.'

'And your husband is doing well?'

'Yes. He is.'

For the most part, her hands were steady as she took out a cigarette, placed it in an ebony holder and waited for the butler, who now stepped forward to light it. Once lit, her lips formed a tight fit around the holder. A breath of smoke rose over the dining table.

Araminta fancied she was about to try hijacking the conversation. She was proved right when Grace said, 'I passed Devlin's intended on the stairs. She's very pretty. And an ideal match.

After all, it couldn't be more convenient for him to marry his nurse.'

'Lucy is a sweet girl,' said Araminta, taking a sip from her glass.

'It's rather romantic, him marrying a nobody.'

'She's not a nobody,' returned Araminta in quite a strident manner. 'She's the woman he loves, and she loves him. That's what makes her a somebody.'

Grace concentrated on the plume of smoke from her cigarette and the halo it formed beneath the overhead lights. 'I suppose so. I haven't seen him yet. Is he well?'

'Yes. He was in the Slough of Despond a while back, that place in *The Pilgrim's Progress* by John Bunyan. You may have read it.'

'I have not.'

'A marshy, dark place, difficult to get out of, and then this nurse came along and helped him out of it. We owe her a great debt.'

Grace responded. 'She is from a lowly background, I presume.'

Araminta gritted her teeth. 'I don't care about that and neither does he. I think they would be good together even if Devlin had no inheritance.'

'I apologise for being so forthright with my opinion. I wasn't criticising. Just wondering.' She gave a little laugh. 'I've so much on my mind.'

'So, it would seem,' returned Araminta. She held on tightly to the narrative. 'The advantage with being wealthy and having influence is that you can afford and obtain a divorce should the need arise. I wonder at this moment in time how many separations are being pursued through the courts, especially in London.'

Mention of divorces and courts brought a startled change in her guest's eyes that told her she'd hit the nail hard on the head. It seemed the word from Deborah was correct. That was perhaps the reason Grace was here, to lick her wounds.

Being of a certain breed, one of those who valued their breeding and the public perception of their lot, Grace recovered her equilibrium and smiled. 'Modern times,' she said as though that explained everything.

Yet Araminta perceived a brittle discomfort, a tightening of the jaw, a sudden jerkiness in her movements.

'I see the table is set for six,' said Grace, after giving the table settings the once-over. 'Devlin and his beloved of course. Who else is expected?'

'Doctor Brakespeare and the Reverend Gregory Sampson will be joining us.'

'A doctor and a vicar! Not too dull, I hope.'

'Not at all. I'm sure you'll find them good company. The Reverend Gregory Sampson is vicar of St Michael's. Doctor Brakespeare is our very much valued resident physician at the Orchard Cottage Hospital.'

'The man in charge of your pet project! I can't wait to meet him. He should be interesting.' Her sudden outburst had an air of excitement that didn't really seem to suit the occasion. A little odd in fact.

'She is,' said Araminta pointedly, a faint smile framing her lips. 'Doctor Frances Brakespeare is a woman. The hospital has much improved since her arrival. She has very modern views and is proving that female doctors are as skilled as their male counterparts.'

'Oh,' said Grace, seemingly taken off guard. 'She sounds very interesting. I'd love to speak to her – and to Lucy... Perhaps I could have a tour of the hospital?'

'I'm sure that both Doctor Brakespeare and Nurse Daniels would oblige you.'

The sound of footsteps and Lucy's voice came from the hallway. So too did the opening of the front door as Frances and Gregory arrived.

What more can I learn from this visit? thought Araminta. She was certain there were things to be learned. Number one was whatever the real reason Grace was here, and it wasn't to visit some long-lost relative.

13

Despite Araminta's unease, once introductions had been made, the evening went well enough, although Devlin maintained an aloof manner, one hand hidden beneath the table, no doubt resting on Lucy's lap.

Lucy, bless her heart, did not show the wariness she must be feeling inside.

Gregory was as disarming as usual.

It amused Araminta to see that Grace was displaying a distinctly feminine interest.

If she had been able to read Grace's mind, she would have perceived her making comparisons between this very amiable man and the one she had married.

'So why are you here?' Devlin's tone was stonily to the point.

For the briefest of moments, Grace was taken aback, though not discomforted. She managed a small laugh.

'I heard of your forthcoming happy event.' She raised a glass of amber-coloured Amontillado. 'I heard you were getting married and wanted to wish you all the best, and seeing as I was coming this way, it seemed a good idea to pop in.'

'And this relative you're visiting?'

Devlin was nothing if not persistent.

Grace maintained her gracious smile, seen by everyone except Devlin. 'Aunt Gertrude. She lives in Bath.'

'I don't recall you having an aunt in Bath.'

'You wouldn't. A colonial, darling. She used to live in India. Now she lives in Bath.'

'Ah,' said Araminta. 'Was she married?' She directed the butler to refill empty glasses.

'Yes, but now a widow.'

'And no children.'

'Sadly, no. I'm her closest relative.'

Araminta resigned herself to not hearing anything more about Grace's matrimonial status, but she knew enough. Respite from an unhappy marriage was reason enough to visit elderly relatives and old friends.

Although still a little in awe of their guest, Lucy displayed a warm friendliness. Her comments were somewhat superficial, confining her remarks to simple subjects such as her admiration for the slinky dress Grace was wearing.

'But yours is so pretty,' Grace responded, her wine glass in one hand, a cigarette holder in the other. 'Simple lines can be very flattering. One doesn't need to spend a fortune.'

'It's the person inside the dress that matters,' exclaimed Devlin somewhat bitingly. 'Clothes do not a lady make.'

Araminta hid her smile. Her son might have been in love with Grace at one time – but certainly not now!

Lucy smiled and said sweet things, but Araminta could see that there was still some discomfort and regretted allowing Grace to come and stay.

To alleviate that discomfort, she retook charge of the conversation and asked Grace what it was like living in London.

'Oh. It's all right. If you've got the energy to keep up with it all. The social scene is quite frantic.'

Lucy was fascinated. 'I would love to go there.'

'You've never been to London?' Grace laughed. 'How strange. I don't think I know anyone who's never been to London.'

'Not everyone wants to go to London. I for one have all I want and need here,' Lucy remarked.

She did it without the slightest sign of sarcasm. Araminta felt like cheering.

'It's a filthy place,' remarked Devlin.

'I wouldn't exactly say that,' Frances interjected. 'It's full of gentlemen wearing bowler hats, pinstriped trousers and carrying rolled-up umbrellas. The centre of the business world. I take it your husband is involved in business?' she asked, the question directed at Grace.

'Yes. Yes, he is,' she said quickly.

'The city where the streets are reputed to be paved with gold – for some,' Devlin said. Nobody could fail to hear the sarcasm in *his* voice.

'What does your husband do?' asked Gregory.

'He divides his time between the city and his estate in Scotland. And he owns a lot of property in London.'

Gregory nodded approvingly. 'Ah. So, he's landed gentry. A knight of the realm. Sorry, I forgot. I do believe Araminta told me as such. Does he ride to hounds?'

There was robust amusement on Gregory's face, a factor that might be allied with irony or just as much with a genuine desire to know more – purely for the sake of knowledge.

'No. He prefers the city,' said Grace from behind a pall of smoke.

'Ah yes. The cut and thrust of business and the culture of the theatre and these new-fangled picture houses that show films from America.'

'I've seen Charlie Chaplin,' said Lucy, her face shining with enthusiasm. 'It's funny. I go with my sister, Nancy, and tell Devlin all about it when I get back.'

Silence blanketed a disinclination to say out loud the reason Devlin could not go.

There was pathos in the situation, yet Araminta took heart in the way Lucy glanced with love at the man she intended to marry.

Grace discerned the same.

'You're a lucky man, Devlin. A match seemingly made in heaven.'

'Yes.'

'The war ruined everything.' She sounded sincere.

He remained quiet, saying little. Only Araminta knew that he was listening very intently.

Grace turned her attention to Frances. 'So, you used to work in London?'

'Yes. I did.' Her face was expressionless. She was still considering whether she would accept the job offered, her secret held tightly to her chest. She had until the New Year to decide. Plenty of time. And anyway she was looking forward to Christmas, log fires, good food and drink and making the hospital look like Santa's grotto.

'And you're now at the local hospital. It must be quite different.'

'It is. I'm in charge. In London, there's precious little chance of gaining a senior position, but perhaps one day...'

Araminta asked herself what Frances meant by that.

Gregory kept smiling.

Grace was speaking. 'How amazing to meet a woman doctor,'

she declared in a gushing manner, which somehow grated on Araminta's nerves. 'I don't recall ever meeting one before.'

'We're rare creatures. Like unicorns.'

'Have you ever considered marrying?'

Frances set down her wine glass and let her lips spread with amusement. 'Indeed, I have.'

'So why haven't you?'

'My fiancé was killed during the last year of the war.'

'I'm sorry.' Embarrassment coupled with apology on Grace's face.

'That was a long time ago.'

'I take it your career is now more important than marriage.'

Frances spread her hand on the table. The ring Gregory had placed there sparkled. She exchanged a look with Gregory that didn't go unnoticed by Grace.

'We both have careers that we love.'

'Oh.' She sounded surprised.

''Tis true,' laughed Gregory, patting his chest and elevating his head backwards. 'I'm so busy reciting the vows at the marriages of other people, that it's the deuce of a job getting around to mine.'

Araminta didn't believe in the men withdrawing to smoke whilst the women chatted alone. Besides, Grace was on what must have been the fifth cigarette this evening, her fingers protected from the nicotine by an elbow-length white satin glove.

'Off to the drawing room for all of us.'

They all trooped off to the drawing room, where they made themselves comfortable in damask-covered chairs and sofas.

Araminta noticed that Grace purposely went out of her way to sit next to Lucy. She could just about hear what was being said.

'I understand that besides looking after Devlin, you have

When the evening finally ended, Araminta escorted her guests to the door.

A lovely evening. That's what they all said.

Frances lingered. 'If your visitor really wants to have a look round, I'm willing to oblige her. Perhaps she could come along with Lucy when she makes her way back tomorrow.'

'I'll bear that in mind, though I can't quite believe my ears. Grace was never of a philanthropic persuasion. A nice girl, but not particularly interested in anything beyond a new dress or a party.'

'Perhaps she's changed.'

Araminta grunted disbelievingly. 'I'm of the old school that believes a leopard incapable of changing their spots.'

'Perhaps this relative she's visiting is ill and a visit to the hospital might put the matter in context.'

Araminta shook her head. 'She's not that sort.'

'Oh well,' said Frances somewhat dismissively. 'Never mind. She's welcome to have a look round, and besides,' she whispered, 'we might be able to persuade her to make a donation.'

'I will do my arm-twisting best,' Araminta added, her grin sending her wrinkles spiralling off in all directions.

After everyone had gone and she was alone in her bedroom, Araminta analysed the evening and her impression of the woman who might have become her daughter-in-law if things had worked out. During their former acquaintanceship, she'd seemed a nice enough girl, but, she thought to herself, that was before she'd married.

Her voice was feathery light when she said, 'And what about your husband? What about your children. You've said so little about them.'

For some reason, Grace had been quite reticent on the subject.

nursing duties at the hospital. You must tell me all about what you do there.'

'It's just nursing.'

Frances interjected: 'It's hardly just nursing. I depend on Lucy to support my work in the family planning clinic.'

'I take it you also administer midwifery services?'

'Of course. It's all part of the job.'

Grace was fascinated. 'It sounds fascinating. I'd love to know more. Would there be any chance of you giving me a guided tour?'

Lucy shrugged her pretty little shoulders. 'As long as Doctor Brakespeare doesn't mind.'

'No. I don't mind.' She exchanged a brief glance with Araminta. Suspicion lurked in those clear blue eyes. It was as though she was trying to understand why a woman like Grace, brought up in the lap of luxury, never having done a day's work in her life, would express an interest in being shown around a hospital.

It occurred to Frances that the visitor from London had not spoken as much about her family as most mothers are inclined to do regarding her two children.

'Do you have children?' Frances asked her.

'Yes. Eloise and Justin. They're eight and ten and both at boarding school.'

'You must miss them.'

'I see them during the holidays. They stay with us in London and also in Scotland. We see them there.'

How sad, thought Frances. She thought of the local women surrounded by children and living on a pittance. Despite their poverty, never in a million years would they contemplate sending their children away from home. They would be unable to understand anyone who did.

***

Correspondence from Deborah arrived after breakfast the following morning.

Araminta took it from the silver tray and waited until she was alone before opening it, though it added little to what she'd already said.

Dear Minty,
  You didn't give me much time, however…
  Wife is quite a socialite.
  Husband is a notorious philanderer.
  Will dig some more.
  Regards, Deborah

Her attention was drawn to the sweeping of headlights breaking through the morning gloom before it set off down the drive.

Alfred was driving Lucy and Grace to the hospital. Lucy had been forced to stay overnight rather than rousing the chauffeur from his bed at the end of the dinner party. A room had been made available, suitably distant from those occupied by her son, though she doubted a little distance would stand in their way. Not that it worried her. They were young. She'd seen too many back in the war years who had lost their sweethearts without ever tasting physical love. 'Seize the day' was her motto.

The sound of the door opening and footsteps drew her attention, along with a draught of colder air coming into the sitting room from the passageway outside.

Devlin tapped his stick along the edge of the door before closing it.

'I heard the car pull away.'

'Yes. Lucy has an early start. It must have been quite a surprise to Grace's system to get out of bed before ten. I recall she was never an early riser.'

'People with nothing to do don't need to get up early.'

She watched him as he made his way to her, his stick brushing the area in front of each piece of furniture only sparingly. He knew this room well.

'You didn't come down to breakfast. Are you planning to go into the office?'

'I decided to have breakfast in my room. As for going into the office, it seems that will have to wait until Alfred gets back.'

Devlin kept himself busy at the quarry office, doing what he could. After all, the responsibility would pass to him when his mother was gone. It made sense to familiarise himself with its running.

'I take it you said goodbye to Lucy earlier this morning.'

'I did.'

'You're aching to know what I thought of Grace.'

Araminta chuckled to herself. 'Last night you were listening intently and although she was doing her best to be gay and carefree, I had the impression she was hiding something – or even here on some kind of fact-finding tour. How did she strike you?'

Devlin leaned on his walking stick; his legs being a little stiffer early in the morning, he stood unnaturally upright – as though they were made of wood.

'Only you can tell me what she looked like – I presume very well?'

'Very well indeed. Very thin too. But you know that's not what I meant. What did you think of what she had to say, and did you detect an undercurrent or cadence to her voice?'

He could imagine his mother's suspicious countenance.

'You're right. I did pay close attention.'

'So, I noticed,' said his mother, sending her pearl drop earrings swinging as she tossed her head. 'You were a picture of alert attention, like a bloodhound sniffing the air.'

Devlin took on a bemused expression. 'I can't say I'm flattered at being compared to a bloodhound, all drooping jowls and bloodshot eyes. Perhaps if you said that I have a sixth sense, I would be flattered, but on reflection, perhaps you are right.'

'Sit down and tell me what you thought.'

Out of habit, she patted the seat of the tapestry armchair closest to her.

There was reason in her habit. He knew she kept the chair in the same spot so he could easily find his way to it. He recalled what it looked like, the same raised texture to the upholstery that he'd known when he was sighted, the cabriole legs like round paws forming dents in the Turkish rug.

He settled himself and began to speak.

'It seemed at first that her laughter was unchanged, but on closer scrutiny I decided otherwise. It was brittle and forced, like a sugary coating covering her nervousness or guilt – or a lie. I did suspect she might have come here to inspect my bride-to-be. That would explain the brittleness to some extent, but I can't believe her jealous of my forthcoming nuptials. Our relationship ended a long time ago. She's here for a reason, I give you that, though not to visit a relative as she told you...'

'At a place called Champley Court.'

'I've never heard of it. Have you?'

'Yes, but it's miles from here, which begs the question...'

'Why she's not staying there.'

'Precisely.'

'Have you not challenged her as to why she chose here?'

'No, but I will when I get the chance. Something else is going on here.'

'Hmm.'

Devlin folded both hands over the handle of his walking stick, head bowed. To an onlooker, it might seem that his unseeing eyes were examining the pattern on the rug. His mother knew that even if he could see it the rug pattern would be the last thing on his mind.

'Does it worry you that she's accompanying Lucy to the hospital this morning?'

'I must admit that I am surprised. My ears detected that dear Grace was gushing fit to burst towards my darling Lucy. It seemed she so wanted to be her friend.'

'And you perceive some ulterior reason for this?'

Devlin shook his head, at the same time running one hand through his shock of glossy hair. 'If I could have seen or touched her face, I might have been able to ascertain her reason – coupled with what I was hearing.'

'To my mind, she did seem over-attentive to your would-be bride.'

'Perhaps she thinks I'm too old for her.'

His mother glared at him before announcing, 'Nonsense. Age is not a barrier and neither...' She fell silent on realising she was about to mention his disability.

'Being blind.'

'Lucy loves you despite your disability.'

'Anyway, I don't think Grace did come to inspect my fiancée. And I'm not entirely sure it was purely to visit this ex-colonial aunt who's landed in Bath. To my mind, she sounded more interested in the hospital – for whatever reason.'

His mother frowned. It wasn't something she'd noticed, but

then, Devlin's hearing had become more astute since losing his sight. 'Why would that be?' she said softly.

Devlin got to his feet. 'I'm going for a walk in the garden. I need to think.'

'It's barely light and still cold.'

'I'll wrap up warm, Mother.' He smiled as he paused by the door, one hand resting on an oak panel, the other on his cane. 'That's what you used to say to me when I was a child. *Wrap up warm*.'

Unseen by her son, a smile of sheer pleasure smoothed out the wrinkles in her face. How she wished they could go back in time.

'I didn't want you to catch a cold then, and I don't now.'

'Thank you for your concern.'

'Just before you go...'

He held the door open and waited for his mother to continue. He could feel her looking at him, pondering how best to put whatever it was she had to say.

'I admit I'm uncomfortable with our visitor. But worrying about what she might be up to is nothing compared to my perception that something is on your mind.'

'I don't know what you mean.' It was said in a clipped tone though not without tenderness. He turned his face firmly to the door so that she could not see his expression.

His mother frowned in his direction. 'Devlin, it has not escaped my attention that you've been a little distracted of late – and that was before Grace arrived. My dear,' she said, her voice softening and quieter, 'something is worrying you. Will you share it with me?'

The air shared their silence before he finally said, 'I sometimes think that I'm being selfish. An older and infirm man, and Lucy, so much younger and full of vitality.'

His mother gasped. 'Devlin! Lucy loves you. Anyone can see that.'

'If they had eyes,' he returned, a marked sarcasm in his tone.

The door closed behind him, leaving his mother stunned to silence as she contemplated whether he was being serious or not.

14

District Nurse Gwen Peebles pressed her hands against her aching back, sighing with satisfaction as she did so. It made a nice break to have a baby arrive only two hours off midday instead of in the wee hours following midnight. Better still that a local woman had got there first before she'd arrived.

The house was small. Just two bedrooms and a big family. That's how it was in Waterloo Terrace.

Sister Peebles stopped rubbing her aching back and strapped her bag beneath the bicycle saddle.

The husband of the new mother came out of his front door looking pleased with himself. Both hands were slouched into his brown corduroys, the knees of which were shiny with wear. He was grinning broadly as he jangled the coins in his pocket.

Gwen waited for him to crow the reason for his merry mood.

'That means I don't 'ave to pay you too much,' he sneered, a look of delight on a face that sweated coal dust.

'I don't suppose you do,' Gwen replied and pretended to be unfazed by what was sure to be said next.

'Old Meg does a good enough job,' he retorted. He withdrew his hands from his baggy pockets and stood looking cock pleased with himself, fists on hips, dirty scarf tied in a knot around his neck. 'Been doing it for years, she 'as. Who needs doctors and nurses when there's old women around like 'er.'

Old Meg had certainly been around a long time. She was eighty if she was a day and didn't look as though she gave much credence to modern hygiene. She was broad in the beam; her full skirts, reminiscent of an earlier age, made her seem even broader.

Gwen wrinkled her nose at the look of them, smeared with grease, stained from lack of washing. As she bent over, her backside with its smattering of cats' hairs, resembled the rear end of a horse. In Gwen's opinion, such women should never go near a birthing.

Once her bag was firmly attached beneath the seat of her bicycle, she patted it as she might a faithful dog. Time for cycling back to the hospital to record the birth, report the circumstances and help herself to a cup of tea and a digestive biscuit.

She was ready to shove off when her attention was diverted to the slamming of the gate set in the high wall of the end house. The gate's wrought-iron bars would, at one time, have been all there was between its garden and the pavement. As an aid to greater privacy, its bars were now obliterated with a solid tin cover. What with the metal gate and the high wall, the house was hidden from the outside world, but the cheap tin plate made quite a racket when it was slammed.

A figure emerged. Tall and wearing dark clothes, he seemed in a hurry. On seeing them, he strode forward in a menacing manner, as though daring them to stand in his way.

Gwen was a brave little soul, would stand up to anyone and

wasn't easily scared, but she saw a pair of small eyes set in a scarred face. His nose was bent to one side, which made his mouth appear lopsided, corners cruelly downturned. All this set above a jutting chin that looked set rigid like plaster of Paris hardened around thin lips that appeared too tense to smile.

The stuff of nightmares, she thought, and shuddered.

In a swift act of self-preservation, she stepped around the other side of her bicycle, swearing under her breath as her stocking caught on something metallic. Her trusty bike would go some way to acting as a shield to whatever was coming her way.

For a split second, the man in front of her seemed about to say something until the father of the newborn stepped forward.

'All right, 'Arry?' He said it somewhat patronisingly, ready to lick the other man's boots if need be.

The scarred face was shaded by the brim of a plain black bowler hat, like a bank manager or businessman might wear. Jacket and trousers were of drab colours that matched each other, though were at odds with his hat – not so much a thing of the banking industry, more like that of a draper or grocer, serviceable but not top-drawer. A muffler was tightly wound around his neck. When the wind caught his open jacket, something silvery glinted from a dark-coloured waistcoat.

All this Gwen noticed, but most of all it was his eyes, which took in the world around, devoured her, though only glanced at her companion.

Two fingers pulled the brim of his hat further down over his face. Then he turned abruptly in the opposite direction and was gone.

He had not responded to the neighbour's cheerful welcome.

'Not the friendliest of neighbours,' she remarked. She eyed the new father as she awaited his response. He looked nervous.

'It's not a problem. He ain't at 'ome much. Lives in London. Comes down now and again to see 'is old mum, though no more than he can 'elp it.'

She recognised the male bravado, his way of dealing with a man who wanted nothing to do with him – or her for that matter.

She took on board what he'd said about the man's mother. 'Poor woman. She must be lonely, holed up behind that high wall. Unless there are other relatives or friends that call in on her.'

A gruff guffaw escaped between the cracked teeth of the father of the new baby. 'There ain't, and even if there was, they wouldn't get much of a welcome. Right old cow she is, and that's a fact.'

'That's very sad,' said Gwen and meant it most sincerely. 'Where I come from in Wales, the whole family make sure they call in and see their elderly relatives. My family certainly does, though mostly the daughters. Not a big surprise, is it? It's my experience that daughters do all the caring.'

'That bloke's changed since he went away to London,' the man said as she cocked her leg over her bicycle and slid a foot into one pedal. 'Unless I didn't know 'im as well as I thought I did. I could get on better with 'im than with 'is mother.' He frowned as a further thought came to him. 'The wife reckons 'is mother is nastier to women than she is to men. Reckons it might be down to the fact that she ain't got no daughters.' He frowned suddenly as he contemplated further. 'Mind you, there was a woman staying there a while ago. Lovely-looking girl. I only seen her the once. Can't rightly recall when. The wife told me she thought it was a friend of 'Arry's.'

Gwen wondered if he might offer more details. But he didn't.

'I'll bid you good day. I'm off to see if the pub's open. Got to wet me new kid's 'ead, ain't I.'

With that he was gone and so was Gwen, off back to the hospital to record the birth in the hospital register and write down how much was owed. Not much, thanks to Midwife Meg, a woman without training but a lifetime's experience – or so she said. Gwen wasn't so sure about that.

15

Whilst Gwen Peebles was cycling back to the hospital, Lady Grace was becoming more and more vexed. Not that she let it show. Her swan-like neck was still creamy above the collar of her fur coat, with no trace of an impatient pink flush.

Frances and Lucy had taken it in turns to give her a guided tour. She made sure to remark how splendid it was and what bricks they were to be part of such a demanding profession. But it wasn't their professional side she wanted to tap into.

But she had to show willing to listen, to take an interest, to make it sound as though this visit really was a pleasure trip, not a quest to find out what her husband had been up to.

'It's no place for the faint-hearted,' Frances said to her. 'Or for those who quite like the uniform. Uniforms get stained with all manner of things. Not just blood.'

'I see.'

At their invitation, Grace had accompanied them around the wards. Every step had brought bile to her throat, with the probable exception of two nursing mothers cuddling their newborn infants. That she could cope with. The old man spitting phlegm into a brass spittoon was another matter entirely. She covered her mouth as she swallowed her nausea. This was not what she was here for. She wanted to talk to someone, to ask about the woman who had been dumped outside the main entrance, who she was, what they'd found out about the person who had left her there.

Thanks to the old man gulping up the contents of his lungs, the sight of sick people, she yearned for some fresh air. The London air was none too pure, but oh, what wouldn't she give for the smell of city streets, the humid warmth of an underground carriage, the trundling comfort of a London taxi. She reminded herself that the underground had never been her travelling method of choice, although she did have a soft spot for it – now that it formed the basis of her fortune.

She began fumbling in her bag, fingers shaking as she sought the silver cigarette case – a birthday present from her husband in the good days before they were married.

Frances knew all the signs of someone uncomfortable with the sights and smells of a hospital ward. 'Are you feeling all right?'

Face a little pale, Grace brought out the items she so needed. 'I'm in need of a cigarette. I think I got up too early this morning.' She tried to laugh and was almost ready to light up when Frances took hold of her hand and suggested she go outside.

'Smoking is not allowed on the wards – not even patients are allowed to smoke.'

'But smoking is healthy – surely?'

Frances shook her head. 'Not in my opinion and I make the rules here.'

'Fine. Your word is law.' Her discerning eyes sought some form of soulmate. 'Would anyone else like to join me?' she asked amiably enough. She offered Lucy a cigarette and warmly asked, 'Would you like one?'

'No, thank you.'

'You don't smoke? I would have thought it a welcome habit. Your stress levels must warrant it, doing the job that you do. Are you sure?'

'Totally sure. I still have to accompany Doctor Brakespeare on her rounds.'

'That's a shame. I would have liked to have a little chat.'

'Perhaps some other time. I might see you later at Orchard Manor?'

'You might.'

The smile that transpired was fleeting and Lucy felt somewhat honoured. She couldn't help being surprised at the friendly attitude of a woman she'd thought would be an enemy.

Grace swayed alluringly as she headed for the porch at the front of the hospital. Heels on shoes of genuine Spanish leather tapped the marble floor. Overhead, the high glass pergola splashed the reception hall with what little daylight there was.

Her jaw set firm and her head down, she made her way to the main door. By the time she got to it, her jaw was aching, along with her head. She had set great store by this visit, but so little had so far been achieved. The whole purpose of coming here was to find out the final moments of the woman whose photo she'd seen in the newspaper. She could have asked of course, but that was something she wished to avoid because then she might be pressed to give a reason for her interest.

No, she decided, this had to be achieved by subtlety.

Feeling frustrated with the outcome of what she had thought would be an easy matter, she lit her cigarette with a silver lighter that matched her cigarette case and blew the resultant smoke with fierce indignation.

Her eyes glazed over as she surveyed December in all its uncertain drabness. It must have looked pretty when the snow had been on the ground a while back. No doubt the wintry scene presented a fine aspect in spring or summer, but at this time of year there was an air of melancholy about it.

'Mind if I join you?' asked a perky voice. Grace glanced at the equally perky face, presuming it to be a patient or someone visiting a patient.

Wrapped up in a shapeless woollen coat, Iris Manning took full advantage of any opportunity. She had seen the cigarette case offered to Nurse Lucy Daniels, saw her refuse too. Up to her. She wouldn't refuse if she was offered one and that was a fact!

Grace continued to gaze at the view via a pall of cigarette smoke.

A cigarette was not immediately offered, but Iris was of a crafty disposition. She began patting herself up and down as though she was seeking a packet of cigarettes that she didn't have. She'd smoked the last one at breakfast time and didn't have any money for another packet.

Her ruse bore fruit. Just as she'd hoped, Grace noticed. The silver cigarette case flicked open and was offered to her.

'Be my guest.'

'Oh, ta. Don't mind if I do.'

She glanced over her shoulder to make sure that nobody had noticed her sneaking out ten minutes earlier than usual for her break.

'I 'ear you're staying with her ladyship.'

'Yes.'

'Enjoying it, are you?'

'It's pleasant enough. Very quiet.' Her tone of voice was slightly clipped. She had no idea who this woman was.

'It's a world unto itself and that's a fact.'

'Is it always quiet?'

'Here or up at Orchard Manor?'

'Both.'

'Well, I can't comment about Orchard Manor. Lucy knows more what goes on there – seeing as she's going to be marrying the son and heir. Got 'er feet under the table, that's for sure. But here, at the hospital, well that's another matter. There's always an emergency or something going on. We do get a bit of excitement now and again. Some things you wouldn't believe.'

On catching the hint of scandal in Iris's voice, Grace was all attention.

'I take it you work here.'

'Yes. I do.'

If the girl worked here, then she might be of assistance. All she had to do was go about it the right way.

'Are you referring to incidents in the distant past?'

'Oh no,' Iris explained. 'Just recently. In the dead of night...'

'Do tell,' whispered Grace, her voice breathless and expression intense.

'Well, there was this woman...'

Grace found herself holding her breath as, without any prompting from her, Iris began to describe what had happened on a chilly December night.

'I think I saw her photo in a newspaper. Brought in dead from the doorstep. Is that right?' She controlled the impatience in her voice, though hope soared.

'It was such a shock,' said Iris, shaking her head whilst looking pleased to be the fount of such knowledge. 'This poor woman was dumped on the doorstep in the middle of the night – and a freezing cold night it was too.'

'That's terrible,' returned Grace and sounded suitably shocked. 'Do they know who she is?'

Iris shook her head before taking a strong and appreciative drawl on her cigarette.

'No.' The response was drawn out; it seemed in a way to emphasise the importance of what she had to impart, a great secret of which only she and she alone knew the full details.

Grace had been brought up to be waited on. It was her experience that lowly people could feel quite elated to be asked about anything.

'Did you see this woman?'

'Oh yes!' Another great puff of cigarette smoke. 'Not until she was dead, mind you. I seen 'er laid out back in the sluice, which is also used as a morgue.' She shook her head. 'Poor soul. Covered in blood she was, on account of the miscarriage.'

'And she had nothing on her that might have led to revealing her identity?'

'Nothing at all... Oh... I lie. There was something. A shell necklace. Just a single shell hanging on a black string.'

Grace held her breath, necessary in controlling her temper. The necklace had been hers.

'So where is this necklace now?'

'I think Doctor Brakespeare's got it, or she's given it to the police. 'Course, they're still looking for the bloke who dumped her yur, but that's more than a bit difficult, seeing as they ain't got a description. He took off before Sister Harrison could get a good look at 'im, though she thought he was unusually tall, legs as long as you like, she reckoned, judging by the way he covered the ground when he made off.'

Daddy Long Legs.

That was what her husband called Harry Squires, a shady type who carried out anything her husband required. It couldn't possibly be anyone else. And the shell hanging on a cord around the woman's neck. Her shell. Given to her as a child and missing from her jewellery box.

No fur coat could alleviate the feeling that her blood had

turned to ice. In the space of little more than fifteen minutes, she had learned all she wanted to know. Her suspicions had been confirmed. There was nothing to stop her from proceeding with a divorce. The future beckoned.

Impatient to get back to London, her gaze fell on the car that had brought her here. The chauffeur was hanging over the car radiator, head buried beneath the bonnet. The clattering of metal against metal, tool against engine, travelled towards her.

Flicking her half-smoked cigarette into the frosty undergrowth and without saying adieu to Iris, she made her way down the slippery steps. She ordered him back into the car, demanding to be taken back to Orchard Manor.

'Now?' he asked, looking surprised she wanted to return so early.

'Now,' she replied, tugging open the door to the rear passenger seat before he had chance to do it for her.

'I can't.' He peered in at her. 'There's a problem with the engine.'

'I need to get back.' It was hard not to scream. She'd been brought up to always be ladylike, including when dealing with servants.

At first, he looked nonplussed, unsure of what to do next. Then an idea came to him. 'Perhaps Doctor Brakespeare can help. She has a car.'

Turning swiftly on her heel, Grace dashed back into the hospital, barged into the doctor's office and declared the problem.

'I must get back. An emergency has occurred.'

Frances apologised that she could not drive her back at this moment in time because a breached birth was expected to be brought in.

'I walked in today, but if you're that determined to get back,

I'll have Wally run round to the vicarage and get Gregory to drive you back to the manor in my car. He can also run you to the railway station. I do hope all is well at home when you get there.'

'It's just something I need to attend to, something I thought was not of any great importance, but my conscience urges me to get home.'

It was all stated in a great rush. To Frances's mind, it sounded like an avalanche of excuses.

Why now? thought Frances. But it wasn't her business to enquire in greater depth, and anyway, she had a hospital to run.

Despite wobbly legs, Wally got round to the vicarage in record time.

The little car Frances had christened Mabel came up the drive like a loyal puppy seeking out the person who loved her most. Gregory was behind the wheel, Wally at his side in the passenger seat.

Frances explained the situation. 'An emergency has occurred. Lady Leinster-Parry needs to get home.'

'Your wish is my command,' Gregory said jokingly. Following a warning look from Frances, he changed his tone. 'I'll get you there as quickly as I can. Orchard Manor first, then the railway station.'

'There's no guarantee that any trains are running,' she said to Lucy as together they watched Frances's beloved little Austin trundle out of the main gate. 'There's been some flooding on the lines. A bit of ice here and there.'

Lucy's eyes sparkled with amusement. 'At least the steam will warm the rails.'

Smiling herself, Frances eyed the comely nurse who never failed to win over even the most curmudgeonly patient. 'How did you get on with her?'

'Surprisingly well. She really seemed keen to have me as a friend.'

Lucy had been surprised at how friendly she'd been, but all the same she'd feared Devlin's former fiancée's reason for the visit. Whatever the reason it didn't matter now. Grace was going back to London. All was well with the world.

* * *

Frances was still in her office at the hospital when Gregory arrived that evening in her car.

'I wasn't expecting you.'

'I thought you might like a ride home. It's a filthy night to be walking.'

He shook the raindrops from his hat as he entered the cosy office, where a gas fire spluttered in protest as she turned it off.

'I cannot resist.'

'Your chariot awaits you, my princess,' he said, enveloping her in his arms and kissing her in sequence, forehead, the tip of her nose and lastly her lips.

She laughingly brushed at the droplets of water on his shoulders.

'Two women in need of a chariot and all in one day. You are a lucky man, are you not?'

Holding his head to one side, Gregory eyed her quizzically.

'She seemed quite troubled. Is there anything you want to tell me? Anything I can help with?'

A crease puckered her forehead. 'I'm not sure. Nobody seems to know for sure why she came here.'

'Here and gone,' said Gregory. 'Let's be off. Mrs Skittings insisted on making us supper tonight. A steaming bowl of rabbit stew awaits us. Oh, and I popped in on your mother. I may have persuaded her to join us for supper.'

Frances looked at him in surprise. 'I shall be amazed if you've managed to do that. She was very ill yesterday.'

'Haven't you said yourself that she's very up and down?'

'Very.'

'Take each day as it comes.'

She kissed his cheek and gazed lovingly up into his eyes. 'You're a miracle worker.'

When he grinned, wrinkles appeared at the sides of his eyes.

He winked. 'It's my stock in trade.'

It made Frances laugh.

16

Whilst back in London, Harry Squires was fit to explode when he saw a picture of Ellen on the front page of a newspaper. The reason was that he knew then and there that his mother had told him a pack of lies.

'Bloody cow!'

He went over the conversation they'd had on that dreadful night when he'd half dragged, half carried Ellen to the cottage hospital.

'They'll see her all right,' his mother had assured him at the time.

His jaw locked when he thought of his mother. Going home to see his old mum was a duty but rarely a pleasure.

The old crow charged him for his time staying in the house that had been his childhood home. Avaricious. That was her. Would do anything for her son – or anyone else for that matter – so long as she was paid for it.

She'd copped dead lucky when he'd asked if Ellen could stay for a few days – at a price of course.

His mother had squinted suspiciously at Ellen's black eye and cut lip and taken hold of her chin between her sharp-nailed fingers.

'She looks a bit battered. Did you do that?' she'd asked him accusingly.

Bubbles of acne and fine marks, long-healed scars suggesting he'd once been cut by a razor – not just once, but enough times to make his flesh pitted and red, striped his face. He could tell a few stories about those marks, how he'd got them, but that was his business and he'd given as good as he'd got.

He'd hit his mother's hand away from Ellen's face. 'No,' he'd said, 'I wouldn't do nothing like that.'

Not believing him, she'd asked Ellen directly.

'No,' she'd said, her normally throaty laugh more subdued than usual. 'I walked into a door.'

His mother had been her usual dismissive self. 'I wouldn't put it past him. There's nothing gentle about my boy.' Her eyes, black as beetles, had not shown one iota of emotion.

'It weren't me.' He'd raised his voice.

His mother had shaken her head as though the stridency of her son's voice hurt her ears. 'Don't shout at me. I'm your mother. Honour your mother and father. That's what the Bible says.'

'I've a care for Ellen.'

'Do you now!' She'd chuckled as she'd said it, but it was true.

Out of all the women he knew who classed themselves as 'entertainers', 'gentlemen's escorts', Ellen was the one he had a soft spot for. Harry was in awe of her refined voice and winning smile, the gleam of her raven-black hair. She was different to all the others, a woman of rounded curves and natural elegance who spoke nicely and acted like a lady; spoke like one too. Dark eyebrows, dark eyes, full lips and a complexion that reminded him of a fresh peach just picked from a tree – or nicked from a stall down Covent Garden. He'd done plenty of the former when he was younger, more of the latter when he'd first come to London.

When she'd begged him to get her away from his boss until her face was recovered and Gerald's temper calmed, he'd caved in. He had no fear of Sir Gerald, but he did like his money. He was well paid for what he did. But Ellen was frightened of Sir Gerald, her lover, the man who kept her on a string.

On pointing out to her that he wouldn't like it, she'd said, 'He won't want to be seen about town in my company with my face looking like this. Might even go out and about with his wife.' She'd said it laughingly because they both knew it was untrue. Sir Gerald loathed his wife. She was just a meal ticket, a source of money that had come with his marriage. 'I'll get back to the house when I'm ready,' she'd promised. The house she referred to was back in London, though not so seedy as some of the other properties Sir Gerald owned. Her rooms were of a decent enough standard for receiving visitors – Gerald in particular.

His mother's initial reluctance had receded once she'd seen the colour of the money – much more money than he usually gave her. He'd left Ellen there. It had seemed the best thing. Nothing could go wrong could it? But it did go wrong.

Sir Gerald Leinster-Parry was a knight of the realm, though Harry was unsure as to what he'd got knighted for. He only knew him as a man about town who was famous amongst a certain kind for frequenting cheap dance halls, music halls and the stage doors of theatres. All of this was kept from his family, who formed the respectable side of his life.

Sir Gerald had an appetite for women. He also liked a drink but did not indulge in gambling unless business ventures were included. He had a thing for buying tall old houses suitable for dividing into boarding houses or small apartments barely big enough to accommodate the families he squeezed into them.

Sometimes a family of four – or more – living in one room. Sir Gerald couldn't resist purchasing a property of potential. It was an ongoing force within him, a challenge to see just how profitable a return he could make from a small investment – the smaller, the better.

He had many contacts to assist him in finding suitable properties, but it was only Harry he trusted to satisfy his appetite for women, not that it was his only assignment. He was also instrumental in collecting overdue rent from the crumbling properties Sir Gerald owned. Sometimes he had to use force, though for the most part people paid up, even if it meant they had to sell something to make ends meet. Sometimes it was wedding rings, small items of value, like teaspoons, a chair, a picture on the wall or a mantel clock, perhaps a fine cashmere shawl snatched there and then from a grandmother's shoulders. Sometimes the items were much more precious than that, even their bodies, their children.

Fog made more noxious by the smoke from a million coal fires softened the harsh outlines of cobbled streets. Gas streetlights fought to alleviate the gloom. He was in the worst part of the city now, the pavements like glass beneath his feet.

A dog ran in front of him outside his favourite watering hole, a pub in a narrow backstreet where he was known and respected.

He caught up on the news from local spivs, thieves and harlots, drank a few pints, was bought a few pints. People showed him respect in the hope of gaining a few coppers themselves.

The following day, it was back to business collecting rents on the foul buildings that some poor souls called home. A few were unable to meet their commitment, pleading with him to give them more time. A destitute widow offered her body, but he declined, not because she wasn't comely but because his mind was elsewhere. He thought of that day he'd gone back to his mother's house in Norton Dene. The journey had taken longer than usual through blinding snow, the locomotive's metal wheels screeching as they fought to make progress on the slippery rails. But still he'd glowed at the prospect of seeing Ellen again.

On arrival at his mother's house, he'd found Ellen, her face slick with sweat, tossing and turning. Even with his meagre knowledge of disease, he knew she had a fever.

'What the bleeding 'ell's going on?' he'd pressed his mother.

'She's miscarrying, you great lummox.'

His jaw had dropped. 'She's in the family way?'

'Don't sound so surprised. Ain't that why you brought her into my house? A fallen woman. A harlot.'

He'd snapped at his mother that he'd not known she was pregnant. 'And not by me,' he'd added in response to the accusation in her mean eyes and the disbelief on her stick-thin lips. It was the truth. 'Will she be all right?'

'Might be,' she'd replied. 'If you can get her to the hospital... Yes. That's the thing. Get 'er to the hospital.'

'The hospital,' he'd repeated, his head spinning, the melting snow on his head mixing with the sweat that was trickling down his face.

'The hospital,' his mother had affirmed more loudly. 'Well, get on with you.'

Here in the warmth of an East London pub, a spit and sawdust place where labourers from the meat market on their way to work drank pints of beer until midnight had come and gone, he downed the first pint quickly and ordered another. The second one was drunk more slowly so he could give himself time to think. Uppermost in his mind was the fact that his mother had told him a pack of lies. His anger was like a fire burning inside him. He wanted to kill her, but she was back in Somerset, and he was here in London. Revenge consumed his heart both for her and for Sir Gerald. He too was to blame. There would be questions as to where Ellen had gone, but he could sort those. The simple excuse was that she'd gone home to her family. He wasn't sure Sir Gerald knew her real address. She'd told him she was from Winchester in Hampshire, but he wasn't sure that was the truth. She'd also said that her father was a doctor or a vicar – on separate occasions. All he did know was that his boss didn't like people running out on him. He only hoped he hadn't read the more downmarket newspapers that had featured her death mask. He'd only ever seen Sir Gerald reading *The Times* or something of that ilk – something upmarket that only refined gentlemen read.

The hue and cry would be too public if he dared attack him. Best to use a more roundabout method. Use his own wicked ways against him. Embarrass him. Gentlemen didn't like their reputations besmirched.

Not that Sir Gerald was much of a gentleman, regardless of the saying that clothes maketh the gentleman. In Harry's opinion, clothes were just a covering. It was the soul lurking inside that really defined a man and Sir Gerald's soul was dark.

17

Back in Norton Dene, Ma Skittings was considering her reputation. Abortions were not something she practised. Nature could be aided but only given a gentle nudge. The injuries of the woman who'd arrived dead at the cottage hospital could only have been caused by physical intervention – that was, something sharp had been introduced into the woman's womb. Ma Skittings had no hard evidence, but she had her suspicions.

In the big house abutting the miners' cottages in Waterloo Terrace, Harry's mother was counting how many bottles of pink pills she had left hidden behind the meat safe in the larder. Satisfied that there were plenty, she adjusted the green metal meat safe so that her hoard was hidden from view.

The larder door banged shut. Just seconds after, a series of knocks came from the front of the house.

She chewed her lips thoughtfully as she considered whether to answer it or not. Was she expecting anyone? Harry had gone back to London days ago, so it wouldn't be him.

Was there any reason the police or anyone else might come asking questions? She decided there were none.

Firm knocking echoed along the stone-floored passageway to the front door.

Determined whoever they were.

'Coming,' she shouted out in a voice that was sweeter than she was feeling.

Grumbling her way all along the passageway, she finally took a firm grip on the door catch and tugged it open.

'Oh,' she said, taking a step back in surprise. 'It's you.'

Violet Squires feared no one – except for Ma Skittings.

'Long time, no see, Violet.'

Ma Skittings lifted her meaty hand. Coins rattled in a small canvas bag that she lifted between them. 'I'm collecting for a funeral and a tombstone for the young woman with no name. She died on the steps of the 'ospital. I take it you heard about it?'

Violet considered denying she'd heard anything, but Norton Dene wasn't that big, and everyone knew what went on within a day of it happening.

'Yes. Yes, I did.'

'Thought you might like to give a few coppers?'

Her penetrating eyes were unsettling and for a moment Violet stood there lost for words. She'd heard Ma Skittings could read people with one look at their eyes and hoped it was all hearsay.

At last, she found her tongue and agreed to donate. 'Won't be a minute.'

'Cold out yur. All right if I come in?'

Violet scowled as Ma Skittings stepped over the threshold and closed the door behind her.

'Nasty and damp out,' she proclaimed.

The woman whose house she had stepped into made no comment. Her mouth was clamped shut. She wished she'd never opened the front door. Now she had to hand over money and

Violet Squires was planning how best to proceed. She had money squirrelled away throughout the house. But it was her money and never meant to be shared.

Her copper change jam jar was half full of farthings, halfpennies and pennies. She kept it under a large jelly mould on a shelf in the kitchen. The jam jar containing silver sixpences, shillings, florins and half-crowns was kept in a hinged footstool in the living room. Paper money, of which there was quite a lot, was kept in a tin cash box hidden at the back of the coal scuttle.

A few coppers from the jam jar in the kitchen would suffice.

Violet was careful with money. She'd dabbled in many a little ruse in the past, including taking loose change from her husband's pockets – and from a few of her previous employers. Her husband had been very well paid being a foreman and undermanager at the mines, although, like her, he'd also been a bit parsimonious, counting out every penny of housekeeping and requiring a record of everything she'd spent. She'd always liked to have some of her own. That was how come she'd ventured into her own bits of business.

In her head, she cursed the steady plod of Ma Skittings following behind her into the kitchen. Was she imagining those sharp eyes boring into the back of her head?

Shaking the unqualified thought aside, she placed herself between the kitchen dresser and her visitor, her back hiding the whereabouts of the jam jar from view. Violet trusted no one.

'Hand me the bag and I'll put some money in,' she said, half turning round and reaching out a grasping hand.

Ma's response was immediate. 'I've got the string of the bag wound around my wrist so I can't do that. You sort out your donation and then put it in the bag.'

Violet's scowl was unseen as she turned back to the dresser. She hated giving money for anything, even for buying food.

The jar had a slot in its tin lid so that when she tipped it up only a few coins made it into the palm of her hand. Too many, she decided, and popped a penny back in.

Jar back in its rightful place, door firmly shut, she offered the coins.

'Much appreciated,' said Ma Skittings. 'Are you sure you can spare it?'

Most thinking people would have picked up on the sarcasm, but Violet was thick-skinned. She'd donated no more than five pennies, would have preferred to keep every single one of them, but congratulated herself that she'd got off lightly. She wouldn't have given anything at all if Ma Skittings hadn't barged into the house and followed her.

She asked herself why she'd allowed that. The straight answer was that refusing might have given rise to gossip – worse still to accusations of somehow being involved. She wanted no police arriving on her doorstep. She only wished her son hadn't brought the woman here in the first place – and she hadn't had to do what she'd done.

Ma Skittings was slow taking her leave.

'Nobody even knows that poor girl's name.' She shook her head despairingly. 'Can't put a name on that stone until we know that.'

'Known only unto God?' Violet offered hopefully.

Ma Skittings gave her a dark look. 'That's on enough tombstones as it is.'

Violet looked at her blankly before it came to her that she was referring to the dead of the Great War. She was right, of course, that many had that same wording engraved on their tombstones.

'The only clue might be the necklace she was wearing.'

'Necklace?'

'Yep. Nothing much. Not jewellery as such. Just a shell hanging on a bit of string or something like that.'

'Not valuable?'

'I don't think so. Mind if I take me weight off me legs a moment,' said Ma Skittings and sat down without invitation. Then started a conversation Violet could well do without. 'How's your 'Arry getting on? Likes living in London, I suppose. Too quiet for a young chap down yur.'

'He'll never come back here,' said Violet, shaking her head vigorously. 'Doing too well up there. He's a man of means, he is. Making his way in the world. Works for a gentleman.'

Ma Skittings was like a dog with a bone and her eyes were as sharp as needles. 'Thought I saw 'im a couple of weeks ago.'

'Really?' Violet shook her head. 'He ain't been down for a while. A month at least.'

'Was it?'

'He only comes here to see me. Make sure I'm all right, especially around Christmas. I expect he'll be down to see me then.'

'That'll be nice for you.' Ma Skittings nodded and accepted the lie. Violet Squires had always been dishonest in word and deed. They'd never been friends, in fact this was the first time she'd ever been in this cold, damp house. It reminded her of a mausoleum, though without the gargoyles and funereal urns.

Still cold though, she thought. *That fire in the grate looks to only have half a shovelful on it. Looks as though she lives in here, in the kitchen. Keeps the other rooms cold and locked.*

She made a mental note never to come here again.

'Well, I'd better be going,' said Ma Skittings, her knees creaking and cracking as she got to her feet. In any other house in town, she would have been offered a cup of tea. Not here though. Still, she was disinclined to accept one. There'd been a chilly reception from the moment the front door had opened.

She stopped at the door, holding it open to let in some fresh air, which might, just might, drown the smell of damp.

'You know the police are looking into the identity of the dead woman.'

If she'd hoped to see Violet blanch, she was disappointed. Violet had always been hard. It had always amazed Ma Skittings how she'd married and given birth to Harry. *Still*, she thought, *it takes all kinds to make a world*. Harry Squires was hardly a welcome addition to humanity. He'd been trouble as a youngster, and she doubted he was much better now. Best for everyone that he stayed in London.

'And the identity of the man who dumped her at the hospital. They're looking into that too. So's the doctor, for that matter. If there's one thing you can count on is that Doctor Brakespeare will hang in there until she knows who was responsible for her death.'

'No doubt.'

Ma Skittings set off down the path promising herself never to enter that chilly, smelly house ever again.

Tugging the strings of the canvas bag from her wrist, she muttered under her breath as she made her way to the vicarage coach house. She looked in on Frances's mother most days, making sure she had a decent meal and doing whatever housework was needed.

She ground what teeth she had left as she pushed open the pine plank door. The warmth of the coach house flooded out and drew her in, the welcoming atmosphere totally opposite to that at the house of Violet Squires.

Coat off, she checked the amount in the collection bag on the table. Without needing to count, she knew Violet's offering had done little to swell the total. 'So why did you go there?' she asked herself.

The answer was that she'd been talking to Sister Peebles, who'd told her about the conversation she'd had with a woman on her rounds. The woman had been pregnant and now she wasn't, had even had the effrontery to hint that she'd got rid of it.

On top of that, Nancy, Ma Skittings' daughter-in-law, who just happened to be a nurse and sister to Nurse Lucy Daniel, had imparted the details about where things stood as regards the dead woman.

'Someone is providing these pills. The police are making enquiries locally, though Doctor Brakespeare thinks they could have been procured through an advert in a national newspaper.'

Nancy had turned a bit sheepish after she'd said that. Ma Skittings had guessed immediately what else might have been said and had instantly taken umbrage.

'Nothing to do with me.'

Her voice had awoken the baby and rattled the ornaments on the mantelpiece.

And that was the reason why she'd set off around the town with a collecting bag to those people who she suspected might have a hand in the matter. She was far from being the only one who dealt in medicines.

It was Sister Peebles who had told her about seeing a man come out of the big house at the end of the terrace, recounting how he had rushed past, even ignoring the neighbour who had spoken to him.

Yet Violet Squires had said her son hadn't visited her and wouldn't be visiting her until Christmas. She'd been lying.

18

Christmas was only ten days off and the return of foul weather seemed a good enough excuse to put up the decorations. Frances gave her permission gladly.

''Tis almost the season to be jolly. Let's bring it forward a bit.'

She was also counting down the days to New Year. That was when she would have to decide about taking the position in London or staying in Norton Dene.

Preparations for the festive season helped raise her spirits. Paper chains were being hung between the hanging lights in the hospital ward, greenery picked from the garden, candles in tiny tin holders were being readied to place on the tree.

Wally was standing on a trestle-style ladder. His old legs wobbled a bit as Lucy handed him the trailing paper chains.

'You all right, Wally?' she asked him.

'I don't like heights. Me legs ain't what they used to be.'

'I'll catch you if you fall,' said Lucy.

'I might chance a broken bone for that,' responded Wally, a grin creasing his wrinkled old face as he looked down at her over his upper arm.

Even Sister Harrison joined in. She moved the lengths of cotton wool she'd threaded onto lengths of white cotton to one side of the ward duty desk. Pleased with the result, she gave them an affectionate pat. 'These are next, Wally. I want them strung up at the windows. It will seem as though snow is falling on the inside, even if there's no more falling outside. I think there should be snow at Christmas.'

She didn't say please or thank you, but Wally had known her a long while and always treated Sister Harrison with respect.

'Yes, Sister Harrison.'

Out in the octagonal hallway off which the wards radiated, Doctor Frances paused on her way back to her office to admire the pine tree Wally had cut down from the garden. Dark green and sombre in the garden, it now stood in what looked to be a clay chimney pot. The pot was decorative, the top serrated by a jagged arrangement reminiscent of a crown.

Very apt, she thought. Doubtless some thought had gone into the choice, the old chimney pot taken from the collection of used and cast-off items Wally hoarded in a shed in the grounds.

Beneath its lower branches sat a cardboard box of decorations waiting for attention – another little job for Wally.

The weather might be cold, but the joy of seeing the tree and decorations warmed the air.

Her office smelled of the gas fire that spluttered in the fire grate.

Two envelopes that had arrived in this morning's post awaited her on the desk.

She fingered the monkey-headed brass letter opener like Aladdin rubbing the brass lamp. Lucy had asked her if she did that for luck. To be honest, she hadn't realised she did it but rather liked the idea.

The first letter was from a recently qualified doctor looking for a job.

I'm particularly interested in women's health...

A male doctor at that. Glancing over his résumé, she could see that he was well qualified.

'Not just yet,' she said with a sigh and determined to write back to him suggesting he get back in touch sometime during the summer. Unless of course she decided to leave. As yet she was still undecided, wishing she could cut herself in half so she could do both. A silly idea.

The other envelope was from the police and enclosed the result of the post-mortem and a statement regarding the shell necklace.

The former was a foregone conclusion – haemorrhage resulting in a miscarriage.

> Residue of substances (tansy and turpentine) were present in the stomach, which in larger quantities would have been solely responsible for the loss of the foetus, which I estimate at being four months gestation. However, the main cause of internal bleeding was due to the insertion of a sharp object...

Frances felt the colour drain from her face and, although she knew she'd read it correctly and had already identified it as the cause, felt compelled to read it again.

She sank into a chair, leaned forward and closed her eyes. It was common amongst abortionists or even for the women concerned to use a knitting needle or a piece of wire to end an unwanted pregnancy. Was it possible this woman had used this method on herself? Or had she had help?

The only person who might know was the man who had dumped the woman at the hospital. If he was her husband, then it might be that the termination had been self-administered. If not, then perhaps he knew the person who had carried out the procedure.

Today, she decided, was not the right time to share the information.

Leaving the letter from the young doctor in need of a job on top of the desk, she placed the other in a desk drawer and locked it.

It might have been easier to find out who had supplied the pills. Tracking down the person responsible for carrying out the abortion was another matter, especially seeing as the dead woman had not been recognised as local.

Let wickedness stay locked away whilst Christmas is upon us, she thought. *Deal with what's closest to hand. Enjoy the small things whilst you can.*

'The tree out in the hall smells lovely,' Frances exclaimed as she walked into the ward. 'And it's quite large. I do hope we have enough decorations.'

Lucy assured her that they did, counting them off on her fingers. 'Tinsel and glass balls, candles and bows made from crêpe paper, and we've got strips just waiting to be glued together to make paper chains.'

It struck Frances that Lucy's cheer seemed a little forced. She was about to ask her if anything was troubling her when Sister Harrison mentioned – not without pride – the pretend parcels she'd made for the tree.

'That sounds very clever,' remarked Frances, genuinely impressed at the senior sister's involvement. 'How did you do that?'

There wasn't often an occasion to praise Sister Harrison about anything apart from her work. She was committed to the hospital running smooth as clockwork. At times, it was hard to realise that she might have other interests or home skills besides her work.

'I made small cardboard boxes and covered them with last year's wrapping paper. I stayed up half the night making them.'

Frances saw an amused look pass between Lucy and Wally, the latter still up the ladder and seemingly enjoying his task.

'Does pretend mean there's nothing in them?' Lucy asked.

'I'm afraid it does.'

'Never mind, if they're purely to decorate the tree. I'm sure they'll look very nice indeed. Are you finished there, Sister?'

Patient notes clipped to a clipboard, and a row of pens in the top pocket of her white jacket, Frances was ready to do a round of the ward.

Sister Harrison left the pile of pretend snow and joined her. She kept two steps behind, as she should. It was her job to await instructions or questions relating to how the patient concerned had slept the night before.

'The women's ward first, I think, Sister, before the Christmas decoration team get there.'

There were six beds in the women's ward, three of them occupied.

Frances opened the first folder from those tucked beneath her arm and stopped by the first bed. She put on her best 'get well soon' smile. 'Mrs Thomas. How are you feeling this morning?'

'As well as can be expected, Doctor.'

'There's no discomfort?'

Mrs Thomas shook her head.

'And there's no bleeding?'

Another shake of her head followed by a jerking of her chin

towards where her lower body lay hidden beneath the bedclothes.

'Nothing down there. I looked earlier.'

'Good,' said Frances. She continued to be intrigued how grown women referred to their private parts. Just a jerk of a chin in this instance towards an area of her body she refrained from naming.

Mrs Thomas looked at her anxiously. 'I'm hoping I won't lose this one. It's hard enough being in the family way without having nothing to show for it at the end, and lordy, lordy, I've been through enough.'

Frances agreed with her. Beryl Thomas was desperate to become a mother and had conceived on several occasions, but none had come to term. All appeared fine until a few months in, and she miscarried. This time, to give her the best chance possible, Frances had insisted that she was admitted to hospital to rest every few weeks so Frances could keep a close eye on what was going on.

Beryl was healthy enough. She had a better life than many women of her age in Norton Dene. Her husband was the owner of a large farm on the edge of town. He also owned acres of trees, straight-trunked firs and Scotch pine – the trunks of which were used to make pit props. They were comfortably off and a devoted couple, but try as they might, there had been no issue from their union – none that lived.

Beryl's eyes were full of entreaty. 'I swear to you, Doctor, that one child will be enough for me. I'm not greedy. Is it too much to ask for?'

'No. It's not.'

Beryl clasped her hands together and muttered a hasty prayer. 'Please, God. Let me keep this one.'

Frances sat on the side of her bed. The medical records she pushed to one side were picked up by Sister Harrison.

Frances reached for the woman's hand and clasped it between both of hers. 'I swear to you that I will do my best. That is why I'm dragging you in here to rest. I'm determined to keep a close eye on you.'

'Thank you, Doctor.'

There was genuine gratefulness in Beryl's openly honest face. She treated everyone with kindness and had admitted to Frances how much she envied those women who could give birth to one child after another.

'Popping them out like peas from a pod.'

Beryl was being funny, but Frances knew there was unending pain beneath the surface. Nobody could deny that it seemed unfair that she couldn't conceive and when she did, her body rejected the things she most wanted.

Over the months they'd been in touch with each other, they had become more like friends than doctor and patient. Frances advised and reassured, and because of that Beryl opened up about her life and her fears.

She had first come to see Frances at the family planning clinic, asking for a word in private. Following on from that, Frances had invited her into her office, asked her to sit down and waited whilst this warm, motherly looking woman clutched her handbag tight and prepared herself for hope – or disappointment.

A short but intense conversation had ensued. Beryl had told of having had three pregnancies all of which had terminated before their time.

Frances had asked her if she'd considered adoption.

She'd shaken her head and almost apologetically said that

although there were doubtless many little souls deserving of a home and the love she could give them, they would not be hers and, somehow, she couldn't countenance raising someone else's child. Besides which, her husband would dearly love a son to work alongside him whilst he was still alive and carry it on when he was dead.

Once the situation was clear, Frances had asked if she minded having an internal examination. Beryl had said that she did not.

It turned out that there was little wrong with her except that her womb was tilted back slightly, and the birth canal was a little narrow.

After Frances had informed her, Beryl's expression had been one of dismay. She'd asked if it meant she would never be able to have children.

Frances had reassured her that it was not impossible, but she would have to keep a close eye on her progress when and if she did get pregnant again.

'Should you see any spotting – bleeding, that is – I want you to come into the hospital for bed rest and so we can keep an eye on you.'

Beryl had agreed to do that.

It was at the beginning of August when Beryl Thomas found herself pregnant for the fourth time. She'd come bounding into the hospital, her face bright with excitement as she'd breathlessly asked Frances when she wanted to admit her into the hospital to rest.

Frances had congratulated her, grasping both hands within hers, almost laughing and crying along with her. She'd advised that she didn't need to come in just yet.

'What I would say is not to overexert yourself. But I would say this, at the slightest sign of spotting – the smallest amount of blood – come in. I won't guarantee that I can prevent a miscarriage, but I will do my best.'

There had been two scares about one month apart, then another had occurred just a few days ago when her husband Archie had brought his wife in. This time, her face had been wet with tears and her manner frantic. Her husband, whose arm she'd been leaning on, had looked worried.

Accepting that it was difficult, Frances advised them to stay calm as anxiety could make things worse. She'd also arranged for a stay in hospital so they could monitor her progress.

To Beryl's great joy and Frances's relief, the bleeding had been minimal. It had now stopped.

'I think you can go home today.'

Beryl looked at her in disbelief. 'I can?'

'I think so. Can you get a message to your husband for him to pick you up?'

'Yes. Yes,' she said enthusiastically before she thought it over and said with worry in her voice and on her face, 'Will I be all right? I don't mind staying in here if I must.'

It was always difficult walking that fine line between what was hoped for and what was possible.

Frances thought carefully on how best to word her advice.

'Christmas is coming. A time to be with loved ones, as long as you're not dashing around making the arrangements or cooking the roast dinner.'

Beryl laughed. 'My sister's come to stay. She's already made a pudding and a cake. And I do have a cook. Mrs Fowler is quite a treasure. She lives in, so I'm well covered, although...' She paused, her eyes taking in the efforts at decorating the ward which was looking more festive by the minute. 'I regret going in a way. I might be missing all the fun.'

She laughed. It was good to hear, and Frances couldn't help but laugh with her.

'Go home and have a good Christmas and, fingers crossed, you'll have your very special Christmas present in the New Year.'

And I will have come to a decision, she thought to herself. *One way or another.*

19

Christmas Day dawned cloaked in fog, and it was icy underfoot. Fortunately, the snow stayed away, which was regretted by small boys who had to make do with slipping and sliding on the patches they'd already made.

Bundled in a warm coat, stout boots and a hat knitted by Sister Harrison and given to her as a Christmas present, Frances bemoaned the fact that she was dressed for snow and there was none.

Dressed in more than one layer of vestments, plus having found a pair of long johns once worn by his father, Gregory sank back from the church porch and into the greater warmth of the chancel, where he gave Frances one of many Christmas kisses.

'I'm glad it's not snowing. I've never known a warm church.'

'You're being churlish,' she said, tapping the cleft in his chin with her index finger. 'People hope for it. It's traditional.'

'Like one of those scenes from a Christmas card, a coach and four standing outside an old inn and the snow coming down in buckets.'

'I love those cards.'

'Snow is best staying on Christmas cards.'

'Humbug,' she said laughingly, though Gregory was far from being mean at any time of year. He just preferred warmer temperatures. The warmer outside the church, the less chilly the old walls and stone floor.

She slid into a pew three rows back from the altar and blew him a kiss before he readied himself for the onslaught.

In minutes, the congregation, some of whom only attended church at Christmas, began filing in.

The braziers blazed away, warming the chancel. Holly, ivy and candles added to the festive cheer.

Frances nodded at those she knew, and they nodded back.

'It's a good turnout,' Lucy whispered from her spot in the Compton-Dixon pew beside Devlin, who was holding her hand tightly.

Araminta was enveloped in a full-length fur coat with wide sleeves and an immense collar that came high on her face, her eyes peering over the top of it like an animal in its burrow.

Devlin remarked that despite the brazier's red hot coals, his feet were cold.

Lucy asked Araminta if she was warm enough. Perhaps she should have heeded her suggestion to bring a blanket.

'No need, my dear.' It was barely perceptible when she shrugged her shoulders beneath the thick fur. 'In fact, I'm feeling a little over encumbered with the skins of half the small creatures of Canada on my back.'

Lucy smiled, hugged Devlin's arm close to her side and squeezed his hand.

Her gaze swept over the congregation, the arched windows and the overhead hammer beams that had held the roof up for centuries. Braziers were needed today to keep the place warm. It would be very different in June when she and Devlin would marry here in front of family, friends and acquaintances of the Compton-Dixon family. The very thought of such a grand occasion, and the prospect that it might never happen, filled her with fear.

Friends of her ladyship would be coming, of course; people Lucy did not know. Friends also of Devlin – old school, university and army friends. She'd met few of them so far and although she'd always been a bright button, full of confidence, due in a way to her dealing with patients and doctors, she felt nervous every time she thought of the wedding. What would they think of her? A nobody who was marrying a somebody, a war hero descended from people with titles.

And what about her little problem?

Another squeeze of her hand by Devlin jerked her back to the here and now.

'All right?' he asked softly.

'Yes. Yes. I was just thinking how lovely everything is.'

'No doubt. Are candles lit?'

'Yes.'

'How big is the tree?'

'Oh, about eight feet tall and covered in tinsel and glass balls.'

'And more candles.'

'Yes.' She gave a little laugh. 'Lots of candles.'

'Good. I'm glad you could make it.'

'So am I.'

Last Christmas, she had been on duty, but there had been fewer staff back then. This year, there were more, and the duty roster was spread less thinly.

Being of Welsh chapel persuasion, Nurse Gwen Peebles had stated her willingness to cover for Christmas Day. Sister Harrison was attending a church closer to home and was scheduled to take over from Nurse Peebles this evening.

'Didn't even know she went to church,' muttered Nancy after enquiring of her sister who was on duty today and this evening. She was attending the service with her husband, Ned Skittings, seated in the aisle in one of the public pews. This was another thing Lucy was finding hard to get used to; sitting in the pew reserved for the Compton-Dixon family rather than with her own family in the public pews.

Worries about her wedding disintegrated as the congregation arose in response to the Reverend Gregory Sampson announcing the first carol – 'Hark the Herald Angels Sing'.

More carols, the sermon and prayers followed, the braziers and candles casting a warm glow, both helping to raise the temperature.

Children were singing lustily, their faces round and pink, their little bodies bundled up in warm winter clothes.

Lucy sang along with everyone else and tried not to worry about the changes she'd detected in her body. *Please God, I mustn't be pregnant. There's a sumptuous wedding planned for June, and I have the biggest part to play. I cannot – I just cannot – let everyone down.*

The Christmas Day service ended with 'Oh Come All Ye Faithful'.

'And now for the pagan-based feast,' said Devlin as they filed out of the church to the rear of everyone else.

He wound his arm around Lucy's waist as they walked past the tombstones of those who had also enjoyed a long-ago Christmas service at the church where they now lay in eternal slumber.

Ahead of them, Devlin's mother was talking to other members of the congregation in her role as lady of the manor.

Devlin tapped his stick along the path, his arm still around her. She tried to force herself to make a jolly comment, but none would come.

'Are you feeling all right, darling? You seem rather quiet.'

She managed to laugh it off. 'I was just thinking that on a freezing-cold day like this I wouldn't mind making toast in front of a roaring fire.'

'If that's what you want, that's what we'll have – although I think my mother and cook won't be best pleased.'

'Then it's a roast with all the trimmings.' Lucy laughed. 'I wouldn't want to upset anyone.'

And, indeed, that was the truth, though she was again thinking about the June wedding. All the invitations had been sent out. All the arrangements already in place.

Devlin had to be the first to be told, but when should she do that?

She took a deep breath, its white steaminess rising on the cold air.

After Christmas. It had to be after Christmas.

* * *

There was another person not at the service who would normally have been sitting with her son Ned, Nancy and their two children. Ma Skittings was otherwise engaged.

Promised Christmas lunch at the vicarage, Ma Skittings had insisted she would look after Frances's mother.

Gregory had prepared everything for the Christmas feast on Christmas Eve after evensong and before the Midnight Mass.

Frances had watched with amusement to see how efficient he was, saucepan in one hand, sermon in the other.

'Can I do anything to help?' she'd asked.

'Can you cast your eyes over the sermon for spelling mistakes and suchlike? My grammar is not always strictly King's English.'

She had taken the sheets of paper and perused as he'd asked her. It wasn't easy to concentrate. Foremost of her concerns was her mother. Holly, ivy and being jolly couldn't obliterate the concern she felt for Mary Devonshire's deteriorating condition. Having her mother join in the festivities would make things perfect. Wouldn't it be wonderful, she'd thought, if her mother could wear a paper hat, pull a cracker, eat her fill and be pink-faced instead of pale as icing sugar.

Together, she and Ma Skittings had worked out a rota of care so that both could indulge in Christmas dinner, one of them sitting with her mother whilst the other indulged in the Christmas meal. It all seemed quite simple. Gregory would keep her meal hot whilst Ma Skittings ate hers, then vice versa.

They'd presented the plan to her mother.

On being told this, her mother had insisted that she would be coming to lunch at the vicarage.

'Me and Ma Skittings are going to sing carols together,' she'd told Frances.

Ma Skittings had slapped her meaty hand onto her equally meaty thigh and added, 'And share a drop of my honey and plum brandy. I had a good harvest this year so plenty of it. I'll bring a bottle for you too, Doctor. I'm sure you'll enjoy it.'

'So will Gregory.' Frances's laughter had been tinged with sadness. Much as she would welcome her mother being able to come downstairs, then, with assistance, walk over to the vicarage as though she wasn't at death's door, it was a tall hope. Or perhaps she was getting better. Perhaps a Christmas miracle was in the offing. That was what Gregory had said. 'They do happen sometimes.'

Surrounded by the magic of Christmas Day, it was possible to believe it.

The bay window of the dining room in the gabled vicarage threw a great pool of golden light onto the frosted ground. The mist had cleared, and in the swiftly gathering darkness of late afternoon, stars were beginning to twinkle.

'Silent night, holy night,' murmured Frances, face turned skywards, her arm linked in his.

They sang it, just the two of them.

Faces pink from cold, they entered the vicarage hallway with its red and black clay terrazzo floor, the smell of food coming out to meet them.

Frances stopped. 'I'd better go to the coach house and see how my mother's doing.'

Just as she started to peel away, the front door of the vicarage opened; its inner light blocked by the wide, tall figure of Ma Skittings.

Frances instantly thought the worst. 'Oh my God.'

Gregory wordlessly rested his hand on her arm as they hurried up the steps.

The overhead light caught the expression on Ma Skittings' face as she stepped back into the hallway. Frances saw that expression and the tight grip around her heart disappeared. It was not a sad tidings expression. Neither was it outright happiness but something in between.

'She's in here,' Ma Skittings said, tilting her head sideways and back to the dining room. 'Couldn't stop 'er. Waiting for 'er dinner, she is.' She nodded at Gregory. 'Better get a move on, Vicar, she's been looking forward to this all day.'

'She managed to get here?' Frances was astounded.

Ma Skittings beamed. 'With a bit of support from a strong right arm. My right arm, in fact.'

In the dining room, where candles glowed on the tree and a fire blazed in the grate, sat Mary Devonshire, Frances's mother.

Her small face peeped out from over the top of a doubled-up blanket, like a blue tit peering out from the hole in a nesting box.

The winged chair she was sitting in dwarfed her tiny form. Frances hadn't been reunited with her that long, though long enough to realise that her mother had shrunk in stature – as old people are wont to do.

'Mother...'

She was about to say that she should be in bed but clamped her mouth over those words. Deep in her soul, she knew that her mother was tasting, not just a meal, but the last moments of her life.

Gregory had taken himself off to the kitchen, from where the clattering of pots and pans rang like a peal of bells.

After discarding her outdoor coat, boots and hat, Frances knelt at her mother's side and took her fragile and freezing hands into hers.

'We sang carols this morning,' said her mother, her eyes twinkling as they hadn't done in a long while. 'And drank plum brandy.'

'Mary,' exclaimed Ma Skittings, her voice booming out with words and laughter. 'You've given me away. I've been telling everybody that I never touch a drop.'

Frances felt the frail body trembling through the thickness of blanket as her mother laughed.

'It sounds as though you've been having a fine time,' Frances exclaimed and gently hugged her. Tears trembled in her eyes, but she held them back. She wanted to share her mother's joy, not wash it away in a flood of tears. This had to be a happy time, one to be remembered.

They had their Christmas dinner, Gregory insisting that because he'd cooked the meal it was also his right to serve it.

'But you've done everything,' Frances protested after he'd forced her to sit.

'Ah,' he said, whilst waving the carving knife and fork. 'Only so far. I'm leaving the dishes. After all, I've got the evening service to contend with.'

There was laughter at that exceptional meal and although her mother couldn't eat very much – just one slice of chicken, one potato, and a spoonful of Christmas pudding to follow, it was a sweet occasion. A glass of Gregory's home-made wine and one or two of what was left of the plum brandy helped wash it down. She noticed her mother had no trouble imbibing wine or brandy.

When it was over, Gregory announced that the bed in the spare room was available. 'Rather than you venturing out again,' he said to Frances's mother. 'Stay here overnight. We'll get you back in the morning. It comes complete with hot-water bottle. And a strong man to take you there.'

Her mother's smile was weak but full of gratitude.

Ma Skittings insisted on staying until she was ready to go to bed.

Tiring easily, it wasn't long before bedtime came.

Gregory picked up the fragile form and the bundled blankets with the greatest of ease. Frances followed him up the stairs to the back bedroom, leaving Ma Skittings to deal with clearing the dishes away.

She sat on the edge of the bed, holding her mother's hand.

'No need for you to stay,' said her mother, her voice barely above a whisper.

'I'll stay here until you fall asleep.' She squeezed her mother's fingers.

They had not removed the blankets she was bundled up in

but covered both them and her small body with the rest of the bedding.

Frances observed that she still looked cold and pale. No more extra blankets could alter that.

She stroked gossamer-fine hair back from her mother's face, noting her eyes were already closed, her breathing shallow.

'Goodnight, Mother,' she whispered and kissed her forehead.

It was then that a thought occurred to her.

'This bed was already made up.'

Gregory was watching from the doorway. 'I wanted you to stay.'

'Alone in this bed?'

He shook his head. 'It's only a few feet from mine. I thought those extra steps – and perhaps sharing a bed would be our Christmas present to each other.'

The light was dim in the room but enough for her to see the affection in his face, the hope in his eyes.

Her mother was already asleep.

She smiled up at this wonderful man. 'I'll be here when you come back from the evening service.'

'Good,' he said, looking sublimely happy. 'Good.'

20

A new year had begun and the wards that had been less full over Christmas at the Orchard Cottage Hospital were filling up again.

Most of the referrals to the hospital came via local doctors and were the result of the winter weather, slips and strains, the first birth of the New Year. Thankfully, the quarries and mines had been closed on Christmas Day, so no time for accidents. However, the Boxing Day meet of the Little Norton Hounds, a fox hound kennels just outside town, had resulted in two casualties. A rider had been dismounted whilst in the process of jumping over a five-bar gate. The other had been bitten by one of the dogs when trying to beat it off from attacking a cat. The cat had escaped up a tree. The man trying to rescue it had needed an anti-rabies injection and antibiotics. It was, however, impossible to bandage the man's buttock, so he was forced to lie face down on the hospital bed while a dressing was supplied and time allowed for the blood to congeal and the pain to ease.

It was on the second of January that a little boy was rushed in by his parents.

Nurse Lucy Daniels carried out a preliminary examination

and knew immediately that he was very poorly indeed. The sweaty look on his face was accompanied by him coughing, spluttering and gasping for breath, his little chest heaving up and down like a pair of bellows.

Lucy called for Sister Gwen Peebles to give her a hand taking him down to a ward containing only one bed – the room reserved for contagious cases. She also instructed one of the student nurses to inform Doctor Brakespeare that she was needed in isolation.

'He's only had measles,' said the father as he ran alongside the trolley on which the seven-year-old lay. 'I keep telling my wife that there's no need to worry. Kids get measles all the time and they get over it.'

The mother was biting her bottom lip, and her eyes were narrowed in a face creased with fear. She too was running alongside the trolley as Gwen Peebles rolled it into the single room.

Lucy, her face ashen, held back and was hardly aware when the parents pushed past her.

Gwen ushered them out of the room. The woman burst into tears as the door to the room closed firmly behind them. Lucy loitered, asking them to follow her, though they hardly noticed.

The man did his best to console his frantic wife, though without much luck.

'I'm telling you. It's nothing to worry about. It's just measles.'

Intent on pushing home his point of view, he almost collided with Frances on her way along the corridor, heading to where she'd been informed a little boy lay with suspected measles complications.

'Are you the doctor?' he asked in a loud, authoritative voice, looking her up and down as though he didn't quite believe it.

'Yes.'

'I want a word.'

'Certainly. After I've seen the patient.'

Lucy was insistent they followed her. 'I might even be able to rustle you up a cup of tea,' she said soothingly.

The prospect of tea seemed to work. To her great relief, she managed to settle them into the waiting room.

Back in the isolation room, Frances was on one side of the bed, Gwen Peebles on the other.

'What's his name?'

'Stephen Brown.'

Frances leaned over him. 'Stephen? Can you hear me?'

There was only a flickering of the closed eyes. The lids were bluish in colour.

Following a close examination, Frances rewound her stethoscope around her neck, sighed and shook her head. 'I'm almost certain it's not encephalitis. That's the good thing.'

Encephalitis was a complication of measles that led to swelling of the brain. There was no cure.

Sister Peebles hesitated before daring to offer her opinion. 'Pneumonia?'

Frances nodded. 'I think so. I believe we have sulphonamides in the pharmacy. I'll assess the dosage. Keep him hydrated and bathe his skin with iced water. Twenty-four hours should see an improvement.'

Or not.

She pushed the unwelcome thought away, left the room and prepared herself to face the parents.

They were seated in the small waiting room adjacent to her office. The man was doing his best to reassure the tearful wife. Two teacups were set on the table, one full, the other only half.

They looked up as she came in and only barely moved apart, staying close a form of consolation and mutual support.

'Mr and Mrs Brown?'

The husband stood up. His wife remained seated and holding onto his arm, her features dwarfed by the expression in her eyes.

'Is he all right?' Mr Brown demanded. 'It is only measles – isn't it?' Mr Brown had reverted to type, the sort convinced he knows better than anyone else.

Frances gave him a stern look. 'I'm afraid your son has pneumonia.'

Mrs Brown gasped.

Mr Brown's jaw dropped. 'But it was only measles. How could he have pneumonia. How could that happen?'

Frances went on to explain that complications could arise, and that pneumonia was only one of them. There were others, some of which led to mortality.

'I've prescribed sulphonamide. At the same time as administering this, we will be attempting to keep him hydrated and nourished as best we can.'

Mrs Brown snatched her hand from her husband, covered her face and shook her head.

Mr Brown, looking more contrite than when he'd first arrived, patted his wife's shoulder. 'Bear up, old girl. Bear up.'

After taking a few details, Frances said she would keep them informed as to their son's progress. They had no telephone at home but gave her the phone number of the cabinet maker who occupied premises at the corner of their street. Frances recognised the name as being that of a coffin maker. She only hoped that they would not need to use his services as well as his telephone.

* * *

Frances was setting her notes in order regarding young Stephen

Brown and other patients when Sister Gwen Peebles knocked at her door.

'Gwen. How can I help you?'

'It's a bit of a story,' said Gwen who closed the door behind her in such a way Frances presumed she was about to impart a secret.

Frances put down her pen and settled back in her chair. 'Then if you're to tell me a story, both of us should make ourselves comfortable.'

With a swishing of starched skirt and apron, Gwen settled herself in the chair on the other side of Frances's desk.

'I've already told you this, but I've been getting things in order in my mind. This upsurge in miscarrying at a very early stage. You already know my view, Doctor, that they're getting something to get rid of their pregnancies. In fact, some of them are almost gloating that it's happened. So, I asked some of them – jokingly – whether they were using stronger gin and hotter baths. There was laughter from those who took it as a big joke. There were others less amused but outspoken about what was going on. A miracle cure for women's monthly cycles, one of them said. As advertised in the paper by some professor of women's ills.'

Frances leaned forward, her expression tight with interest. '"Women's ills". I've heard that phrase before. A furtive way of describing an unwanted pregnancy and, for a fee, offering a way to "cure" the little problem.'

Gwen Peebles nodded. 'Yes and I've found out a bit more. They've been getting pills through this advert in the *Norton Dene Times*. You send off a postal order stating name and address and get a bottle of pills in return. It's as simple as that.'

'So, we have the address! We can literally go knocking on the door!'

Gwen shook her head. 'No. We can't. It's a London address.

That's where they send their postal orders. Then it's posted on to them from someone in the local vicinity.'

Brow furrowed with thought, Frances leaned forward, playing with her fountain pen as she considered what to do next.

'We need a copy of that advertisement.'

'I have a copy here.'

Gwen handed a page of classifieds over to Frances.

'I've circled the advertisement I think is relevant.'

Frances took the piece of newspaper, her gaze skimming over adverts for housekeepers, maids and accommodation until alighting on the advertisement Sister Gwen Peebles had circled which referred to women's 'out of sort' illnesses.

Guaranteed Cure for calming women's monthly hysteria.

Professor P. Y. Regance, graduate of the Bayeaux Medical School in France and Andorra University, has many years' experience in female physiology...

'Charlatan! That's the only qualification this person has. As far as I know, there is no medical school in Bayeaux, and I doubt mountainous little Andorra has a university.'

She fell to silence, her grey eyes dark with concern.

Gwen sat watching her, not making further comment, waiting for Frances to suggest what to do next.

Once she'd taken the first part of the advert in, Frances read the rest out loud: '"Should the prescription route fail to alter Nature's courses, then a face-to-face consultation is available with Professor Regance at our London clinic. Extra fees will be incurred."'

'I don't doubt extra fees will be incurred,' said Frances. With a look of disgust, she threw the scrap of newspaper from her hand as though it was soiled with something quite disgusting. As far as she was concerned, it was disgusting and both annoyed and worried her. Quack doctors had been around for centuries, but never, she guessed, had they made as much money as they could now from advertising their wares. Their nets were spread wide, and many fish were swimming into them.

* * *

On the following evening, Frances was out in the reception hall when Lucy came by with a cup of tea.

'Pop it in on my desk, please.'

At first, she didn't notice that her face had turned pale and followed Lucy into her office.

The desk being covered in paperwork, Lucy made room on the blotting pad for the cup and saucer. As she did, columns of classified advertisements caught her eye, one of which had been circled in black ink.

She read it quickly, her heart thudding against her ribs. Was this the miracle she desperately wanted?

Or did she?

Her blood felt as though it had congealed around her lower limbs.

What would her ladyship think of her? What a peasant, they would say. Just went to show that you couldn't make a silk purse from a sow's ear!

Her breath came quickly as she took in what the advert said. Nature's courses! Nature's courses! Well, she certainly knew what that meant and it was easy to guess what was being offered. Pills to bring on a miscarriage. And then everybody would be happy! Devlin and his mother would have the grand wedding Araminta was planning. They likely would not welcome this baby arriving at such an inconvenient time.

Frances came breezing in, ready for her cup of tea and not noticing that the scrap of paper was gone from her desk.

Lucy screwed it up, clenching it tightly in her fist. Now to alter the subject.

'Do you think Stephen Brown will recover?'

'We can only do our best.'

'He's beginning to look better. Less flushed.'

'Then he's on the mend. Thankfully.'

After taking a sip of tea, Frances picked up her pen and moved a small heap of piles in front of her. 'Might as well get on with these. Thanks for the tea.'

It was a dismissal Lucy was willing to take. Frances did not see her push the crumpled-up piece of paper into the pocket of her uniform.

Feeling guilty, she took a deep breath outside the doctor's office. What she'd done was underhanded, though hardly dishonest. The piece of newspaper had been headed for the wastepaper basket.

Once outside, she bumped into Sister Harrison, who would be taking over the shift from Sister Peebles within the hour.

'I hear we have a case of pneumonia in a child as a result of measles,' proclaimed Sister Harrison.

'Yes. His name's Stephen Brown. He's in isolation.'

'I should think so too. Away from the clinic. We don't want him anywhere near our expectant mothers, do we now.'

Lucy felt as though a torrent of ice-cold water had been poured over her.

Sister Harrison noticed. 'Is something wrong, Nurse Daniels?'

Just for once, Lucy wasn't bemused by Sister Harrison addressing her so formally. She'd often wanted to say, *Please,*

Sister, call me Lucy and I'll call you Edith. Today, Sister Harrison had stated something far more important. She'd reminded Lucy of the latest findings on measles and its effects on the unborn foetus – premature birth or underweight at best, but it could be far worse.

'No. Nothing,' she responded. The icy shivers she was experiencing had nothing to do with the winter weather.

She carried out her remaining duties like clockwork, just as if somebody had wound up a key in her back and she was jolting along from one task to another. Unknowingly, Sister Harrison had given her an extra reason not to have this baby. She had lately exposed herself to Stephen Brown and the possibility of the child being affected by measles. She couldn't go through with it but couldn't tell anyone. She would act as though nothing was wrong, but in the meantime, she would send off for the pills – or even ask for a face-to-face encounter.

In her heart of hearts, she wanted this baby, but she also wanted to be accepted in Devlin's world. A society wedding was the pinnacle of that acceptance – at least that's how it seemed to her.

Tomorrow she would consult the only local person who might help her and keep her secret. She had to do something.

21

Lucy chose her time well. Going direct to Ma Skittings' place would be noticed especially if Nancy or the children were there.

It was her day off and around midday she made her way to the vicarage coach house where her sister's mother-in-law would be preparing a meal for Doctor Brakespeare's mother. The doctor herself would be at the hospital, so now seemed the best chance.

Wrapped up against the lingering cold, she made her way there, passing a bunch of snowdrops that were showing their delicate heads above the dank dirt.

To reach the coach house meant going past the vicarage. If the vicar was at home, he would be in his study, which she recalled was at the rear of the substantial house that had been built back in the nineteenth century.

Aware of the sound of her footsteps clumping on the flagstone path, she walked on the soles of her feet and was almost holding her breath as she crept past the vicarage, its big bay window looking out on the world. She only hoped that the vicar was not on the other side of it, although on reflection he might not be suspicious at all. After all, she was related to Ma Skittings, via the marriage of her sister Nancy to Ned Skittings.

She told herself to stop being so nervous. She had every right to be here.

The heavy iron knocker on the coach house door was loud. Loud enough to wake the dead, she thought.

Ma Skittings looked taken aback when she saw Lucy standing there. Almost, but not quite.

'Lucy. Nice to see you. Come on in.'

Not 'why are you here', or 'what a surprise', just an instant invitation to come inside. Such warmth made Lucy feel almost guilty that she had such an awkward question to ask. She stopped holding her handbag in a stranglehold.

The interior of the coach house was warm by virtue of the coal-fired range, aided by another range in the kitchen. Everything inside was just as Lucy remembered it from the days when she and Nancy had been asked to clean and look after it prior to the arrival of the town's only female doctor.

The smell of home cooking wafted in from the kitchen.

Lucy inhaled appreciatively. 'Something smells delicious.'

'Parsnip and honey soup.'

Ma Skittings leaned over a black cast-iron pot from the hob at the side of the fire and gave it a stir. 'I've got bread baking in the range,' she said, jerking her head in the general direction of the kitchen, where the bread oven was set into the wall alongside the larger coal-fired range. 'You can take a loaf with you if you like.'

'That would be nice.' Lucy paused. She'd rehearsed three times the scene that should come next but was still unready. 'How's Mrs Devonshire?'

She already knew that the doctor's mother was very ill. The fact that Ma Skittings came here on a regular basis was enough to tell her just how ill she was.

'Waiting for her lunch.'

'She's lucky to have you here. She's not getting any better, so I hear.'

Still bent over the pot, Ma Skittings paused in her stirring and looked over her shoulder at Lucy. 'But you already know that. So, my girl, what are you here for?'

Lucy's eyelids fluttered in response to the unblinking eyes of the woman who could read people as easily as some could read a book.

Overwhelmed by the scrutiny, Lucy sank onto a high-backed Windsor chair, its arms worn smooth over the years by the hands that had rested there.

Ma Skittings straightened and looked directly at her, wooden spoon dangling at her side. She waited.

'I... came here... because... well...' She took a deep breath, her fingers interlaced in a wiry clasp.

Ma Skittings shook her head, her keen eyes seeing everything – or at least that was the way it seemed to Lucy. 'Hanging onto it won't do any good. Might as well spill it out.'

Startled by the inferred insight, as though she knew there was a secret, a problem that needed to come out, Lucy raised her chin. Her mouth was dry, but there was no turning back. She had to share her secret with someone trustworthy and nobody fitted the bill as well as Ma Skittings.

She took a deep breath, then said, 'I have a... little problem.'

'Ah!' The old leather armchair with its crinkled skin and tasselled cushions creaked as Ma Skittings settled herself. 'A woman's problem, I suppose.'

Lucy nodded.

'How far gone?'

There it was. Right from the start Ma Skittings knew.

'Only about two months. I thought...'

'Why do I get the impression that this new life growing within you is not welcome. You're engaged. You're getting married. Have you had a change of heart? You're marrying the father, aren't you?'

'Yes, but... the timing is wrong.'

'Wrong?' That one word carried an aura of accusation. 'My dear, is there ever a right time? Now tell me why you feel this way.'

Lucy licked her bottom lip. The words were there, but she was having trouble getting them in some order. 'Her ladyship has organised this wonderful wedding for June. We've had a hand in it too – Devlin and I, and I don't want to spoil things.'

Ma Skittings cocked her head to one side. She had the look of an inquisitive owl, eyes unblinking with statement and questions. 'And an early baby will spoil it. How about bringing the date forward?'

Lucy shook her head emphatically. 'I can't do that. What would people think of me?'

'What will Devlin think of you? Isn't that what really matters?'

Lucy picked at a stray thread on her coat sleeve. 'I know what you're saying, but you see...' She raised her head swiftly. 'I'll be letting him down. He wants to show me off, to proclaim to the world – his world and that of his mother – that I might be ordinary, but I can act the part of the lady. Cancelling the wedding in June would cause scandal.' She shook her head. 'I don't want to do that.'

Ma Skittings saw the pleading in her face, the anxiety in her eyes. She narrowed her own. Lucy was hardly the first girl caught out before her wedding day.

'Blow the wedding. Tell the truth and bring the date forward.'

Lucy gasped. 'But what will they all think of me? I feel I'd be letting him down. Him and the rest of the family. Her ladyship has invited a lot of her friends, rich and important people from London and suchlike. Local gentry too.'

Ma Skittings chuckled. 'You could go ahead anyway. You wouldn't be the first to walk down the aisle with a big belly. Imagine their faces if you left it until June.' Ma Skittings chuckled again.

'I can't. Don't you see how it looks? Some of them must already think that Devlin's marrying beneath him. Me being in the family way would be proof of that.'

Ma Skittings sighed and clasped her work-worn hands on her lap. 'So, you feel unworthy. You've got it in mind that you're marrying above yourself, and everything must be perfect just so the wedding guests think well of you. What does your intended think?'

Lucy looked down at her tangled fingers and bit her bottom lip. 'I haven't told him.'

'Can you speak up, girl? You're squeaking like a little mouse, and I know you've never been one to squeak. Speak up.' Ma Skittings' voice was loud enough to make Lucy jump. Which was as she'd intended. She wanted to wake her up to reality.

'I haven't told him.' She said it more resolutely, holding herself more upright and looking as though she was braver than she was feeling.

'Then perhaps you should before you do anything drastic.'

'But I don't want to let him down.'

Ma Skittings eyed Lucy's lovely face. How could any man not love her? But then Devlin couldn't see her face. But if he loved her, family wouldn't matter.

'I wondered if you could give me something...'

Ma Skittings turned away. 'I can't help you. Now I must get on. Mrs Devonshire is waiting for her lunch.'

Lucy felt a surge of anger coupled with disappointment. Never had Ma Skittings snubbed her like this or refused to help when she needed it.

'But if you can't give me anything, what should I do?' she pleaded.

A bowl of hot soup in hand, the only thing she could get Mrs Devonshire to eat of late, Ma Skittings headed for the stairs without answering – not until her foot was on the bottom tread. Then she turned round.

'Tell the father first. He has a right.'

Then she left her there, the sound of her footfall signalling the finality of their conversation. Lucy was left by herself, alone, contemplating her options but basically distraught.

Aware that their meeting was over and without gain, she left the coach house and ran back along the path past the vicarage without looking right or left.

If she had, she would have seen the tall figure of the Reverend Gregory Sampson standing at the bay window, watching and wondering why she was there.

Gregory's eyes fixed on her. The young nurse was almost running, a handkerchief held to her lower face as though she was trying to stem a sob. He thought about going to the front door and calling out after her and offering if he could help her in some way. Judging by her stance, the handkerchief held to her mouth, she obviously had a problem. As a vicar, he was used to reading people's disposition even before they let on what they were worried about. It was a skill he'd honed over the years.

Rather than shout out after her, he decided not to intervene. Whatever was the matter he might hear about it later from his darling Frances. Tonight, they were dining together, not, for once, at the vicarage, but at the coach house.

Because of her mother's diminishing health, Frances was

wary of leaving her mother alone, so this evening he was going round there to dine. She'd told him in an optimistic manner that it was to give Ma Skittings a break, but he was wiser than that. Her mother was fading fast, but he discerned there was something else on her mind. Her career made heavy demands on her time and on her feelings too and it wasn't easy keeping a balance. It took a lot of strength to soldier on.

As for himself, he'd attended enough sick and dying people to be able to tell when they were not long for this world. So, he respected the doctor's stance, the way she juggled both her professional and her personal responsibilities.

I will be her strength, he promised himself, almost like a prayer. *I will respect her wishes and will be there whenever I am needed.*

Whilst her mother slept upstairs, they would eat, drink and entertain with witty comments and intimate thoughts.

The food and drink were very important, of course, and being a man at ease in the kitchen, he had prepared a casserole, a rhubarb crumble and a bottle of decent wine.

'And you'll leave the dishes for me, I suppose,' grumbled Mrs Cross, his housekeeper.

'No need. I'm taking them over to the coach house tonight. Ma Skittings is a bit too busy to cook much.'

'Humph. I'm being pushed aside in favour of Ma Skittings, am I?'

'You're the most important woman in my life, Mrs Cross. I count on your support.'

A girlish blush came to her fifty-year-old face. Mrs Cross was easily persuaded. Having long ago accepted his usefulness in the kitchen, she quite liked having nothing much else but housework to do.

His mind returned to Frances. As always, he ran through a

few subjects for discourse: the leak in the church roof, the flower committee, forthcoming christenings, weddings and funerals. The latter was in the majority at this time of year. Now what middle-of-the-road subjects could he resort to? There was the ongoing investigation into the incident at the hospital before Christmas, but even that was fading into memory. It was also a sad subject. Mentioning that he'd seen Lucy coming out of the coach house and running along the path might strike up some interest and alleviate the more sombre subject of Mrs Devonshire.

Yes, he decided, he would mention it this evening, perhaps over a pre-dinner drink.

22

The mist was of a thick white variety that clung damply to one's hair, the sprinkled droplets sparkling like sequins over a dark coat.

The windscreen wipers of Frances's little car kept the wetness at bay, though the inside needed a constant swipe of a cloth to stop it from misting up.

Just in case there was an overnight frost, Frances drove the car into the garage and shut the double wooden doors.

Although the snows of midwinter had receded – at least for now – the chill she was experiencing, and the prospect of a coal fire made her speed towards the front door.

On closing the door, Frances was amused to see that Ma Skittings had her coat on.

'How come you always know when I'm about to come in the front door?' she asked laughingly.

'Instinct. Dogs and cats 'ave it and so do I.'

'I think that's what's called a sixth sense.'

'It's my sense,' stated Ma Skittings with a lofty lift of her head.

Frances took off her coat and gave it a good shake before

hanging it on a hook at the side of the fire. She then asked the question that one day she would hate to hear the answer to.

'How's Mrs Devonshire – my mother – today?' She'd got into the habit of referring to her mother as Mrs Devonshire before adding the word 'mother'.

'Slept a lot. Had half a dozen spoonfuls of soup for lunch and 'alf a slice of bread, plus a cup of tea at four o'clock.'

Frances knew without Ma Skittings saying that her mother would only have drunk half a cupful of tea. Half of everything, or sometimes less. Her consumption of food had long been small and was getting smaller.

'Oh well. Perhaps she'll have a bit more this evening. Something light?'

'I've made your mother a bowl of custard. She's had no appetite today, but she might like something sweet and easily digested.'

There was a flatness to the way she said it, matter-of-fact but in a strange way without emotion.

'I see.'

Her mother's appetite had gone downhill. Gone was that sweet time at Christmas when she'd insisted on getting up and indulging in the Christmas lunch Gregory had prepared. What a treasure he was. Besides cooking, he'd also had to organise and officiate at the Christmas services. Most of the cooking had been aided by Ma Skittings and she'd taken charge of the washing up.

Frances thanked Ma Skittings for the bowl of custard. As she took it, her attention was drawn to the dining table of scrubbed pine, big enough to seat six. A setting for two people was laid out complete with wine glasses.

She smiled. 'Thank you for setting the table.'

'No need. It didn't take much effort, and I know the vicar is coming round tonight.' She beamed, her smile displaying a lack of teeth. 'You could do with a treat.'

Ma Skittings' brows were beetled over her all-knowing eyes, and she made no further progress towards the front door.

'Is something wrong?'

Ma Skittings looked affronted but easily collected herself. 'You know she's fading away.'

'Yes.'

She did not leave but grimaced into the room, not really looking at anything. Frances perceived she might be considering something that she did not want to bring into the open, chewing over whatever was in her mind.

Ma Skittings had decided to keep the reason for Lucy's visit a secret. It was only fair. Devlin Compton-Dixon should be the first to know the reason at the bottom of her reluctance.

She buttoned her coat and pulled her hat down more firmly on her straggly grey hair. Fashion and presentation were never a big priority in her world. 'I'll be off then.'

'Thank you again.'

Fresh air wafted into the warm room before the door closed, sending tongues of yellow flames in the fireplace licking over those coals not yet glowing.

Her mother's bedroom was as warm as downstairs, the curtains closed against the night and an extra blanket placed on top of the eiderdown. She knew without checking that there would also be a hot-water bottle at her mother's feet.

A face made small by age and illness lay white and still upon the pillow. Her eyes were closed, her lips a pale mauve colour. Thankfully, her breathing was regular. Frances breathed a sigh of relief.

'Mother,' she said softly as she set down the bowl of custard on the bedside table. 'Ma Skittings made you some custard. Are you up to it?'

Her question resulted in a deep, long sigh. For a moment, Frances held her breath. The sigh was reminiscent of the last breath of someone dying. She'd heard plenty of those in her time.

'Nooo.' The response was long, drawn out and barely above a whisper.

'Mother?' She caressed her mother's cheek, then ran her fingers through the fluffy grey hair, fanning it back from her face. 'Is there anything I can get you?'

A slight movement, the smallest shake of her head.

'Would you like me to read to you?'

Even to her own ears, the question seemed mildly amusing. Like a mother reading a bedtime story to a child, only in this case the roles were reversed. The child, now grown, was suggesting she read to the mother.

The only response was her mother snuggling down deeper into the bedclothes.

'No. I'm tired.' A pause for breath. 'You put your feet up.' Another pause for breath. 'You've had a hard day.' Strangled breath catching in a diseased throat. The disease of the lungs had travelled upwards into the throat. It might yet go further, though was enough already to kill her.

'Would you like me to lie down with you for a while? Just until you fall asleep.'

Another long-drawn-out sigh. Another small shake of the head.

Her mouth was moving, but her words were swallowed back in or said so quietly Frances failed to hear.

'I didn't catch what you said, Mother.'

A thin finger, the flesh barely covering the bone, rose weakly and, bending like a claw, beckoned her closer.

In a bid to hear, Frances turned her head sideways so that her ear was against her mother's mouth.

The thin lips parted. Words and breath were barely distinguishable, yet Frances heard.

'Dying is hard work. I never knew it could be so hard.'

Frances almost choked. It wasn't the first time a patient had made a similar comment. Wishing they wouldn't wake up in the morning was another one she'd heard the most from someone in pain. But this was her mother and although they hadn't shared many years together, it was still as if a steel needle had pierced her heart. She would dearly love more time.

With some difficulty, she regained her composure and proceeded to tuck the bedding in around the frail body lying on her side at the centre of the bed.

'I'll leave the custard on the table for you just in case you fancy it later. In my opinion, I prefer it cold to hot. Would that be all right with you?'

Her mother gave a mumbled response that sounded like agreement and, much as Frances would have liked to hear more, she knew it wouldn't happen. When strength went, voice soon followed.

After washing and changing into a dark blue off-the-shoulder dress, she went back downstairs, her thoughts in disarray. For a start, why had she put on this dress and the pearl necklace Ralph, her former sweetheart, had given her? There didn't have to be any reason, but it just felt the right thing to do in order to go on living, to enjoy life. Tonight, she felt like dressing up like a princess and, just for a while, enter another world and leave her worries behind. She needed that just to keep her sanity.

'I bear gifts,' declared Gregory as she let him in. 'Chicken casserole, plus rhubarb pie. Have you cream? Or custard. Sauce Anglaise.' He added the French description of custard with a flourish.

Frances said that she did. 'Cream for preference.'

The truth was, she couldn't countenance serving custard. It would be like having her mother present at the table, a reminder that happiness wasn't a foregone conclusion.

'Cream is fine with me.'

Gregory looked at the prettily laid table. A tiny bunch of snowdrops peeped over the top of a small glass, the kind used for tots of rum.

'Someone's been busy,' he said before turning to her. His eyes swept over her creamy shoulders and dark satin bodice. 'And you, my darling, are a sight for sore eyes.'

His expression and comment were sincere. She smiled and poured them both a drink. 'I felt I needed to come out of myself tonight.'

As they clinked glasses, he tilted his head to one side as he smiled on her face.

'To you, my favourite doctor.'

'Thank you. I'm so glad you came round tonight. You light up my world at a difficult time.'

His eyebrows rose quizzically. 'How is she?'

'Sleeping, I think. She's comfortable. Ma Skittings has made sure of that.'

'That isn't what I meant.'

Frances maintained a weak smile and shook her head. 'I don't think it will be long and even though I've cared for other patients who were dying, this time it affects me more. I wasn't sure that it would. If I'm honest, I didn't think I would care as much as I do.'

'Understandable.' He led her to the sofa. 'You were parted

when you were born. You've lived separate lives, but the bond is still strong. Stronger than you could have imagined.'

The warmth of his hand on her shoulder was comforting. She moved closer and rested her head against his neck.

'I can't help feeling guilty. I feel I should be here all the time.'

'Ma Skittings is here during the day.'

'Yes, but she's not trained in medicine.'

'I suppose having a nurse in might help. Are you planning to do that?'

'I had considered it, but I've no plan to put it into action. Besides, my mother is very comfortable with Ma Skittings.'

'I thought you might have been planning to engage a nurse, seeing as Lucy was here earlier.'

'Lucy?' Frances's closed eyes popped open. 'Are you sure?'

'Yes. I saw her go into the coach house and come out again.'

'Mrs Skittings didn't mention her calling in.'

'Have I got the wrong end of the stick?'

'I think you have.'

Gregory shrugged. 'Perhaps it was a family matter. I must admit she didn't look very happy.'

Frances raised her head from his shoulder and looked into his eyes, a small frown hanging on her forehead. 'It's strange that Ma Skittings didn't say anything. She usually tells me everything that's happened during the day.'

'Perhaps it's very personal. You could ask her.'

She sat up straight. 'I would ask, but don't want her to think I'm prying. As you say, it may be something personal.'

'You could ask Lucy.'

Her frown was undiminished. 'No. I don't think so. I've no wish to intrude.'

'You've heard no rumours at the hospital?'

'Should I?'

'It's just that she looked so miserable, not at all her usual bouncy self.'

'Oh dear. You've made me feel so guilty. The trouble is that of late I've been wrapped up worrying about my mother here and at the hospital I've got a little boy who's very ill. He's got pneumonia which developed from measles. Another day or two and we should know whether he'll get over it. And other patients of course. It varies from day to day. Then there's still the ongoing investigation into the dead woman who was dumped at the hospital. Thanks for doing the funeral service.'

The funeral had occurred only the day before.

'At least she's had a Christian burial. Do you yet have a name? If no relative is found and she remains without a name, I'll pay for a headstone – even if we still have no name.'

'We do not, but I get the feeling we're getting closer. It all stems from those pink pills we found on her. Not that the pills caused her death. Something sharp did that.' Her voice lowered on those last few words.

Gregory grimaced, then poured them another drink whilst the food he'd brought stayed warm in the oven. 'Do you think the supplier of these pills might know who she is?'

'There's a fair chance. We've seen an advertisement placed in London. The supplier claims to be an expert, some kind of doctor, though I suspect the stated credentials are fraudulent. Sister Peebles has heard rumours of local women who have used the same pills.'

'And did this woman use these pills?'

'She might have done to begin with, but at some point she had a physical intervention – a cack-handed abortion – and that was what killed her.'

'Poor woman. A curse on the culprit in London.'

Frances shook her head. 'Yes, I agree, but on the other hand I can't help thinking that the whole scenario with the woman who died is closer to home. She wasn't from around here, but there had to be some reason she was here. Someone locally must have known her. Who brought her to the hospital? Who was responsible for the physical intrusion?'

'Are you any good at jigsaws?'

She laughed. 'I think so. Get the bits around the edge in place first, then tackle the heart of the puzzle.'

'That's a good plan. Very sensible. Where do you go from here? How do you get from the edge of the puzzle to the heart of it?'

She laughed and slugged back her drink. 'It's conjecture, but to my mind there could have been a time lapse between her taking the pills and then having a termination by internal intrusion – someone in Norton Dene.'

'Someone with medical knowledge?'

'Not necessarily. Women have always assisted at the births of other women and intervened when asked. It's a knowledge handed down from one generation to another and dates back to long before the establishment of a credible medical profession.'

'So, it could be anyone, but specifically a woman.'

'Yes. That's what I think. At some point, we might find out who it is. I do hope we do.'

Gregory refilled their glasses. 'In the meantime, let's have dinner. I must admit I could eat a horse.'

'Me too.'

'No horses available, but I can offer you chicken casserole.'

'That's fine.'

She felt his eyes on her once she was sat at the table.

'Is anything wrong?'

'Oh, it's just...'

She recognised that she was about to dodge his question when earlier she had decided to tell him about London.

She took a deep breath. 'There is something.'

'Do you mind telling me what it is?'

There was no escape. Once she'd opened her mouth, the words she needed to say tumbled out.

The silence of indecision and awkwardness hung in the air between them.

For the first time ever, Gregory's air of amusement fled from his face.

'But you haven't made a decision yet?'

She shook her head. 'No. Not yet.'

It was a foregone conclusion that after dinner they would have made love in front of the fire. But not now.

He looked down into his empty glass, lips that perpetually smiled slightly pursed, brow slightly crumpled.

'I would like to think that our relationship might influence your decision, but I know you better than that. When do you have to make your mind up?'

'It was supposed to be by the end of this month, but I've told them I can't do that. I have my mother to consider.'

Gregory sighed, raised his eyes and looked deeply into hers. 'Then it's one day at a time from now on.'

23

Sister Edith Harrison was secreted behind a set of curtained screens, giving advice prior to fitting a contraceptive device.

Some women changed their minds once they were behind those screens. Some felt guilty that they had not asked their husband's permission. Others looked at what was going inside them and turned pale.

Sister Harrison had never been inclined to a sympathetic tone of voice and didn't now.

'You won't feel a thing,' she said to those who baulked at the thought of a foreign body being inserted into their private parts. To those who had second thoughts about not telling their husbands, she said, 'It's your body. You're the one who gives birth, not them. A few minutes' pleasure. That's what they get. The pain is yours and yours alone.'

Getting straight to the point worked with most of them. The others turned tail and ran for the exit.

Once the last patient had been seen, Sister Harrison came out from behind the screen, more than ready for a cup of tea and a biscuit in the staffroom.

Bleak Times at Orchard Cottage Hospital

She'd expected to see that all the chairs were empty, but one was still occupied and this woman was in no need of any form of contraception – not yet anyway.

She recognised the woman as the one who was unfortunate enough not to be able to bring her pregnancies to full term. Doctor Brakespeare had advised a stay in hospital each time a miscarriage seemed probable.

It occurred to her she was having a worrying moment.

'Mrs Thomas. Is there something I can do for you? Is everything all right?'

She scrutinised the bloated body – nothing unusual for a woman not far off from giving birth.

Mrs Thomas beamed. 'No. Not at all.'

'You're not showing, are you?'

Showing was the term hospital staff normally used if blood was being shed. Not a good sign. It meant the baby was coming but too early and likely to lead to complications.

Mrs Thomas shook her head again. 'No. Everything is fine.'

Sister Harrison frowned. 'Did you wish to discuss contraceptive arrangements after you've given birth?'

Mrs Thomas looked askance. 'Oh. Not really. I haven't given it much thought. Not yet anyway,' she said, an embarrassed laugh rolling off her tongue.

Sister Harrison had the distinct impression she was going round in circles. Mrs Thomas's presence was a bit premature for anything the clinic could offer, so why was she here?

'I've been to the mother and baby clinic.'

'Ah. Well, that makes sense. You'll be joining them before very long with your new baby. A bit early yet though.'

'I know.'

Mrs Thomas sighed in a contented manner.

Before Sister Harrison could pry any further, she upturned her plump face.

'I come here as much as I can, just in case anything does happen.'

Sister Harrison frowned. 'You come to the family planning clinic and to the mother and baby unit – in case something happens?'

She stated it carefully, thus giving Mrs Thomas the chance to explain further.

'I sit out in reception sometimes during the day. It was lovely when the Christmas tree was out there. Not so nice now, of course, but I don't mind. At least I'm here if I start losing another baby so you can take action straight away.' She shook her head and this time when she looked up at Sister Harrison, her eyes were wet with unshed tears. 'So, I come here as much as I can. You're not going to send me away, are you? I can come here?'

Rarely was Sister Harrison lost for words, but she was now. It was the first time she'd heard of anyone visiting the hospital just in case disaster threatened. Coming in if something was wrong was one thing. Camping here – almost – was unheard of.

'I think you should go home now.' Sister Harrison placed a hand on the woman's shoulder, then took hold of her elbow. 'I'll see you to the door. Just come back when your waters break. It won't be long now.'

She didn't let go of Mrs Thomas until they were down the bottom of the steps. Even then, Sister Harrison remained there watching until Mrs Thomas had disappeared out of the gate.

She headed to the staffroom for a cup of tea and a custard cream biscuit, thinking about Mrs Thomas. The funny thing was, she'd shown no trace of anxiety, merely a forthright stoicism that she was doing the right thing. It made her smile. With an attitude like that, she was bound to achieve her goal.

She was still smiling when she'd finished her tea and was on her way back to the wards. Doctor Brakespeare was coming from the other direction.

'Sister Harrison. Something's obviously tickled your fancy.'

'I am amused,' she said, and swiftly wiped the smile from her face before telling Frances about Mrs Thomas and her actions.

Frances smiled too. 'I thought I'd seen her around. Still, I can't blame her. She's lost other babies and is determined not to lose this one. It also gladdens me that she's taken on board my advice. I wish every woman we got in here would do the same.'

'You don't want me to stop her from coming in?'

'If it eases her mind, then I've no objection. It won't be long now until she gives birth. Who knows, everything might fall into place at the right time – and in the right place, come to that. In fact, Sister, her actions make me feel quite perky. On top of that, the little boy whose measles led to pneumonia has also recovered. A couple of days and he can go home. An event to raise all our spirits. Today is a happy day.'

Sister Harrison agreed with her that it was.

* * *

Ma Skittings was sitting by the fire, feeling more downhearted than she'd felt in a long while. Doctor Brakespeare would be home soon and expecting her to be readying herself to go home. Not tonight. She hadn't put her coat on but was sitting in the chair, hands clasped in her lap and her steely gaze on the fire.

Her thoughts went back to Lucy's predicament and her asking about getting rid of the unborn child she was carrying. Yes, she could have provided something, but just because she could didn't mean that she should.

Lucy's attitude about the forthcoming wedding both worried

and surprised her. Up until now, she'd thought everything was going swimmingly and had never guessed that Lucy was harbouring a feeling that she was not good enough.

There was no doubt about it, she had to do her best to reassure her that all would be well. That Devlin loved her for who she was and if the wedding had to be brought forward, then so be it. But was she the best person to reassure her that all would be well? Getting someone else to speak to her would mean betraying her secret, but then, it was for the girl's own good. That's what Ma Skittings told herself.

Her musings were terminated by the sound of the latch and a key turning in the front door.

In a rush to escape the wet and dark of early evening – which was lingering firmly in midwinter – Frances and the cold came in together.

Ma Skittings saw the doctor's face pale and her jaw drop. At first, she wondered why until realising that here she was sitting in an armchair staring blankly into the fire.

Frances stood there motionless.

Before she could enquire whether her mother was in this world or the next, Ma Skittings was on her feet.

'Doctor. I need a word with you.'

'My mother?'

'She's fine. It's something else I want to discuss with you.'

'Yes. Yes of course,' said Frances, shaking the wetness from her coat before hanging it up.

Ma Skittings smacked her big square hands on her thighs. 'It's about Lucy.'

Frances sank into the other armchair and listened to what was being said about Lucy being pregnant and the effect it might have on the wedding.

'It's making her feel as though she's letting the side down – as in the toffs and upper crust that would be coming to her wedding – or won't be as it turns out. Not in June anyways.'

'That explains a lot. She's looked a bit drawn of late. Has she told Devlin?'

'Not when I spoke to her.'

'She must discuss it with him. I'm sure he'll be happy to bring the wedding forward.'

Ma Skittings' eyes were shrewishly narrowed. 'It ain't 'im she's worried about. It's this big posh wedding and all these posh people. Her ladyship too. I never thought I would say it, but the dear girl feels out of her depth.'

Frances poured herself a stiff brandy and offered a glass to Ma Skittings.

'I see,' she said. There was a slight upwards curve to one corner of her mouth. She knew what was being asked of her. 'You don't want me to speak to Lucy. You want me to speak to her ladyship.'

Ma Skittings knocked the whole measure of brandy back before nodding her head.

'I figure you could do it better than me, and besides, I don't move in them circles. I ain't entered that 'ouse since I was in service there to the old folk.'

Frances knew she was referring to her ladyship's parents.

'I should have seen that something was worrying her, but quite honestly I didn't.' She shook her head. 'It makes me feel quite guilty.' She frowned as she thought through what she should do next. Raising the subject with her ladyship was something of a challenge. She knew how much she was looking forward to this June wedding and that she'd put a lot of thought into it. 'I think I need to have a word with Lucy first.'

Ma Skittings got to her feet and reached for her coat and her 'cow banger' hat, so called because it was the sort farmers whacked the rears of their cows with to get them in or out of the milking shed. 'I'm sorry to lumber you with this, Doctor, but I couldn't think of any other way.'

'I understand.' Frances felt the older woman's strong gaze, looked up and met her eyes. 'What is it?'

'She asked me if I had anything I could give her to get rid of the baby. I told her no.'

Frances raised one querulous eyebrow. 'Do you?'

Ma Skittings shook her head. 'Nothing stringent.'

'Not like the advertisement in the paper for pills or...' she paused '...other methods of stabilising a woman's monthly health.'

'I have heard as such.'

Of course she had. Ma Skittings knew those who operated their illegal trade in the shadows, catering for patients – women mostly – who had large families or weren't married. Most had little or no medical knowledge or had been struck off for drunkenness or other things that made them ill equipped for the medical profession. She also had her suspicions about Mrs Squires, but there was no evidence that she'd terminated the child of the woman left on the hospital steps. And there was no way she could ask her.

Unwilling to trust herself not to mention her suspicions regarding Mrs Squires, a woman she heartily disliked, Ma Skittings headed for the front door.

'I've given your mother a bit of rice pudding. She ate some of it. She likes the dollop of honey I puts on it.'

Frances smiled. 'I bet she does.'

'I'll be off then.'

She vanished into the night, leaving a cold draught from outside that made the flames in the grate flicker before they straightened and burned upright again.

24

The crafty old sod! That's what Harry Squires was thinking but wouldn't dare say out loud whilst Sir Gerald was in earshot.

The boss had flogged one of his properties to an unsuspecting woman who probably thought she was getting a great deal. She couldn't know how run-down it was; leaky guttering, blocked drains and so much woodworm, there was a danger of the staircases collapsing.

Not your problem, mate, Harry said to himself. He was paid well and for the most part that was all that mattered. Except for her. Ellen. He felt an emptiness in his heart where he'd carried her for so long – not that she'd ever noticed.

Sir Gerald had once joked that he was in love with somebody who wouldn't give him the time of day. It was probably true, but that didn't mean he couldn't love her from afar.

The smoke in the Cockpit Club was thick with the stench of cigars, sweat, blood and money. It was members only and Sir Gerald Leinster-Parry was most definitely a member.

The facility for cockfighting was confined to the large underground cellar beneath the club itself. Upstairs, it looked to all intents and purposes like any other gentlemen's club, smartly attired waiters gliding between the tables, mirrors on the walls, bulbous-shaped chandeliers sparkling like giant diadems.

The cellars beneath it were a place where anything could be betted on or bought and sold.

Harry was not allowed upstairs. It was his job to act as bodyguard to Sir Gerald whilst he was down here. Once he moved upstairs with the rest of those who called themselves gentlemen, Harry would be ordered outside. He merely had to wait and get Sir Gerald home – 'back into the chilly arms of my wife,' as Sir Gerald described his bosom companion – the one whose name appeared on the marriage certificate.

The building which housed the Cockpit Club and the gentlemen's club on the other floors was also owned by Sir Gerald.

As was his habit and by order of the boss, Harry waited outside, close to where he'd parked the Bentley, and took out a cigarette. Smoking was not allowed inside the car, so outside it had to be.

To stave off the chill, he polished one of the oversized headlamps with the sleeve of his coat. He liked the Bentley, especially the headlamps which he thought looked like frogs' eyes perpetually staring ahead into the night.

The cigarette smoke circled his head. Before it was completely burned out, he opened the car door. The smell of leather was also that of luxury. What a gorgeous interior it was, though his mightiness didn't deserve it. Just as he'd not deserved Ellen.

With a wicked grin, Harry stubbed out the lit cigarette on the sumptuous upholstery. He could imagine that smug face shattering when he viewed the damage. All hell would break loose on the shoulders of the perpetrator – him. Not that he'd be around for the anger, the terrible fury that would be unleashed.

The police officer he knew had been glad of the tip-off regarding the Cockpit Club. Illicit goings-on the police had not known about. A raid would net many so-called respectable men – Sir Gerald amongst them. This was Harry's revenge. Embarrass those who thought themselves above the law.

He gave the headlamp closest to him an affectionate pat. 'Goodbye, mate. I'm off now.'

His long spidery legs swiftly covered the ground away from the Cockpit Club. He was heading for the narrow streets and rougher parts of the city. He kept up the speedy pace until smothered in the falling fog of a London night.

When a black car sped past him, followed by another, then a Black Maria, the latter without windows like a van but used to transport prisoners, he flattened himself against a garden wall and watched knowing all that he was seeing was down to him.

The skidding of tyres on a wet road was followed by the tramping of boots and the screech of police whistles.

The Cockpit Club was about to be raided, and Sir Gerald and his cronies were going to be arrested – or at least embarrassed. That was the trouble with the rich. They could pay their way out.

A taxi, dark and unlit in the gloom, came slowly to a stop where Harry was standing. The rear window was wound down. A head appeared, a veiled woman who beckoned him to come closer.

'Mr Squires. I've been looking for you.'

Despite the veil, he recognised Sir Gerald's wife.

He considered beating it but decided not to. He was interested in whatever she had to say.

He nodded at the cabbie before grasping the door handle and getting into the back seat.

Grace was wearing black, very appropriate in the circumstances.

'I saw a police car go past just now. More than one in fact. They pulled up outside the Cockpit Club. Is there something I should know?'

He couldn't say for sure, but thought he saw a smile smothered in part by the black veil she wore.

'Let's put it this way, you may need to pay to get your husband out of jail.'

'Certainly not. I'd prefer him to rot there.'

Harry made a sound that was half grunt, half laughter.

'You and me both.'

'Might I ask why?'

After a few minutes' consideration, he decided to enlighten her. He told her about Ellen's relationship with Sir Gerald and dying outside the entrance to a hospital. 'And he didn't care. Threw her aside like an old shoe.'

'Ellen Grant. Yes. I saw the article and photo in the newspaper.' She paused. 'It sounds as though you cared for her.'

He nodded and went on to explain that his revenge was on behalf of Ellen, who had resolved to get rid of the child she was carrying.

'No offence to you,' he added.

'No offence taken. You and I both have reason to relish his demise.'

Cracking his knuckles and staring wide-eyed like a man about to kill, Harry spilled what he was thinking.

'I'd like to kill whoever supplied her with them pills.'

He heard the faint rustle of silk as she turned her face to him.

'It wasn't the pills that killed her.'

He started at the sound of Lady Grace's voice. The words she'd spoken were like bullets lodging in his brain.

Even though she was but a shadowy presence in the darkness, Harry stared at her.

He asked her what she meant.

'I understand from a friend of mine at Norton Dene that Ellen's miscarriage was not brought on by pills alone. She underwent a primitive operation. A sharp object was used. It had to have been done by someone locally.'

Harry felt as though a boxer had slammed a fist into the side of his head.

'Are you sure?' His voice was no more than a croak in his throat.

'Yes. I learned it from the hospital. Some vile backstreet abortionist was responsible.'

Digesting the words, he thought back to that night, his mother telling him that Ellen had taken something and entreating him to get her to the nearest hospital.

Stiff and bloodless; that's how he felt. His body had petrified, turned into something that was no longer flesh.

'Don't you want to ask me what I'm going to do with the property I bought?'

'Not my business,' he replied. 'I've got what I wanted.'

'What will you do now?'

'I can't stay in London – I'll get out for a while. Word will get round that I snitched to the police. Wouldn't get a job for love nor money – not in my line of work.'

'Where will you go?'

He didn't answer straight away because he was busily putting two and two together.

'For now I'll go home to me old mum,' he said in a cold and purposeful manner.

'Home is where the heart is.'

He almost laughed out loud. If only she knew.

He was going back to Norton Dene to make right what had

gone so wrong. There were more scores to be settled, some more pleasant than others.

* * *

As expected, Sir Gerald did not spend much time in custody, in fact he'd fled out of the back door of the property and climbed over a wall at the end of the garden. That was where the contingent of police who'd arrived in the next street were waiting for him. By nine o'clock the next morning his solicitor, Sir Alex Fordham, had got him out – not so much by lawful means but generously greasing the right hands.

He arrived home at his London house, a white painted terraced in the most expensive part of Knightsbridge, dishevelled and smelling of blood, dirt, brandy and the antiseptic smell of a prison cell.

Unsmiling, Grace looked at him without any movement at all until she wrinkled her nose. 'You smell disgusting.'

A lock of dark hair flopped over the middle of his temple. It looked dejected, greasy and lank.

'I'm going up to change.'

He made for the hallway and the staircase that led upstairs.

Grace followed him.

Aware of this, Gerald paused with one foot on the bottom tread.

'I can tell from your face that you have something quite profound to say.'

'Yes. I've had enough of your obnoxious behaviour, Gerald. I'm filing for divorce.'

For no more than a minute, he stared at her before throwing back his leonine head and laughing.

'You think it's funny?'

In one ferocious bound, he had left the stairs and was gripping her shoulders.

'Yes. I do. I suffer this marriage for the sake of propriety. The fact that it is just a façade is convenient for me. It gets me invited to places I might not be invited to if it wasn't for being married to a titled, though poverty-stricken military family like yours. In short, it is convenient that this marriage continues.'

Despite the ferocity in his eyes, she forced herself not to tremble or wonder how bruised her arms would be thanks to his iron grip.

'Hardly poverty stricken. You spent enough of my money to keep me poverty stricken.' She took a deep breath and held her head high. 'But things have changed. I don't care. I am filing for divorce. I've taken advice.'

'Oh, have you now. Well let's get this straight, my darling, you will get no financial support from me. Is that clear?'

A slow smile crossed her face. 'I have my own money.'

'Oh yes,' he cried laughingly. 'The little bit of allowance your father left you. I am your husband…'

'I've invested it.'

Contempt came with a sarcastic sneer. 'That's laughable. You know nothing about such matters.'

This was the moment she would prove herself, shock him with what she had achieved.

'I've bought that old house of yours on Sears Street.'

'You bought it!' He looked as though he was going to collapse with laughter now. 'My dear woman, that place is falling to bits. You'll never get any decent tenants in there. The scum of the earth only!' Loud guffaws shook the loose flesh that middle age had brought to his once firm jaw.

'I'm not letting it out. I'm giving everyone notice that it's being pulled down.'

The laughter died. Gerald gave her a sidelong look. 'A rebuild? That'll cost you a packet,' he scoffed. 'Nobody will lend a woman money to rebuild. I'll certainly see to that if you continue demanding a divorce.'

Grace had expressive eyes, and when she hung her head and looked up from beneath dark, fluttering eyelashes, he had to admit that she could melt the hardest of hearts.

Now, she thought, to land the bombshell – such a bombshell that he hadn't seen coming.

'I talk to people, Gerald. I talk to ordinary people. I make it my duty not to overlook the meek of this earth. So...' Now she couldn't help smiling as she prepared to deliver the death blow. 'I spoke to some men working on the underground. They told me there was a new route going through and a few of the old houses thereabouts – around Sears Street – would need to be bought and then pulled down. So, I bought yours, Gerald, at a very good price. And I've resold it to the Underground. They paid me a lot of money, so, you see, you no longer have a hold over me or the children.'

He looked dumbfounded, but she knew how quickly he could turn.

Wrapped up in what had happened to him at the hands of the police, he hadn't noticed the piece of luggage at the bottom of the stairs until now.

'What's that?' he asked in his usual churlish manner.

'Luggage. I'll send for the rest at a later date.'

Gerald's jaw dropped. He would have said more, but the butler came to tell her that the taxi was outside awaiting her pleasure.

Recovering from his self-imposed stupor, Gerald demanded to know where she was going.

'To see a friend and apologise for my behaviour when I last visited. Goodbye, Gerald. I hope never to see you again.'

Then she was gone, off in the taxi and then the train to Norton Dene, where she would give Doctor Brakespeare, Araminta and the police the information they sought.

The only thing she couldn't help them with was the identity of whoever it was who had carried out the abortion. That was something she did not know, but perhaps what she had to offer might help.

25

A telegram arrived at Orchard Manor from Lady Grace Leinster-Parry.

```
Dear Araminta,
    I hope you can put me up for a night or
two. I believe I have some explaining to
do and an apology is in order; Writing a
letter to you simply would not suffice.
    Sincerely, Grace.
```

Araminta conveyed the details of the telegram to her son, who looked surprised.

'Well, there's a turn-up for the books.' Devlin kept staring straight ahead as he voiced his opinion. 'I didn't think she was particularly rude when she stayed before. A little distracted may be.'

'Marriage problems?'

'Is that an assumption, Mother, or your gut instinct?'

'I was always one for gut instinct,' his mother laughingly

retorted. 'But husbands are always a trial. Prickly and self-centred.'

'I cannot possibly comment. I've never been a husband and neither have I had a husband.'

His answer amused Araminta. 'You should ask Lucy's opinion of what she expects from you as a husband and father.'

He managed a rather tight smile. 'Perhaps I should. Husband first though. We'll cross the fatherhood bridge when we come to it, though the husband bit is also a bridge yet to cross.'

Araminta found her son's retort just a little bit careless and feared asking him whether he was having second thoughts just in case she didn't like the answer. Lucy hadn't called in for a few days, even though the weather was far more clement than prior to Christmas, but, of course, the hospital was busy again. Well, she wasn't one to let the grass grow under her feet.

'I've invited Lucy to stay for dinner this evening,' she said to Devlin.

He stiffened slightly, hands clasped one on top of the other over his walking cane.

'Is there any particular reason for that?'

'She and Grace seemed to get on quite well. She asked if she could come down and I cannot refuse. I really want to know what she needs to explain about her behaviour. In fact,' she said, with a twinkle in her eye, 'I can't help thinking it's something quite salacious.'

'Mother, if you lived in more modest means in town, you'd out-gossip most of the women there!'

'I'll take that as a compliment. Now. Down to brass tacks. Do you think Grace's comment about making an apology has something to do with Lucy? You know Lucy was nervous that she was only visiting us to give her the once-over.'

'Mother, I've no idea.'

His mother's thoughts were already reforming. 'Or, as I said earlier, she has marriage problems.' She sipped tea from her cup and then with narrow eyes looked over the rim at him. 'I did hear that Sir Gerald is not the nicest of men.'

Devlin sighed. 'Does it matter whether it's an act of jealousy or personal problems?'

'No. I suppose not. That's what we're going to find out.'

* * *

As before, Alfred was sent to pick Lady Grace Leinster-Parry up from the station. A room had been prepared. Dinner was organised.

Araminta was feeling just the teeny-weeniest bit guilty that she hadn't informed Lucy that Grace was coming back for another visit. More so, she'd informed her that Alfred would pick her up but hadn't said that he would do this before picking Grace up at the station. She depended on Grace to break the ice and told herself that it couldn't fail. Two young women, one about ten years older than the other and both half of a relationship with her son. She was depending on their closeness in age to bridge any perceived gap between them.

Oh well, she thought, smiling to herself in a secretive, mischievous way, *I've ploughed the field and scattered the seeds. Let's just see what grows.*

* * *

Wrapped up in her own thoughts, specifically about when to tell Devlin of her condition, Lucy didn't notice that they were en route to the railway station until they drew up in front of it.

'What are we doing here?' she asked once she'd emerged from her gloomy thoughts.

'We're picking up Lady Leinster-Parry, miss.'

'She's coming to stay again?' This came as a complete surprise.

'Apparently so, Miss Daniels.'

'I hadn't heard that.'

'It was short notice,' Alfred replied, ever the loyal servant, the man who just did whatever her ladyship pleased.

Alfred got out to greet the train and take charge of the luggage, whilst Lucy sat there, unsure what to make of it. What was Grace doing here? It certainly wasn't to inspect the intended wife of Devlin Compton-Dixon. She'd already done that on her first visit and they had rubbed along quite well. Lucy had enjoyed talking with her about the hospital and accompanying her on a guided tour, showing her the wards, the facilities and telling her of Doctor Brakespeare's modern thinking.

Grace came into view, smartly dressed and picking her way over the cobbles so that the heels of her shoes didn't get trapped and she wouldn't stumble.

Alfred was following on behind, carrying her luggage – just one suitcase on this occasion.

Having set down the suitcase, Alfred opened the rear passenger door so Grace could slide in with a rustle of silk amidst a cloud of perfume.

Grace pulled up the net veil at the front of her hat – a tulip-shaped one in dark burgundy. She looked radiant. Lucy said hello and Grace responded.

'Lucy. It's wonderful to see you again.' She sounded exuberant.

'It's good to see you too. I trust you are well.'

'Very well.'

'It's quite a surprise to see you again. I didn't know you were coming.'

'I know it must have come as something of a surprise, but coming down again was something I had to do. I've apologies to make.'

'Do you?'

Lucy wasn't quite sure to what she was referring.

Grace took a deep breath before enlightening her.

'Do forgive me for dashing off that day. Things had got to a head, things that I had to sort out. That's why I'm here. I want to explain and apologise to you and to Lady Minty. Araminta,' she said quickly in response to Lucy's puzzled expression. 'Few people know Lady Compton-Dixon as Minty. Just those who've known her for years.'

Lucy was taken aback by an exuberance Grace had not shown on their first meeting. Warmth and friendship were flooding out of her and whatever she'd come to apologise for, Lucy had the impression she'd turned some kind of corner in her life. If that was so, then the effect on her demeanour was much altered.

As the car took the road to Orchard Manor between drab verges and the bare branches of stark trees, Grace grabbed both Lucy's hands. It was something of a surprise.

'Lucy, my first apology is for running off that day. I don't know whether you recall, but I went outside for a cigarette. One of your staff followed me out. We had quite a chat. She told me about the woman who'd died. That nothing was known about her, and that the police were investigating, and Doctor Brakespeare was desperate to put the matter to rest.'

The warmth and exuberance that had flooded out of her was diminished as a sad expression took hold.

'You see, I knew who she was. Her name was Ellen Grant. She wore a simple necklace, a shell hanging from a leather frond.'

She paused, all the better for the effectiveness of what she said next. 'That shell was mine. My father gave it to me when I was a child. I used to keep it in my jewellery box, but it disappeared. My husband gave it to Ellen Grant. She was my husband's mistress – or one of them.'

Lucy froze. 'Doctor Brakespeare was adamant that she'd had—'

Grace shushed her. The glass between Alfred in the front and them in the back was wide open. She leaned forward and slid it shut before saying, 'The child she was carrying was his.'

The memory of seeing the poor woman's bloodied skirts was brought vividly to mind.

'She'd been operated on by an amateur with something sharp. Could he have known? Could he have paid for it?'

Grace nodded. At the same time, her hands tightened over Lucy's hands. 'It's more than likely. I saw Ellen's face in the newspaper and recognised her immediately. You see, my husband takes great delight in flaunting his women, even introducing them to me. He thinks it quite droll.'

'That's terrible. How could he do such a horrible thing?' Lucy couldn't help comparing this man with Devlin. They were worlds apart.

'Very easily, I'm afraid. That's the kind of man he is.'

'And he stole your keepsake.'

'Yes. And describing it as a keepsake is very accurate. He knew how much I treasured it, which made him gloat even more. It wasn't the first piece to go missing from my jewellery box, and although it wasn't gold and diamonds, it was the most precious.' Her voice had softened.

Although she was becoming slightly nauseous, Lucy couldn't help being curious. 'I don't quite understand why you've come.'

'I told you. To apologise. I wasn't myself you see. Araminta must have noticed and also Devlin. Did he say anything to you?'

Lucy shook her head. 'No, though I haven't seen him for a few days. He hasn't been quite himself of late. His legs hurt a bit in this weather.'

It wasn't strictly true, but she needed some kind of excuse for his recent rather distant behaviour.

Grace smiled. 'He's such a good man. I truly wish you all the best in your life together. He deserves someone good like you. I hope you'll invite me to the wedding.' She tilted her head to the side, one finger twirling the elaborate kiss curl that looked stuck to the side of her face. She carried on speaking, going over the old history. 'It was always going to turn out the way it did. You suit him so much better. I saw from the start that you two were made for each other. When did you say the wedding is?'

'June.'

'Have you chosen the dress yet?'

'No.'

There was a churning in Lucy's stomach. Something acidic was coming to the surface. She covered her mouth with one hand as the car bumped over a series of potholes, the movement making her feel seriously sick.

She felt Grace looking at her, her manicured eyebrows meeting in a delicate frown. 'Are you all right, darling?'

Lucy reached for the door handle. 'I need to get out. I'm going to be sick.'

Alfred stopped the car in response to Grace's loud hailing.

Lucy staggered out, gagging until she'd spit no more than an egg cupful of bile onto the muddy road. The churning inside continued.

Grace was still in the car leaning out of the door, looking

concerned and asking if she was all right, one dainty foot hovering above a clump of sodden wet grass.

Lucy dabbed at her mouth with a handkerchief. The foul taste had lessened, but a residual bitterness remained.

Grace held her head to one side and appraised what she was seeing before her eyes. Without saying anything else, she glanced at Alfred still sitting in the driver's seat and slammed the passenger door. Taking hold of Lucy's elbow, she led her some distance from the car so they wouldn't be overheard.

'Correct me if I'm wrong, darling, but I don't think June is a good time for a wedding. I strongly advise that you bring it forward – don't you?'

Lucy stared at her. Denial was useless. Grace was already a mother. She'd had two children. She knew all the signs. That was all it took. Someone hitting the nail on the head and all the pent-up emotions broke into a flood of tears.

Unable to find her voice at first, she nodded before uttering her response.

'Yes.'

'How far gone are you?'

'No more than two months, perhaps a little more.'

Grace tossed her head with an air of nonchalance. 'Oh well. It's hardly the end of the world.'

'It's the wedding. All those posh people. What will they think of me? And her ladyship. She's done so much. I feel I'm letting her down.' There was pleading in her eyes.

Grace sighed and shook her head as she might at one of her children when they'd said something silly. 'I haven't known you very long, Lucy, but think it's long enough for you to allow me to call you a silly goose. Might I point out, darling, that a wedding encompasses one day. It's not a marriage.'

Lucy's eyes were like overlarge moonstones as she looked up

at Grace, an elegant woman who had been born into that upper class she feared to offend. 'It's all very well for you to say that. You're not me.'

Grace's steamy breath rose in a plume of white when she sighed, turned her head and stared into the distance. 'I had the most expensive wedding you could imagine. The great and good – not so good, if I'm honest – were there. The price of my dress was enough to buy some deserving soul a house. My father spent a fortune – but then he could afford it. Champagne, caviar, silks, satins and a five-piece band playing dance music. That was fifteen years ago.'

'It sounds very special.'

'Yes. It does, doesn't it. Roses all the way – only there was nothing rosy about my marriage. You see, my husband wed me for status and on marriage some of my money, was, of course, transferred to him. I mean, women are incapable of taking charge of their own finances, are they? They haven't a head for business. That was the deal. I had a little of it but then my uncle recently left me a lot more.' She shook her head in a determined manner. 'I have no intention of him taking that. I've held on to all of it.'

There was a bitter twisting to Grace's mouth. Her gaze flitted between Lucy and the distant rise of the Wiltshire Downs, and the white horse embedded in its flanks.

'That's very unfair.'

'Yes. Isn't it just. Those fifteen years were the worst of my life, but such were the legalities and financial restrictions, I could not escape. But now, purely by speaking to the right people – those who are not upper class, I have brokered my own future. I now have my own money and will shortly be consigning my husband to the past. I've employed the best law firm to file for divorce. Things should progress quickly.' She laughed. 'I'm certainly paying Meek and Harper enough money for the privilege.'

'Is your husband very angry?'

Grace shrugged. 'I don't care if he is.' Her face darkened. 'That woman who died on the steps of the hospital. You're certain it was a miscarriage?'

'Yes. Doctor is certain she'd had an abortion.'

'Poor woman. Ellen Grant. Sweet name. Sweet person – not that I knew her well. Poor girl couldn't have realised that she was only one of his love interests, though love is far from the right word to use. And he used. He used people and threw them aside when he was finished with them. I'm using the past tense, though I doubt anything will change. He can't help himself.'

Open-mouthed, Lucy fixed her eyes on the fabulous Grace who she'd thought so astonishingly confident, gorgeous, elegant. The surest of herself person she'd ever met.

'That's why I'm visiting Araminta,' Grace said, puffing more smoke into the chill air. 'I want to apologise for my uncharacteristic behaviour when I was last here. I must also thank that person at the hospital who joined me for a smoke and gave me the details about Ellen Grant's death.'

Lucy contemplated what she was hearing and made a note to inform Doctor Brakespeare of the woman's name.

Instead, she asked more about the dead woman. 'Why didn't you tell someone back then that her name was Ellen Grant?'

'My feelings were muddled. There was jealousy, anger and fear that I would be locked in this unhappy marriage for ever. I had to think, you see.'

'I'll inform the doctor and the vicar – he's had a tombstone erected over her grave, but as yet there is no name on it,' Lucy explained in response to Grace's questioning look.

Grace sighed as she unloaded the half-smoked cigarette from

its holder. 'That's very good of him. I'd like to donate if I may. I owe Ellen a debt of honour. Hearing what happened to her finally made me take charge of my life and sue for divorce. That and an inheritance from a darling uncle, my father's brother.'

'Divorce is a terrible thing,' Lucy said. 'I think you're very brave. I don't think I could face doing something like that.'

'Yes. People talk. Look down their noses, but my status in society will see me through. "The slings and arrows of outrageous fortune".' Grace shook her head as she tapped a cigarette into an ebony holder and lit up, the flame from her lighter a welcome glow in the grey day.

She turned to face Lucy, her eyes narrowing as she attempted to ascertain the attraction between two opposites – a man and a woman from different sides of the track. She didn't need to think about it too much. She'd analysed and made her decision.

'I don't think you will ever need to file for divorce. Devlin certainly isn't marrying you for your money.'

Lucy's laugh produced a soft gurgle in her throat. 'He'd be very disappointed if that was the case. Except for my wages as a nurse, I'm penniless.'

A kind look transformed Grace's eyes. She liked Lucy and felt a powerful urge to take her under her wing and impart some of the confidence she herself showed but didn't always feel. She'd always been good at keeping a stiff upper lip, not showing how she really felt.

'So why do you think he wants you to be his wife?' Her voice was softly cajoling. She looked amused.

Lucy thought she knew, but it seemed somehow pretentious putting what she thought – what she wanted the reason to be – into words.

Sensing as such, Grace did it for her.

'He loves you. Devlin loves you and you cannot believe how

incredibly jealous that makes me. You see, I knew a time when he loved me, so I know the kind of man he is. Events got in the way of our relationship, but that was then. I couldn't cope with him as he is now, not being able to see his way around a room, but then, I'm of more of a selfish disposition. But you, I can see that you are unselfish. You've given him your love regardless of his shortcomings. He cannot see your face and will never see the faces of his children. But you're there for him. You're made for each other. Bring the marriage forward and damn what everyone else thinks. That, my darling, is my advice. Marry him in haste. I guarantee you won't repent at leisure – well, you might – but it will be a very pleasant repentance with half a dozen children around you.'

Lucy felt more light-hearted than she had in weeks. The importance she'd put on the attitudes of would-be wedding guests were no more than dandelion floss, fluffy and flying on the merest puff of wind.

'Thank you,' she said softly.

Grace didn't answer but was smiling. She too was feeling lighter in spirit. The dark weight she'd carried for so long was falling from her shoulders.

26

The car pulled up outside the palatial entrance of Orchard Manor. Wind-blown twigs danced and fluttered over the drive and gathered in drifts on the marble steps leading to the mahogany double doors. The light from an ornate lantern of Italian design helped to counterbalance the greyness of the day.

Alfred got out of the car and opened the rear passenger door. Grace alighted first. Lucy followed; her head suddenly tilted back to examine the grand old house anew. For the first time ever, she found herself ready to accept that this really could be her home for the rest of her days.

Nellie, one of the housemaids, greeted them both.

'Good evening, Lady Grace.' She took Grace's coat and suitcase before throwing a smile at Lucy. 'Miss Lucy. Mr Devlin is in his rooms. Will you be going along there?'

'Yes. I will.' She said it with a wonderful feeling that she hadn't felt for a long time.

'Shall I take tea or coffee along, say in about ten minutes?'

Lucy exchanged a swift conspiratory glance with Grace. 'Make it fifteen minutes. I need to discuss something with him first. And then see if you can find a bottle of champagne in the cellar.'

Nellie's face lit up. 'Certainly, Miss Lucy.'

Grace smiled and took her leave, saying nothing more but following Nellie upstairs.

Lucy peeled off along the chilly side corridor leading to Devlin's suite of rooms. She tapped on the door before entering.

A coal fire glowed in the grate and a bevy of table lamps cast amber light over the upholstered chairs, the low tables, and the red Turkish rugs.

Devlin was standing at the window with his back to her and didn't turn round as she entered. The stiffness of his stance was instantly worrying.

'Devlin,' she asked softly. 'Is anything wrong?'

He didn't turn round. 'I'm glad you're here. I need to talk to you.'

No kiss, rushing over and throwing his arms around her. She so wanted to feel his arms and to know that everything would be well between them. Instead, she sensed a certain aloofness.

'You sound quite ominous, darling,' she said in a light-hearted manner. She laughed. 'Sorry. I travelled here with Grace. She calls everyone darling.'

For some reason, her laugh made him turn away from the window, and although he couldn't see her, she sensed he was trying to gauge her mood. It was almost as though he wanted to see her laughing before he said a word.

'You want to have a talk with me.'

'Yes. I do.'

She hadn't a clue what he wanted to talk to her about, but she was ready to listen.

'I'll sit on the green sofa here in front of the fire. Will you join me? Then you can tell me what you want me to know.'

'I would prefer to stand.'

Alarm bells rang. Lucy prepared herself for whatever it was he had to say, but after calming herself settled for, 'I need to talk to you too.'

Perhaps it was her tone of voice that made the stiff stance suddenly melt, but she did get the definite impression that his shoulders were less squared, his jaw less rigid.

'All right.' He took a deep breath. 'Lucy. I want you to consider what I say very carefully. I have a very pertinent question to ask. Do you promise to answer me honestly?'

Her chest felt tight as she wondered what the question might be. She couldn't guess and because of that felt a little wobbly, her thoughts darting here, there and everywhere but without any conclusion. 'Of course I will.'

The beat of her heart seemed to increase, throbbing against her ribcage. It wasn't really. She was a nurse so knew it wasn't, but emotion, especially love, could easily affect the physical self.

She remained seated, looking up at him, waiting for whatever it was he had to say and equally impatient to impart her own news.

He remained standing, the daylight outside forming a backdrop behind him. 'Lucy. I want to ask you if you truly love me. That is all I want to know.'

A breath caught in Lucy's throat. His question was unexpected. Perhaps her sojourn with Grace on the journey here coloured her anticipation of what he meant asking this particular question; that she was from the lower ranks, and he should marry someone of similar background to himself. 'Of course I do.'

'Just to make sure, there is another question I want to ask you, but first I have to declare how I feel.'

Fearing the worst but hoping for the best, she clasped her

hands behind her back and crossed her fingers. Please let it be something she wanted to hear.

'Lucy. I love you dearly. I'm passionate about you, but I must know that you're not marrying me out of pity. I would hate that most of all. Even marrying me for money I could stand, but pity...' He threw his head back, an action of exasperation.

'No.' Such was her surprise that her voice rang out loud and clear. 'No!'

Initial surprise was countered by elation. In declaring this fear he'd harboured, he had unwittingly opened the door to how she should proceed with her news in a way that would convince him how she really felt.

'Please come and sit with me, Devlin. Please. There's something I have to tell you that may upset our wedding plans.'

Even though he couldn't see her doing it, she patted the soft velvet seat beside her and positioned a cushion so that he had something comfortable at his back.

At first, he made no move until she said, 'Please. I won't give you my news until you're sitting beside me. It's far too important. You need to know this and once known, it will, hopefully, put your fear to rest.'

If one could swell with courageous confidence, this was that moment.

She straightened her back. If Devlin could have done, he would have seen a resolute expression on her face and a slight smile curving the corners of her mouth. She felt confident and ready to declare her news.

He sat down beside her, his hands still folded over the silver horse head that topped his walking stick.

His face was turned towards her. His eyelids flickered above his sightless eyes.

She took a deep breath. 'I won't be marrying you in June.'

The statement seemed to make no impact at first. His expression remained immobile. So much so that she *did* begin to pity him.

'I want to get married as quickly as possible – if you still want me.'

His lips moved as though the words were in his head but refused to come to his mouth.

Lucy took hold of his hands, then let one go and took only his right hand, which she placed on her belly.

'I do hope your mother won't be too disappointed, but her grandchild can't possibly wait until the wedding ceremony is over in order for him or her to make its appearance.'

At first, it was just his jaw that dropped, but then he dropped his head and rested it in her lap, his hand against her belly.

'Oh, my dear God,' he whispered. 'My darling Lucy. I am blessed. Blessed indeed.'

'We are blessed,' she whispered, stroking his hair whilst noting a tear trickling down his cheek and feeling its twin trickling down her own.

27

It was just after midday when Sister Peebles was yet again visiting the shabby houses of Waterloo Terrace.

Delivering babies was always a happy event, even when the mother was already worn out with childbearing and surrounded by children close in age.

On this occasion, she was in a ramshackle house in the same terrace changing an old man's dressings.

The man had been injured in a mining accident some months back and his wounds were slow to heal. Not surprising, she thought, seeing as he'd refused to visit a doctor, a hospital or done anything else to ease his suffering. A stubborn man, thought Gwen, but then there were plenty of those.

The accident had opened his flesh all the way down his shinbone and pus was still seeping from the wound. He'd been lucky that it hadn't been broken.

Gwen frowned at the yellowish seepage and wrinkled her nose. The smell was noxious, and she had done all she could with what she had. If things didn't improve soon, Mr Underwood, the man concerned, was likely to lose his leg.

To alleviate the shock, she jokingly said, 'Do you want to drag me 'round here every day, Mr Underwood? I've got other people to see besides you, and that's a fact.'

He countered by saying that his wife would look after him and that he would heal well enough if he rested in his favourite chair.

She fixed him with a no-nonsense warning look that wouldn't have shamed a sergeant major. 'Are you bathing your leg every day like I told you?'

'On warm days I do.'

He avoided looking in her eyes. His wife sat on a wooden dining chair, plump arms folded over plump belly.

'You should be rolling up your trousers every day.'

The old man pulled a face reminiscent of a punctured leather football. 'It's too cold. I feels the cold, I do.'

'Too cold to roll your trousers up? That's no excuse. You're still wearing your combinations, aren't you?'

'They got holes in the crotch.'

'Darn them.'

'And on the knees.'

'Wear a dressing gown.'

'I ain't got one.'

His wife butted in. 'His dressing gown is at the pawnbroker's. I brought down the army surcoat from off our bed, but he let the dog use it for a bed. That's 'im. That's my Jim. Always been a stubborn old sod.'

A tier of chins wobbled as Mrs Underwood jerked her podgy chin at the black and white terrier underneath a battered oak dining table. He was curled up on it, ears twitching as though avidly listening to the human conversation.

Losing patience, it was hard for Gwen not to swallow the

threatening gasp of horror. 'It's not hygienic for the dog to be lying on it. Dogs have germs.'

'Huh,' snorted Mrs Underwood. 'You just try gettin' 'im off. Let me show you.'

The dog opened one eye and growled threateningly when she tried to drag the coat from beneath it.

'See what I mean,' she yelled, hand hastily withdrawn when the dog bared its teeth.

Mr Underwood beamed. 'One dog, one master. And I don't mind 'im laying on me coat.'

'Silly old sod,' his wife grumbled in her peevish manner, bottom lip downturned, chin resting on her chest.

Gwen sighed as an old saying from Welsh chapel ran through her mind: *God helps them who help themselves.*

The rest of the saying, *but God help those who help themselves*, which referred to someone stealing – more specifically shoplifting – didn't matter.

'Mr Underwood, if you don't keep your wound clean, you could end up losing a leg. Now that's not very nice, is it now?'

He cackled and, to her great surprise, Mrs Underwood cackled too but with more reservation.

'Tipping you the wink, Sister Peebles...' He did just that, winking at her as though a great joke was about to be spouted. 'If I loses me leg, then the mine's got to pay me a bit of compensation. Means I won't 'ave to do a stroke for the rest of me days.'

The shock of his statement stayed her flow of explanation. Surely, he hadn't understood her properly. She tried again to emphasise the seriousness of the situation.

'All very well, but do you really want to go through surgery? And what about afterwards, you won't be able to walk without the use of a crutch.'

His continuing mirth came as something of a surprise. So did his next statement.

'I'll put up with pain if it means I ain't got to work. As for walking with a crutch, so long as it gets me to the pub of a night, that's all that matters.'

Not for the first time in her nursing career, Gwen felt at a loss. Regardless of all the training she'd had and the appetite to do good, she felt useless, as though she had wasted her time. Basically, she had concluded that the healing of the sick could only be carried out if the patient wanted to be healed. In Mr Underwood's case, it seemed he was willing to accept disablement so long as it got him some money and he no longer needed to work.

Why do I bother? she thought to herself and felt deeply despondent. As her old dad, a lay preacher as well as a miner, used to say, human beings were strange cattle.

As she wondered what to do next, she scrutinised the scruffy house, the wallpaper peeling from the walls, the bodies of dead flies stuck to the strip of sticky paper hanging from the ceiling, the mouse droppings along the sideboard. Enough reason to take a bit of money and enjoy what life remained. In Mr Underwood's case, not much.

Once she'd packed away the ointment and dressings, she was escorted to the front door by Mrs Underwood, who shuffled along behind her smelling of cooked cabbage and fried onions and gabbling on about one neighbour or another. The woman was a voracious gossip.

'Thinks she's lady of the manor, she do! Time was she'd give her services for nothing, but now...' It was all garbled in the local dialect, a mishmash of country words and shortenings of proper words.

'And then there's that son of 'ers...'

Gwen had lost track of which of the neighbours she was

running down. On and on it went, even as Gwen was swinging her leg over her bicycle.

Gwen was about to push off and escape Mrs Underwood's tirade when she saw a figure bounding towards the big house at the end of the road. Her hands tightened over the handlebars, her gaze fixed on the loping, lanky figure, one she recognised.

Fallen to an abrupt silence, Mrs Underwood stood next to her. Like Gwen, her gaze was fixed on his black garb and his big feet. There was something intimidating about the furtive way he glanced in their direction, swiftly looking away before the metal gate clanged shut behind him.

'Who is that man?' asked Gwen.

Mrs Underwood answered, 'That be Harry Squires. His mother's Mrs Squires.' She pulled a face. 'Not neighbourly at all. Won't give you the drippings of 'er nose that one!'

The latter comment was one she'd heard before – not the nicest terminology but apt for a mean person. Gwen decided there and then to make use of the gossipy Mrs Underwood, poke her a bit in the hope of finding out more.

Gwen was as friendly as she could be with a woman who smelled of boiled cabbage – a little distance – enough so she could keep her breakfast down. 'I think someone told me that he was in the company of a young woman when I last saw him. Is she there now?' She waited expectantly for an answer.

'Not that I know of, not today if you knows what I mean,' Mrs Underwood replied, flattered at being able to offer information.

'A while back. Before Christmas.'

'Ah, now yur asking. I've seen other young women go into 'er place, but only one in the company of 'Arry. Nice-looking she was, though a bit wan about the face.'

'Other young women visit there?'

'Nothing wrong with that, is there,' she suddenly snapped. 'Got every right to visit 'er, ain't they?'

There was a marked change in Mrs Underwood's manner. She'd not liked being asked about other young women visiting that house. Gwen's curiosity was piqued. There'd been a question mark before about the woman who lived in that house. She'd heard as much from Lucy, who'd had a conversation with Ma Skittings, and what Ma Skittings didn't know wasn't worth knowing.

So, what was going on there to cause Mrs Underwood to snap at her like her husband's nasty dog? Her conclusion was that she'd found what she was looking for. Mrs Squires had a little business going, one that involved young women in trouble. This part of town was peopled by those who were not always on the right side of the law.

Gossipy Mrs Underwood had pulled down the shutters. Asking more questions would be pointless, thought Gwen and knew it for sure when the smelly woman turned and headed back to her decrepit-looking house without looking back.

Her curiosity roused, Gwen decided that she couldn't leave this matter alone. She cycled towards the end of the street and the house that was so unlike all the others, better quality and hidden behind a high wall.

She stopped outside, noted the wrought-iron garden gate was covered on the inside by a layer of tin, thus obstructing any nosy parkers looking in. *Like me*, she thought. The only reason for going to all that trouble had to be because there was something to hide.

Now what? Should she go barging in? Or should she merely report her suspicions to Doctor Brakespeare, who would then, no doubt, pass the information on to the police?

Nobody had told her outright that Mrs Squires was an abortionist or, at the very least, a supplier of the pink pills, but she was very sure. How to prove it?

Perhaps if she followed her?

As she sat astride her bike pondering, a sudden thought popped into her head. Propping her bicycle upright, she reached behind her and rummaged in her saddlebag, her fingers eventually touching a folded-up piece of newspaper. Unfolding it, she found the pretty face of the unknown woman lying pale and cold, her photo taken by a cameraman hired by the police. They now knew her identity, but she could pretend that she did not.

Paper in hand, she considered her options. There were several considerations. For a start, Mrs Squires might lie and demand she leave the premises. Ditto her son, who, by the looks of his scarred face, might be more aggressive about her leaving.

With its grey stone façade and high garden wall, the house itself bore a formidable look, not the sort you wanted to enter in daylight, and most definitely not at night. Who knows what ghosts were lurking there?

Gwen shuddered. First, she needed to know for sure that the photo portrayed the same woman who had been seen with Harry Squires.

Mrs Underwood would know.

After turning her bike around, she pedalled back to the Underwoods' mean terraced house. Mrs Underwood finally appeared in response to Gwen's resonant knocking on the door. She didn't look pleased that she was back.

Before she had chance to query her return, Gwen held the piece of newspaper in front of her eyes.

'Is this the woman you saw with Harry Squires? Please, Mrs Underwood. It's very important.'

Small eyes peered out of layers of wrinkles and fat at the photo.

'She looks dead.'

'She is dead. Dead and buried. We want to find out who she is – or was. Someone must know. I think Mr Squires might know. Did you not see this in the newspaper, Mrs Underwood?'

Mrs Underwood shook her head. 'I don't read papers. Neither does my old man.'

Gwen guessed that neither of them could read or write. They were hardly the only ones around here. But the photograph didn't need her to be able to read or write.

The small eyes narrowed some more as she leaned closer.

For a moment, Gwen was concerned that she wouldn't get an answer – but then she did.

''Course, she was live when I saw 'er, but that's 'er all right. That's the young woman.'

Gwen was almost inclined to hug and kiss her – almost. The smell of cabbage and general filth stopped her. 'Thank you. Thank you very much, Mrs Underwood. You're a treasure.'

So great was her excitement that she stopped outside the Squires' house again, parked her bike and pushed open the gate. The metal sheet covering the wrought iron clanged behind her.

Bang, bang, bang went the knocker. She put all her effort into the knocking and when nobody came immediately to answer, she gave it another good bash.

It was Mrs Squires who came to the door, a big woman dressed in layers of purple; dress, long cardigan and a turban wrapped around her head. Hooped earrings dangled from her ears and a ring twinkled on each finger. To Gwen's mind, she looked like a fairground fortune teller.

Sooty black brows beetled on her face and there was open hostility in the hooded eyes above a nose as hooked as the beak of a parrot.

'Are you the district nurse?'

'Yes.'

'Did I ask for you to call?'

'No. I came here of my own volition to ask if you knew this woman.' She thrust the newspaper cutting towards the woman's fat face.

Mrs Squires gave the photograph only the most cursory glance.

'Should I?'

'Yes. A neighbour said she saw this woman with your son, saw her come into this house in fact. Can you confirm that to be true?'

Gwen congratulated herself that she'd sought comment from Mrs Underwood before coming here. She had proof. Fragile proof, but Mrs Squires did not know that. It was enough to inform her that she couldn't lie. That somebody could bear witness.

All the same, it appeared that Mrs Squires was reluctant to respond. She was looking for excuses.

'She looks dead.'

That same observation that she'd had from Mrs Underwood.

Gwen sighed heavily before saying, 'Yes. She is dead. She died when miscarrying a child brought on by an abortion. Did you carry out that abortion, Mrs Squires?'

There was only the slightest flicker of comprehension on the woman's face.

Gwen decided to tell what she now knew. 'Her name is – or was – Ellen Grant. Do you remember her now? And don't lie. I've been informed that she was here.'

The smug expression was replaced with wariness. 'I don't know anything about that.'

'You're saying you did not carry out an abortion?'

'I don't do things like that. It's illegal.'

'Yes,' said Gwen. 'It is.'

'And even if I did, you'd have to prove it.'

In her long career, Sister Gwen Peebles had met many people she'd wanted to punch, but never more so than this woman. She was right of course; she couldn't prove that she'd carried out the abortion.

Determined to get to the bottom of this, Gwen pressed on regardless. 'Shortly after the abortion, Ellen Grant was dumped outside the cottage hospital as though she were nothing but a bag of rubbish being thrown away. Are you saying you know nothing about that?'

'I weren't her keeper. She was a free woman who could go where she liked. I don't know where she went. She just went.'

She attempted to close the door, but Gwen's foot stopped it from closing.

'Who carried out the abortion, Mrs Squires? Was it you?'

With a hefty shove that dislodged Gwen's foot, the door was slammed shut.

Gwen retrieved her hat which had fallen to the floor, feeling that she had something important to relate to Doctor Brakespeare. She'd found the likely perpetrator of what was, in law, a crime.

* * *

In the dimness of his mother's house, the grim place where he'd grown up, Harry came out from the shadows. Rage was etched on his face and his fists were clenched. He'd heard everything and his blood was boiling.

Turning round to face him, his mother closed her gaping mouth when she saw the terrible fierceness in his eyes.

'You told me the pills killed my Ellen. That woman said

otherwise. You used something sharp, and nasty didn't you, you cut her insides, and she bled to death!'

'She was just…'

'You cow. You murderer. You murdered my Ellen!'

So obsessed was he with the image of that night, the blood, the cold, he was not aware that his hands were around his mother's throat, that she was clawing at his hands and that his knuckles were red with blood.

'You killed her. You killed her!'

He said it over and over again and there was a red mist in front of his eyes. His hands were still vicelike around her neck when he realised her body had gone limp. There was a lumpen thud as he let her fall to the ground. He stood over her and looked at her. He'd strangled the breath out of her.

He felt nothing for her. No regret.

What next?

It did cross his mind to bury her out in the garden, but what with the tangled undergrowth and the frozen ground, that would take too long. Instead, he would leave her where she'd fallen.

Decision made, he gathered all he needed, including the money the old crone kept in her various safe places around the house, and took off. London beckoned, the city where he could lose himself in the crowd. Things would have settled down a bit and vengeance was still due for Sir Gerald. Setting the police on him and the other nobs at the club was not enough and he was the one to dish it out.

28

The monthly meeting of the hospital committee consisted mainly of agreeing the accounts and approval to take on another doctor who would be junior to Frances.

It seemed the enquiry from the recently qualified doctor had come at a crucial time. Several of the old general practitioners who had lived and practised their skills here most of their lives had retired and more patients were applying to the hospital panel. She couldn't possibly deal with all of them alone, and besides, she hadn't dismissed the London job out of hand. There was a certain excitement to climbing the career ladder. However, there was her mother to consider and Gregory.

Gregory was her rock. Her mother depended on her.

The letter from the young doctor who had written before Christmas was passed round. There were grunts and tight-lipped musings about his qualifications being all well and good, but perhaps it might be a good idea to advertise and see who else might be interested?

'There's every chance that Doctor Reeves might still be our

choice, but we must keep an open mind. I'd be inclined to advertise. Just to make sure.'

'Quite right,' said Araminta as she slammed her file shut. 'Wind the meeting up, Cedric.'

Cedric was the new bank manager, who closed the meeting by smacking the desk with the palm of his hand. 'I declare this meeting adjourned.'

The gentlemen of the committee showed due homage to her ladyship by tapping the brims of their hats.

Frances and Araminta were last to leave. On their way, they passed the gentlemen's cloakroom. From within, unguarded male voices filtered out into their earshot.

'At least this doctor who's applied is a man. We don't want another woman doctor, do we now.'

'Certainly not. It goes against the natural order of things.'

Frances and Araminta stopped and exchanged looks.

'I've a mind to barge in there and give them a piece of my mind,' said Araminta.

Frances pulled a face. 'I wonder how long we'll have to wait until we overcome male prejudice.'

'Never,' declared Araminta as, with head held high, she proceeded to the exit. 'They've held the whip hand for centuries. They're not going to let go easily.'

'Would you care for a cup of tea before you leave?'

Araminta cocked an arched eyebrow. 'Do you have sherry?'

Frances recalled half a bottle left over from Christmas hidden away in a filing cabinet. 'I believe I do.'

'Just as Izzy did. Your guardian was my friend. You too are my friend.'

They toasted each other and followed that with a toast to the women's movement, to which both Araminta and Izzy had belonged. Then to the ongoing success of the hospital, which had improved a great deal since Frances had been in charge.

Araminta lifted her aristocratic chin to a lofty height. 'I still recall their faces at your interview when the committee had to be told that Francis with an "i" is male and Frances with an "e" is feminine. Just goes to show the level of male intelligence,' said Araminta, raising her glass again before taking a sip.

Frances smiled. 'And that was just the beginning. The family planning clinic did cause a bit of a stir. They'd never heard the likes of such a thing.'

'Good. I like upsetting the male establishment. Did you know that I took over the financial side of my husband's life when we married? Figures just seemed a jumble of nonsense to him.' She shook her head. 'No number of beatings as a boy could drum the subject into him. He was relieved when I took over. A weight off his mind.'

'Shared responsibilities based on individual skills, not gender.'

A faraway look came to her ladyship's face. 'We were equals in our marriage, thus it was a happy one.'

'And does Devlin take after his father?'

Araminta smiled a rueful but affectionate smile. 'In some ways. He's considerate and sometimes overthinks situations. I think Lucy will be good for him.'

'She's been to see me. I believe I gave her the right advice.'

'You did and I'm grateful that you did.'

'She told me the wedding's been brought forward on account of her condition.'

'All those invitations I sent out!' Laughter danced in Araminta's eyes. 'I've now sent out cancellations to most of the guests. My son and Lucy want a quiet wedding without fuss. Devlin stressed that it be without fuss. A smaller wedding but a happy one.'

'You'll become a grandmother.'

'I'll drink to that.'

Frances refilled their glasses. The thought came to her that whereas she'd drunk two glasses Araminta – Minty – had drunk three. She looked to be getting quite tiddly and judging by the pinkness of her cheeks was thoroughly enjoying herself.

'Here's to my grandchild.'

'Be assured that I will look after Lucy to the best of my ability.' Frances hoped Lucy was no longer worried about her brush with the boy suffering from the after-effects of measles. It seemed she had not mentioned anything to Devlin's mother so neither would she.

'I know you will. I wouldn't have it any other way. The very best of Harley Street are incomparable to you, my dear. Now, whilst on the subject of marriage, are you and our wonderful vicar ever going to walk down the aisle?'

It was a question Frances would prefer not to answer. 'We never seem to have the time to have a serious discussion about it. We're both so busy.'

Araminta looked bemused. 'That is certainly so, but the dear man, if he's ever going to stand before the altar rather than officiating, needs to get round to it. Neither of you are getting any younger – if you don't mind me saying so, my dear.'

Frances placed her empty sherry glass onto the edge of her desk. Discussions about them marrying had rarely passed between her and Gregory of late. Yes, they were both busy, but there was also a kind of wall between them, a reluctance to speak about it. 'I have my mother to think about for now.'

Araminta gave her a shrewd, narrow-eyed look. 'I think you're making an excuse, but never mind. Let's change the subject, shall we? How are the police getting on with the investigation of that woman who died. I understand her name was Ellen Grant and she hailed from London.'

'I've passed what I know to the police. The rest is up to them.'

It struck Frances as quite surprising that Araminta was aware of the woman's identity and asked her outright.

'I wasn't aware that as yet it was general knowledge. Do you have a covert information service that I don't know about?' she asked laughingly.

A lifetime of wrinkles creased around Araminta's eyes. 'In a way, yes, I do. I didn't hear of her identity locally. Grace told me.'

'Grace who Devlin was once engaged to?' Frances raised her eyebrows. It had been surprising enough when his ex-fiancée had turned up, seemingly out of the blue, but what was the connection between her and the dead woman?

Araminta nodded in a secretive but rather self-satisfied way. At the same time, she smoothed the fox fur that hung around her shoulders, running a finger in a line just above its glassy eyes and snap shut mouth.

'I'm sure she won't mind you knowing this, but she's divorcing her husband. Ellen Grant was one of the reasons.'

'Ah.' It was hardly the first time Frances had brushed with divorce, mostly in London. In Norton Dene, the adage of marriage being for life still held. Plus, nobody in this town could afford to end their marriage. Divorce was confined to monied people. London lawyers had the advantage there. 'It's not likely to be easy for her.'

'You know, Frances, it's amazing what a woman can do when she puts her mind to it.'

Frances rose from her chair at the same time as Araminta did, leaning on her walking stick – a recent addition to aid her creaking knees. However, she was one of the most powerful women she'd ever encountered. Izzy, her guardian/stepmother, was another.

'Formidable women.' Frances smiled at the fond memories of just how wonderful life had been in that house full of women and ideas when a thirst for freedom and challenge held sway over dependence on a man.

Her feelings softened when Gregory came to mind. There was a time when she'd thought nobody could replace Ralph, but that was before she'd come to Norton Dene, before she'd met Gregory.

29

Frances didn't even have time to take her coat off before realising that something wasn't quite right. She'd got back early to the coach house, hoping to have afternoon tea with her mother and had fully expected to bump into Ma Skittings even before she went up to her mother.

The ranges were still chugging and chucking out heat. The smell of freshly baked bread and some sort of meaty casserole hung heavy on the air. All were evidence of human habitation, but an air of emptiness pervaded.

The living room and kitchen were empty. Calling out for Ma Skittings got no response.

Where the devil was she?

Her next shout was up the stairs. No response from there either.

Perhaps...

Had her mother passed over and Ma Skittings had gone looking for her?

She reined in the panic, reminding herself that she was a doctor and should keep a clear head.

Taking two steps at a time, she ran upstairs. Breathless, not so much with the effort of running upstairs but with the sudden fear that the end had come.

As it was, she found her mother's bed empty, the bedclothes thrown back in disarray.

'Oh my God.'

Frances ran back down the stairs and dashed out of the door without closing it behind her.

There were no lights on in the vicarage, which meant that Gregory was out, so neither her mother nor Ma Skittings would be in there.

The road outside was empty. Not a soul in sight. Her feet stayed rooted to the spot as she considered which direction to go in. The centre of town seemed the best option simply because there would be people there who might have seen her mother or Ma Skittings.

Ma Skittings' house was also in that direction. Her mother had said she'd felt better that morning and had wondered out loud whether Mrs Skittings would like to take a turn with her.

'The weather's changing.'

'It's still cold.'

'I could wrap up warm.'

Frances had disregarded the remark, convinced that her mother was incapable of leaving the front door behind, let along walking out of the gate.

'Frances.'

The voice was thin, like a canary that has sang its heart out and could sing no more.

It was followed by a far stronger one. On hearing it, her worst fears vanished.

There was Ma Skittings, bold as brass and well wrapped up in her old coat and hat. Frances felt an instant wave of relief flood over her, even though her mother was bundled up beneath blankets being pushed along in a wheelbarrow.

On seeing her surprised expression, Ma Skittings explained.

'She wanted a bit of fresh air and we've no wheelchair, but this wheelbarrow works a treat!'

Her mother was no more than a nose and a pair of eyes above the blankets, a thick woolly hat pulled low on her forehead, a scarlet scarf covering her mouth.

Frances shook her head in disbelief.

Ma Skittings remarked that she was home early.

'Yes. I managed to get away.'

'Oh, sorry, Doctor. It must have startled you when you found us both gone.'

'Yes. It did,' said Frances, gritting her teeth to stop from shouting. There was no point in making a mountain out of a molehill. 'So, you've been for a walk.' She said it lightly and not without pleasure. Her mother's face had more colour than it had for a long time.

'Your mother saw a few sparrows and blackbirds outside the window. They were fluttering about as though spring had come. They're wrong, mind you, but it's the smell in the air. The feeling that winter might be over at last – at least for today. So, I got the wheelbarrow from out back and made it nice and cosy for her majesty to get in! Next best thing to a coach and four – or at least a pony and trap.' Loud laughter came from Ma Skittings and weaker laughter from her mother.

The promising patches of blue sky were clouding over. 'I think we should go back now.'

'Don't be such a spoilsport! Your mother and me went round to Nancy and Ned's place for tea and cake. It's not often we get to play truant.' Ma Skittings sidled up close to her. 'You work hard, Doctor. Don't you worry about me and your mother. We've 'ad our little jaunt around the block, so to speak, but now we'll get on back. Some of those potatoes I've left in the sack outside the kitchen won't peel themselves. And that mutton stew should be just about done. I need to get back and your mother has had her fair share of fresh air. You ain't though, so take your time getting back. It'll do you good.'

Frances was tempted to say that she was the doctor, the one who gave health advice, but she didn't. Instead she stood with her mouth open, watching the pair of them amble off, Ma Skittings laughing and making jokes. Her mother's voice could be heard now and again, though faintly.

She felt strangely lost being left there. People were going in and out of the shops in the high street. Most of them acknowledged her with a polite nod or smile. One or two of the few men out and about at this time of day seemed more awkward about seeing her.

Her footsteps took on a mind of their own, one step in front of another until she found herself standing in front of the war memorial. It dominated the triangle of grass in the centre of the town. For most of the year, it was surrounded by flowers. In March, there would be daffodils, wallflowers after that, and tulips, then summer blooms. At this time of year, the delicate heads of snowdrops, cowslips and crocus hinted at the displays to come.

When it was first constructed, the stone would have been as white as a cold marble sepulchre. But that was getting on for twenty years ago after the end of the Great War. Thanks to time and the weather, it had become besmirched with dirty streaks running like black tears against the white stone. She decided it deserved to look like that. There was no glory in war and only sadness in death.

Engraved into the stone were the names of those who had

perished. It didn't matter that their names were picked out in gilt; they would have much preferred to be alive than lying in some foreign field – in pieces. Home with family, friends, down at the pub, playing football or cricket – anything but being dead.

In peacetime, those men would have worked in quarrying or mining, long-standing industries in this part of Somerset. If she'd mentioned to anyone from London, specifically about mining, they would have cited South Wales and the north of England as the main source of black gold – as she'd heard it called.

Her eyes dropped to another name, one she still cherished even though she had left him long behind.

This town and its war memorial were the last remaining link between her and Ralph, her fiancé who had died in the muddy battlefields of northern France. She'd come to this town not expecting to stay, or at least only long enough to lick her wounds and find a position back in London, a career position where she could put her skills to wider use.

The fact that his name was on there at all was down to the Reverend Gregory Sampson. Some years following the war, he had been involved in selecting one of the fallen from all the services to be buried as The Unknown Warrior in Westminster Abbey. All of them should have been unknown – except he had found a locket on one of them, a name and a photograph of a woman he recalled from a field hospital. That woman had been her. The identifiable man had been Ralph. Out of conscience, and his memory of her, Gregory had had the name inscribed on the memorial.

She'd never quite believed that her coming here and his involvement with the interment of Ralph was pure coincidence, but it no longer mattered. Perhaps, she'd once said to Gregory, it might be divine providence.

She'd not only come here and found Ralph's name carved in

stone she'd also found him. And Gregory wanted to marry her, although work had intervened. Setting up the family planning facility had been a dream she'd longed for after devouring any printed matter about Professor Marie Stopes in Britain and Margaret Sanger in the United States. Like her guardian, Izzy, before her, she'd acquired a burning desire to change women's lives.

As for divine providence, perhaps that might have had some bearing on standing here. Ralph, Gregory, her mother; each discovered in this town.

A feeling of great calm descended on her.

The delicate smell of damp earth preparing for spring was as pungent in the air as the smell of petrol coming from the pumps standing like soldiers on sentry duty.

Despite those unconnected smells, her mind travelled back to a different time, a different location, in fact a different country.

Winter was still in the air, but her mind was counterbalancing greyness, cold and feeble sunshine with a cherished memory of a day at the height of summer, a hayfield in France and a cloud of red poppies.

They had been lovers, her and Ralph, hanging onto each other and their passion amid a cruel and bloody war. Time, she decided, took no prisoners. If it didn't happen when it was supposed to, it would never happen. It had applied to Ralph. It might also apply to Gregory.

Thinking of weddings cast her thoughts in Lucy's direction. She and Devlin had broken new ground. The fact that they would become parents this coming year had broken through whatever reservations they'd had. A happy couple, she thought. Everything had turned out right and Devlin for one seemed almost relieved that they would not be having a big society event. Lucy agreed with him.

'I don't mind a small wedding,' she'd told Frances, her eyes sparkling with joy. 'It's my marriage that matters.'

Frances had agreed that it was indeed all that mattered.

Her thoughts went back to Gregory. Yes, she still had her mother to look after, but was that the true reason why she was so hesitant about her future?

The hospital and the lately established clinic had a lot to do with it. Not just the pressure of medicine, but the fact that she couldn't help getting involved in the personal lives of the women who came to ask her advice.

'I despair,' she'd said to Sister Edith Harrison, a doughty sort who she'd been wary of when she'd first arrived at the hospital but was now a rock she could lean on. 'I understood a marriage was made in heaven. Some of these women are living in hell.'

'It's their choice, Doctor. You're here to give them medical advice. That's all. They won't thank you for meddling in their lives.'

'But they could be so much more. Do so much more.'

'They're women. They've got the husband they were told they needed. He's the one who brings in the wage. All they have to do is keep house and give him children.'

'No longer in charge of their own lives, not even their bodies. Sounds more like a prison to me.'

The conversation with Sister Harrison had taken place following a husband's refusal to give permission for his wife to be fitted with an IUD, a device manufactured from rubber that would prevent his wife from getting pregnant. The poor woman already had five children. She had the look of a woman of forty-five, but she was not yet twenty-eight.

All of these things had made Frances feel as though she was carrying a blacksmith's anvil on each shoulder. How would it be if she married Gregory? One consolation was that at least she was knowledgeable about contraception. Another was that Gregory knew better than to dictate what she should or shouldn't do with her own body. There would be discussions between them, at least that's what she liked to think.

* * *

Frances waved as she passed the vicarage. A day of chilly sunshine had grown into a pleasant evening.

She felt a sense of homecoming when she entered the coach house. It was nowhere near as grand as the vicarage, but she loved its cosy character, its flagstone floors, the constant heat from the kitchen range warming the thick walls and floors.

Home, she thought. The coach house was home. Norton Dene was home.

The smell of home-made cooking greeted her as she swung open the door.

Ma Skittings was in the kitchen using a pair of bellows to get the coals glowing hot.

'You're not to worry about your mother.'

'I'm not?' It was a surprising statement, given even before a good evening or how was your day today.

'No,' returned the formidable, thickset woman. 'Your mother's already taken to her bed. It's all that fresh air. And I've cooked her fried liver and onions for her supper. Only chicken liver, mind you. Her disposition can't cope with anything stronger.'

'Is she very tired?'

'She'll sleep well tonight.'

'I was quite surprised to see you out and about in town – as for the wheelbarrow... loaded in there like a sack of turnips.'

A pair of kind, intelligent eyes looked at her from above a

soup ladle. 'Just because she's dying don't mean she can't have one last shot at enjoying herself.'

'It is cold outside.'

'Not as cold as the grave. What does it matter now? Let her live until the very last breath. Life is wonderful no matter what it is.'

'Even if she died tonight?'

Ma Skittings shrugged. 'Then you can say she lived up until the very last.'

'I think I might take her supper up to her.'

'No.' Ma Skittings shook her head. Her frown was deep and so was the grim line of her mouth. 'You can't. It's forbidden.'

'Forbidden?' Frances raised her eyebrows in surprise. 'By whom?'

The grim façade disappeared. Her face was like the sun coming out from behind a cloud.

'Because you've dinner at the vicarage. 'Alf seven and don't be late.'

30

Thin clouds ranged in ragged strips across a sky that was turning to indigo and sprinkled with stars. Fresh from her bath and wearing a dress that made her feel feminine, Frances skipped up the three steps leading to the broad door of the vicarage.

Light from within flooded over her, and a broad arm and strong hand dragged her in. Gregory's warm palms lingered on her shoulders as he took her coat.

Once her coat was hung up and her hat whisked from her head, he kissed her cheek. 'My. Your cheek is cold enough to freeze my lips off. Now come on in. A small glass of wine will bring the roses to your cheeks. Two will make them blossom as though it's high summer.'

She laughed and kissed his cheek. Sombre moods had no chance of persisting when one was in the company of Gregory Sampson.

Brimming with bonhomie, he guided her into the dining room, where the robust heat from rosy, red coals made the walls glow. He guided her into a green velvet tub chair.

'Bath Chaps tonight – my version of it anyway,' he said with considerable pride. 'One ham knuckle covered in honey and breadcrumbs. I thought it jolly good, though Mrs Cross frowned at my efforts. Told me in no uncertain terms that honey didn't figure in the traditional recipe. She's been with me long enough by now to know I enjoy cooking. But she's of the old school and doesn't think men should be allowed in the kitchen. How's Ma Skittings doing with looking after your place?'

'She's very good with my mother and she's readily available at this time of year. What things will be like in the summer, I really can't say...'

She stopped abruptly. What happened in the summer all depended on whether her mother was still around by then.

Before coming to the vicarage, she'd looked in on her mother. Her breathing had been slow but peaceful. There was pinkness in her cheeks, the last vestige of her trip out. She looked as though she would have a peaceful night's sleep and for that she was grateful.

'Fancy a refill?' The wine bottle hovered over her glass.

'Not for the moment.'

He leaned over and kissed her lips. 'I've had a good day. I've got good news in fact. Her ladyship has asked me to officiate at her son's wedding to one, Nurse Lucy Daniels.'

'I never doubted it.'

'Now tell me your news. I can tell you're bursting to fill me in on the details.'

Frances laughed. 'Where shall I start. Oh yes, I entered the coach house to find that both my mother and Ma Skittings were not around.'

Gregory gave one of his wide-eyed looks of surprise that made him look like an owl blinded by daylight. 'And where were those intrepid little minxes...'

Frances gave him a shrewish look.

'Sorry. You must have been worried.'

She nodded. 'I was. I raced like a hare into the town centre. That was where I found them.'

'Not indulging in a quick pint at the Red Lion, were they?'

Another shrewish look and he apologised again.

'Of course not. So where were they?'

'Well, you know that wheelbarrow that you keep at the back of the coach house.'

'I do.'

'Ma Skittings was pushing it, and my mother was riding in it.'

The straight face she had tried to maintain broke into chuckling amusement.

Gregory joined her. 'Wheeling her along like a load of compost.'

'Something like that.'

Frances forgot her earlier concern about her mother being out and about in the cold. She had to admit it was funny, and that Ma Skittings and her mother would be troopers until the end.

'I worried at first. And then I thought, well, why not? Let them have their fun.'

'Just as we do,' said Gregory, his breath tickling her ear.

She slapped his shoulder playfully before planting a kiss on his welcoming lips.

'Stop making fun. I was worried.'

He spread his hands wide, humour remaining in his wide grin and that impish look.

'Look at it this way. You've got to admire the fact that your mother still has an adventurous spirit. You have to admire Ma Skittings for her inventive use of a simple garden wheelbarrow. Nobody gives a second thought to taking a baby out in a pram to get some fresh air and put a bit of colour in their cheeks. Very clever.'

Gregory's humour never failed to be infectious. After a long day at the hospital – or half the night on occasion – he lifted her spirits.

His fingers curved around hers as he took her glass, then pulled her to her feet.

'Come on. Let's not let the meal get cold.'

As usual, the food was good. Gregory admitted that cooking was his way of relaxing.

'It helps me to forget some of the troubles and confessions that come my way. I may not be a Catholic priest, but old habits die hard – if that makes sense.'

'The Reformation happened a long time ago.'

He took a long draught of wine before eyeing her over the rim of the glass. 'People still sometimes feel a need to unburden themselves of their troubles. Sins, if you like.'

Frances thought of her conversation with Araminta, of Grace who'd suffered a horrendous marriage and was now able to sue for divorce and was fighting for custody of her children. Thinking of children brought on a concern local to home.

'You know that Lucy is in the family way, do you? You're still allowing her to marry in church even though you know that?'

Gregory sighed, leaned back in his chair and, whilst quaffing more wine, raised his eyes thoughtfully in the direction of the large oriel window. It was criss-crossed with lead bars, bright splashes of colour at its highest point. Sunshine at the right time of year made those panes sparkle. Right now, there was only darkness outside.

'My darling Frances, half the brides that walk down the aisle of St Michael's are in the family way. In fact, that number might be much more. It depends on circumstances.'

Gregory covered her hand with his. She in turn covered his

before he did the same again so that their hands were stacked in quiet unity.

For a moment, they were engrossed in their own thoughts until Gregory said, 'Let's get Devlin and Lucy married and then reconsider our own circumstances, the prospect of you ever agreeing to become my wife.'

Frances laughed as though he was merely cracking another joke, though she thought not.

'A lot of water could go under the bridge between now and then. A lot could happen.'

* * *

The unexpected happens when you least expect it. That was what Frances thought the next morning when she went into her mother's room and saw her lying there, peaceful and not breathing.

She sat on the side of the bed, looking down at her, her wispy hair splayed around her head like the petals of a flower or the rays of the sun.

Her mother had passed away and although it was a sad occasion, Frances couldn't help thinking of the day before when Ma Skittings was pushing her along in a wheelbarrow. She'd looked so happy, and Ma had been right. She'd lived her life until the very last. The thought of that scene made Frances smile but also cry at the unfairness of life.

There would be no feeling the warm summer sun on her face and breathing in the scent of roses coming from the vicarage garden.

She brushed the tears away, feeling an immense sadness that they had not been reunited earlier in her life. What fun they might have had – if the wheelbarrow episode was anything to go by.

But there. Life, God or whatever, ordained how many years were due.

News of her mother's passing spread from Ma Skittings to her daughter-in-law, Nancy, to Lucy, who informed Sister Harrison, who in turn told everyone else.

Frances flitted in and out of the hospital ensuring that she wasn't needed, that the Orchard Cottage Hospital could run without her. Sister Harrison was adamant that she could manage very well.

'I wish Doctor Reeves had already started. It would have been useful.'

It had been decided not to advertise the position seeing as someone had applied directly. The board had taken the view that his enthusiasm to apply direct to a small cottage hospital rather than a big city institution was a definite plus.

The new doctor wasn't starting for another month. She'd had second thoughts about him, how would she feel sharing some of the responsibility with someone else. In circumstances such as this, she knew that it was the right thing to do and would give her more free time to pursue whatever else she wanted. Even the idea of marriage was becoming more attractive. Everyone needed someone to love, someone to feel warm and breathing next to you in bed.

'I'm so sorry for your loss,' said Sister Harrison. 'But rest assured I'll take care of arrangements for your mother.'

It had seemed as though she was going to say something else, but whatever was happening beyond Frances's shoulder had attracted her attention.

Two police officers removed their helmets as they entered and respectfully saluted the two women.

Sympathetic to how Frances might be feeling, Sister Harrison stepped forward.

'Can I help you?' she asked in her most superior voice.

The police officer fetched a small notebook and pencil from out of his pocket and read whatever it was that was written there.

'Only if you're the district nurse.'

Sister Harrison frowned at him. 'No. That would be Sister Peebles.'

Frances was intrigued. 'May I ask you what you want her for?'

Gwen had told her of her visit to the house at the end of a lowly street in a rough part of town and the scar-faced man who she'd seen there.

The most senior of the policemen, a sergeant judging by the stripes on his sleeve, cleared his throat. 'We've found a dead woman in a house at the end of Waterloo Terrace and understand that your Sister Peebles was asking questions about Mrs Squires and her son. Where is she?'

'Is she under arrest?'

'Only if she murdered the old girl. Though I doubt she did, not unless she's got hands strong enough to crush a human throat.'

Frances gasped. Sister Harrison's jaw dropped.

'We just want her confirmation That's all. Thanks to her depiction of events and her description of Harry Squires, the dead woman's son, we need look no further. We know him of old before he moved away to London. And good riddance to him. It's over to the London police to apprehend him. Nothing more we can do.'

'You mean he murdered his mother.' Frances found this very upsetting, especially seeing as her own mother was only lately deceased.

Frances escorted them from the premises, Sister Harrison at her side.

'Do you know, Sister Harrison, once upon a time I believed coming here would be a very peaceful transition compared to London. It seems I was wrong.'

Sister Harrison heaved her mighty breasts in a matter-of-fact sigh. 'Things can only improve.'

Frances jerked her chin in a curt nod. 'I most certainly hope it does.'

'Your mother's at peace now.'

'I certainly hope so.'

'And you've a wedding to look forward to.'

'Most certainly.'

* * *

Lucy stroked the wide satin ribbon that held together the box which had arrived by special delivery. It was a large box and had a luxury sheen, plus the name Selfridges emblazoned on the lid.

'I didn't know quite what you would need, my darling, but Selfridges employ people who pick what's relevant for you. So that's what I did. Sorry it wasn't me.'

Dazzled by its luxurious appearance, a luxury she had not been born to enjoy, Lucy slowly undid the satin bow and pulled the top of the box from the lower half. Inside, she found the most exquisite baby clothes – everything she could ever want – and more besides.

One beautiful item after another: matinee jackets, nightgowns and the softest Turkish towelling nappies for the expected baby.

There was also a card.

To my beloved.

Just three words, but enough to have her burst into tears.

'It's all so beautiful.'

She threw her arms around Devlin, her shoulders heaving with sobs.

'Did they do a good job? I mean, is there anything else I should have asked them for?'

She shook her head, tears filling her eyes. 'Everything is perfect. Everything.'

And it was.

Except for one little thing that Lucy had buried deep inside. One little thing that might or might not affect her and Devlin's happiness.

31

Although she wasn't that well known in the town, the funeral of Mary Devonshire was as well attended as could be expected. She was the mother of Doctor Brakespeare and that was good enough for her patients and other townspeople.

Frances looked around at all those who had come to pay their respects. Patients who had hardly known her mother, but valued their doctor, touched her arm when offering their sympathies.

'May she rest in peace.'

'I really feel for you.'

'My heartfelt condolences.'

She accepted their comments with a pale smile and slight inclination of her head.

There were more wreaths and flowers than she'd expected, her own contribution a mass of yellow and blue amongst dark green foliage.

The coffin seemed so small. It was also hard to accept that it held the body of her mother, a woman who had only belatedly entered her life. If only they'd had a little more time to get to know each other. If only...

She brushed away a tear and swallowed the sadness she felt inside, avoided eyeing the coffin and instead perused the occupants of the pews.

We all look like crows, thought Frances as she looked around the church. Everyone was dressed in black. Her eyes returned to the colourful flowers lying on top of the coffin. The brass handles glinted.

They sang the first hymn – 'Guide Me, O Thou Great Redeemer' – the notes of Cwm Rhondda flying upwards into the rafters. Everyone seemed to like that hymn.

A bleak wind rustled the early daffodils out in the churchyard as the living gathered around the open grave.

The wind dropped as the coffin was lowered into the ground.

Her eyes met Gregory's as he intoned the final committal. 'Ashes to ashes…'

The amen from subdued voices was like the whispering of grasses in a subtle breeze.

There was another prepared grave close by. Glances that turned that way were accompanied with low murmurs. One or two made a blunt comment. On the morrow Mrs Squires was being laid to rest. Ma Skittings was the only person to attend the funeral along with a police officer and an employee of the coroner's court.

Daughter-in-law Nancy asked her why she'd bothered.

'I didn't like 'er and neither did anybody else. That's why I came. It's only right, and besides she wasn't always a bad lot – well, only most of the time.'

* * *

Early lambs were being born in the fields skirting the town.

Daffodils, their heads barely open, were poking through the verges around the war memorial.

Three new babies had been born at the hospital, their arrival bringing joy and the capacity to forget the dark events of midwinter. Each baby was weighed, measured and inspected to see that all was well, a job that Lucy relished.

'And how are our latest patients?' asked Frances once the babies were safely suckling at their mothers' bosoms.

Lucy didn't answer.

Frances looked at her. Her face was quite drawn and there was a faraway, contemplative look in her eyes. Frances sensed something was wrong.

'Lucy? Did you hear what I said?'

'Oh. Sorry.'

She looked as though she'd been awoken from a deep sleep.

'What is it, Lucy?'

Wide-eyed, Lucy turned and looked at her, pretty face far paler than it usually was.

'I'm a bit worried.'

'About the wedding?'

She thought she already knew the answer but had a care for Lucy's feelings. This was a situation that needed careful handling.

Lucy shook her head. 'No.'

Frances laid her hand gently on Lucy's arm. 'Let me finish my round and then we can have a cup of tea and a quiet chat in my office.'

It was an hour later when they were sat in the quiet privacy of the office. Frances insisted on pouring the tea from a white porcelain pot decorated with dark green ivy leaves. The cups were of the same pattern, a present at Christmas from Araminta.

Lucy took a sip of tea. 'I haven't been quite myself, have I?'

'It's to be expected. You're an expectant mother. Have you been sick in the mornings?'

'Sometimes.'

'But that's not what's worrying you.'

Lucy shook her head.

'You're worrying about the boy who was brought in with a bad bout of pneumonia that had begun as measles. It's the measles you're worrying about and how it might have affected your baby.'

Lucy nodded. 'I know we've already discussed it and that my contact with the boy was minimal, but still, I can't stop worrying. You see,' she said, 'I was worrying about cancelling the posh wedding in June. I hated the thought of letting everyone down, especially Devlin's mother. But then everything turned out right. Fate seemed to lend a hand, and I was over the moon. I was so happy, but then I had this awful feeling that something might come along and spoil things.'

She hung her head and although there were no tears, Frances knew she was crying inside.

She searched for the right words that might bring some solace. 'Lucy, you must cope with this. I can't cope for you. Neither can I guarantee that your baby wasn't affected, but my gut feeling is that you weren't in contact with the boy long enough.'

She'd been as reassuring as she could be, but sensed her words had not had as great an effect as she'd hoped and had a rethink as to why this was.

'You think you don't deserve such happiness, but you do.'

'It seems too perfect.'

'I wouldn't say that. Things will go wrong. That's how life is. But your baby?' She shook her head. 'It's your duty to keep healthy and worry-free. That's what you can do for your baby.'

* * *

On her next day off, Frances visited her mother's grave. Gregory told her that he'd had both her mother's maiden name and married name engraved on the headstone, though it would be some time before it was completed and erected by the stonemasons. The headstone had not yet been placed on the grave, where bouquets and wreaths of flowers lay.

There was another mound next to it, that of the infamous Mrs Squires. There were no flowers on her grave only a sprig of holly which might have been blown from a nearby tree.

Mrs Squires, the abortionist. There was no headstone on her grave either. Frances would have preferred the awful woman not to be buried next to her mother, but they weren't here to mind.

'You're probably wondering where that holly came from.'

Frances turned to face the familiar form of Ma Skittings.

'It's traditional. I put it on there. Something sharp and prickly like her. The devil will see the holly and take her to hell.'

Ma Skittings' face was expressionless, as blank as a flagstone slab.

Surprised at her sudden appearance and her comment, Frances asked her if that was true. 'About it being an old custom.'

Merriment replaced the blankness. 'Might not be. I ain't that old, so I wouldn't know. It just blew down from the tree.' She grinned. 'There again, the devil knows 'is own. He don't need a human hand to guide him.'

She came to stand beside Frances. Together they regarded her mother's grave.

'I wish I'd known her sooner in my life,' Frances said softly.

'Wishes are so much hot air. You can't turn the clocks back.'

Ma Skittings dragged the centre of her coat over her belly,

glanced at the last resting place of Mrs Squires and turned back to Frances.

'Any idea whether the police have tracked her son down?'

Frances shook her head. 'No. London is a big place, but at least they know his name. I suppose they can ask around.'

'Sounds to me you don't care one way or another.'

Frances thought about it. 'I didn't know him or his mother.'

'And yet you can't help thinking of your own mother and that poor soul who died at the hands of Mrs Squires.'

Frances looked at her in surprise. 'How did you know that?'

That funny lopsided grin before she replied.

'That's who you are. I know your soul, Doctor Brakespeare, and it's a good one.'

* * *

Miles away in London, Harry Squires had gone banging on the door of the handsome house where Sir Gerald Leinster-Parry lived with his wife. He'd found out from gossip that the wife had moved out and was divorcing the old roué. It also turned out that Sir Gerald hadn't been at home since the day before.

Harry knew the police would be looking for him. He also knew it wouldn't be wise to have a high profile, to linger in this affluent area where money and status were everything.

He made his way to the Cockpit Club, which the police had raided. Fat chance they had of getting that closed. It was frequented by people of note, everyone from landed gentry to judges and a good few in between.

The club was as busy as ever, Bentley and Rolls-Royce limousines dropping off their esteemed – and decidedly crooked – owners. Under orders from their masters not to hang around, some of the chauffeurs drove off to where they had proximity to a telephone. Armed with the number of this phone, their employers could arrange collection once they'd had their fill of gambling and girls.

After brushing off his suit and setting his hat straight, Harry ambled across the road to the grand frontage, his eyes raking those cars left outside, looking for Sir Gerald's Bentley.

It wasn't there.

So where next?

There was only one place, the house in Sears Place where Ellen used to live. He ground his teeth when he thought of Ellen. In his mind, he firmly believed that she'd favoured him, but Harry was something of a fantasist. In actuality it couldn't be true. He wasn't able to give her the lavish presents that Sir Gerald had given her. He wasn't able take her to the theatre or to smart restaurants to dine. In his mind, it didn't matter. In his mind, he was the one she had loved; it was just that she couldn't show it. That was what he told himself.

He had lifted enough of his mother's money to take a cab but decided not to. He walked all the way to the house in Sears Place, fists thrust deep into his pockets, anger bubbling inside him.

The broad streets and elegant houses of the more fashionable and expensive areas gave way to older buildings that had once been houses, though long converted to multiple occupation.

Ellen had lived in a tall house here. She'd had a suite of rooms. There'd been other women there too, some with children, but few men. Except for those who visited. In times past, they'd called such a place a stew and often a brothel. Harry used to collect rents from here and other places roundabout. It was one of many owned by Sir Gerald.

The moment he entered Sears Place; he knew something was wrong. Thick dust rose from behind the building where underground trains rattled past, their passing shaking loose windowpanes and making doors rattle in their frames.

There was no sign of a Bentley, Rolls-Royce or any other make of car. Men were hammering sheets of ply over the windows on the ground floor and at road level two workmen were hammering a sign into place which obliterated the front door.

Harry read only the first line of the notice…

'Acquired by London Underground.'

He waylaid the man wielding the hammer, who turned round, his black eyebrows fixed into a deep vee. His manner was less aggressive on scrutinising Harry's scarred, tough-man appearance. Here was one not to upset.

'Sorry to trouble you, mate, but what's going on yur? Where's all the people gone that lived yur?'

'Moved out.'

He made as if to turn back to his job.

'Where they gone?'

Chancing his luck that Harry couldn't be tougher than him, the man lurched into him, so close that his nose was only inches away. 'Ask the bleedin' Underground.' He flung a meaty hand in the direction of the sign. 'Now shove off, will ya? I've got a job to do.'

Harry thought about asking if the owner was about but changed his mind. No point. He'd get the same reply, and the sausage-shaped fingers would flap once again towards the sign. He so wanted to break those fingers. But not now. Nothing was as important as getting even with Sir Gerald.

There was nothing more he could do here. All he could do was hang around outside the Cockpit Club or Sir Gerald's house.

The Cockpit Club was the closest, but didn't really get lively until a thick, foggy London night had fallen. Men of Sir Gerald's standing preferred to take their fun at night. It would be a while before darkness fell so he decided to take a detour; go to the house first, hang around outside, wait until he appeared, then tackle him, beat him, kill him. That's what he wanted to do.

First to get there. He was almost amused on his decision to use the underground, the fastest route back to the hallowed houses of the titled and wealthy.

The crowds thronged around the entrance to the station. Small, large, male and female, surged like an avalanche of many-sized boulders down the stairs, parted at the bottom to purchase tickets before resuming their journey. Like a flood tide, he thought, a flood tide of humanity heading for the underground burrow.

The station smelled. Overhead lights flickered and flashes of blue spat from the cables that powered the trains.

Like sardines in a can, the mass of humanity huddled together, not meeting the eyes of the person next to them. Each was absorbed in their own world, making their own plans, aching to get on the train and off at the other end, the place where they wished to go.

He heard a woman say to the man next to her that she was fed up with this journey and, more so, this run-down station.

The man agreed with her. 'The station's falling to bits. The line's falling to bits. I sometimes wonder whether I'll get 'ome to the missus in one piece.'

Such was the mood of those trying to get where they wanted to be that the conversation around him remained muted and, for the most part, uninteresting.

Shudders, squeals and rattling preceded the arrival of an ancient underground train, a black blanket of smoke sitting on its roof as it creaked like a tired old man from out of the tunnel and into the station.

People on the platform surged forward without giving enough time to the people getting off. There were shouts and scuffles, a few punches were thrown. Women jostled as much as men.

'Excuse me. I am a lady you know.'

Whoever the woman was, her voice died as a tide of impatient travellers moved to get into a carriage before it pulled away.

Having no intention of being polite to men or women, Harry pushed his way through and got on board.

Others crowded in behind him, but in the interests of expediency, he held his place close to the folding doors. Sometimes a policeman got on board, pushing his way through those passengers who had not been lucky enough to get a seat. Every so often he stopped by someone who, to his mind at least, looked a bit suspicious. Harry had allowed for this, hence standing close to the doors, so, if need be, he could get a swift getaway.

To his relief, there was no constabulary presence this evening. The train doors closed. With another squeal of springs and a grinding of brakes, the train began to ease away from the platform and into the labyrinthine network of burrows that made up part of the London underground. The ill-lit station was left behind. They entered the blackness of the tunnel.

People lurched from side to side as they always did but suddenly more so, their bodies falling from side to side, slamming against each other, falling onto seated passengers, crashing into the closed doors and upright rails.

An almighty bang, as loud as any cannon, reverberated through the carriage. The floor vibrated beneath them, boxes and cases fell from the overhead luggage racks, cracking onto heads, laps and leaving blood on foreheads.

Screams and shouts inside were accompanied by a shower of

sparks cascading like the display of huge Roman candles sparkling against the windows.

The train hurtled on, the noise and light display increasing from sparkling display to outstanding crescendo as the train increased its rolling motion and people rolled like pebbles from side to side.

Shouts and screams intensified. Wherever the conductor was, the man who checked tickets, he wasn't around now.

Harry was slammed against the door which he'd thought would be his escape route if needed. No matter what he did, the door would not open, but then he wasn't sure whether it would be best closed or open.

With a final flash of sparks and a ripping of metal, the train rolled against the tunnel wall, windows smashing, the whole carriage lifting and then tilting onto its side. Thick black smoke billowed, followed by flames that leaped up from beneath the carriage, enveloping all those within.

The screams were fierce, though not for long as the interior of the carriage burst into flames and the train, travelling on its side now, thundered and crashed. Not all the carriages had burst into flame, just the one Harry Squires had been travelling in.

32

News of the underground crash had little impact on the town of Norton Dene. A few people had read about it or heard a news snippet on the wireless, but not many. Things that were happening in Norton Dene interested them most. Life went on in what Londoners might consider a humdrum manner.

Wednesday morning and Doctor Reeves was trailing along behind Frances as she explained the layout of the hospital, the wards, the staffroom, doctor's office and pharmacy.

He had not been due to begin at the hospital until the following month, but Frances had persuaded him to come earlier.

'Several of us have been invited to a very important wedding. I need to leave a doctor in charge of things. If you could be so obliging?'

He'd gushed his acceptance and thus had arrived earlier in the week. No permanent accommodation had been arranged as yet, so Frances had offered him her spare room.

'You also have an offer from the manor house, but my abode,

although smaller and not nearly so grand, is closer to the hospital.'

Much to her relief, he'd jumped at the chance, arriving at the coach house carrying only one piece of luggage and raising his hat in greeting. All this was related by Ma Skittings who had changed the bedding in the spare room and cleaned the place from top to bottom. She'd also provided him with a hot meal after his train journey from Paddington.

Declining an invitation from Gregory that night, she'd had Ma Skittings set the table for two.

Gregory had been disappointed and more than willing to have both her and the new doctor to dinner that evening.

Frances again declined the offer.

'I would like to have a tête-à-tête with him alone before we meet on a social level – I can't explain why. I think we need to work together a while before we switch from a professional to a personal relationship.'

Gregory told her that he understood. Inwardly, he conceded that she was still a little tender following the death of her mother. The familiar, as in friends, would help soothe her feelings.

Her first impression of Doctor Reeves was that he looked too young to be a doctor until she reminded herself that she was approaching her mid-thirties.

It wasn't just the look of him that made her feel old, perhaps also a little inadequate. Doctor Reeves was twenty-nine, newly qualified and fired up with the confidence of a young man who had passed the exams and was now determined to use that knowledge to change the world. None of his patients would die. They would all be saved. Such was his belief in a combination of modern medicine and himself.

If azure meant something more intense than blue, then it ably described the colour of his eyes. His hair was black, and his complexion consisted of patches of ruddy cheeks leaching into lightly tanned skin.

She took him to the isolation room, which was presently occupied by a miner whose lungs were gone beyond repair.

Doctor Reeves merely nodded and said that he understood when she went into detail about how coal dust settled in men's lungs, turning into a black treacle not dissimilar to molasses.

In passing, she introduced him first to Sister Harrison, Sister Peebles and Iris Manning, who thrust herself forward to shake his hand.

A curtain swished as Lucy pulled it back, bedpan in hand.

'And this is Nurse Daniels.'

It was as though Lucy was the star turn on a stage, coming as she did from behind the set of curtains that surrounded a bed.

'My word,' he said softly and offered his hand to be shaken. 'I'm Doctor Reeves. Perhaps when we know each other better, you might call me Claude.'

Lucy's bright eyes looked from him to Frances. Behind her was Sister Harrison, a look of condemnation on her face. 'You may call me Nurse Daniels until the weekend. After that, you may call me Nurse Compton-Dixon.'

More swishing sounds, not from curtains this time, but from Lucy turning swiftly and heading off to the sluice room.

A look of surprise smothered Doctor Reeves' cockier look.

Frances was amused. 'Lucy is about to be married. That's why I've put you in charge of the hospital on Saturday.'

'Well. She is quite a corker.' The young doctor seemed unrepentant. 'A chap can't be condemned for trying.'

Frances pursed her mouth into an amused moue. 'You will be if Lady Compton-Dixon, the bridegroom's mother and chair of the hospital management committee, gets to hear of it.'

'Bit of an upstart,' said Sister Harrison once Doctor Reeves had moved off to follow Sister Peebles on a tour of the pharmacy. 'I will certainly be keeping an eye on him. I know what doctors can be like with young nurses.'

'Indeed,' said Frances, a smile tickling the corners of her lips.

* * *

It was gone midday on the first Saturday in March and today was the day that Devlin Compton-Dixon was marrying Lucy Daniels. Those not invited began gathering outside St Michael's Church, surmising why the wedding had been brought forward. Not that the town's population were that surprised and did not condemn; close to open countryside, 'jumping the broomstick' was recalled by many. Expecting before marriage had been common.

Slates on the church roof looked as though they'd been dusted with icing sugar. There had been a frost the night before. Winter had not quite done with them yet, though a sickly sun was doing its best to pierce a few stray clouds.

Onlookers knew the time for the wedding was nigh when the vicar, the Reverend Gregory Sampson, appeared in the church porch attired in his vestments. The book of common prayer was clutched to his chest against his white robe. His golden hair was like a halo around his head.

The crowd had seen the first guests entering beneath the lychgate and walking the quarry-tiled path into the church. Among them was Doctor Frances Brakespeare, adults and children of the Skittings family, members of the hospital committee, Sister Harrison and Sister Peebles. There were also a few of the shopkeepers in the high street and some of the servants from Orchard Manor.

The undertaker and his family were long-time friends and guests. They arrived in the highly polished black hearse which was also used as an ambulance when needed. Lady Compton-Dixon's Bentley would be used to bring her, Devlin and honoured guests.

Gregory greeted everyone, reserving a kiss for Frances and whispering that she looked very nice indeed.

'Just something from the back of the wardrobe,' she whispered back, which was rubbish. She'd purposely gone to London to buy something special and had taken Lucy with her. Pulling all the stops out was, she thought, a good way to reassure Lucy and concentrate her mind on the wedding. Whatever came after that was neither here nor there. First the wedding, then giving birth to her baby. She sincerely hoped that Lucy would indeed cast care aside – at least for today.

The church was, as is the nature of churches, just a bit chilly, but Gregory had had the presence of mind to light the braziers that had been lit for Christmas. Judging by the amount of white ash tumbling onto the floor, he'd lit them early that morning.

Nods of greeting and recognition passed between the burgeoning congregation.

Heads turned as the slamming of a car door sounded from outside, heralding the arrival of Lady Araminta Compton-Dixon.

Thanks to her newly acquired walking stick, she walked steadily down the aisle on the arm of her son, Devlin. Behind them came Gaston, a fellow officer he'd fought with in France who was there as best man.

Another car door sounded from outside. A second car had arrived.

Curiosity turned the heads of the congregation. Framed by the Norman arch connecting the vestibule to the aisle, three figures appeared, one an adult, plus two children. Low mutterings and whispers ran through the congregation at the sight of

Grace Leinster-Parry accompanied by her children, who looked a bit taken aback as to why they were there.

Before turning her head fully to the altar where Gregory was waiting to officiate, Frances returned Grace's smile, one that on this occasion shone in her eyes. Compared to their first visit, she seemed to be blooming.

She was still a woman beautifully turned out. Her outfit was pale pink bordered with grey, pink roses clung to a dark grey band around a cerise-coloured hat. Still elegant. Still beautiful and she glided rather than walked. But Frances detected a new warmth that hadn't been too obvious on their first meeting – not that she'd had much to do with her.

Frances refrained from staring and evaluating further. She knew from Araminta that there'd been changes in Grace's life, mostly to do with the momentous decision to leave her husband. She'd taken the plunge and was happier for it. Being a doctor rather than a lawyer, she didn't have a clue about the current rules regarding divorce, although Araminta had mentioned that the finalities were imminent.

Still, that was divorce and this was a wedding. For most people the former rarely followed the latter.

She vanquished the disparate thoughts from her mind and mentally wished Grace all the best. Eyes forward, Frances!

Ahead of her, closer to the altar, Araminta settled herself in the family pew and bowed her head over her hands which were clasped on the back of the pew in front. Lady of the manor, thought Frances, as suited to her position as any doyenne in times gone by.

Her gaze continued to travel. There was Gregory, his hands placed either side of the lectern, a brass eagle with folded wings. Devlin stood before the altar with his best man. Even though the war they'd fought in and suffered was long over, both wore the uniforms of officers. She had to admit that they looked very handsome. Whoever had cleaned Devlin's uniform had done a very good job. He most certainly looked the dashing groom.

Frances heard the coos of delight as Lucy came down the aisle on old Wally's arm. Her own parents dead and brother-in-law invited as a guest; she had opted for someone who under normal circumstances wouldn't have been invited. Wally looked very proud indeed to have been allocated as honorary father.

The dress from London was a dream of cream silk overlaid with lace. A circlet of pink silk rosebuds kept her veil in place. Flowers from the hothouses at Orchard Manor House formed her bouquet.

'No bridesmaids,' someone whispered.

Frances smiled at the comment. Lucy had decided that this was for her and Devlin. Just the two of them. Just as it would be for the rest of their lives.

* * *

'I now pronounce you man and wife.'

The Wedding March was belted out on the organ by a Mrs Parker, wife of the greengrocer.

Frances waited until the mass of the congregation had exited the church, men mopping at sweaty brows, women's gloved hands fanning their faces beneath the brims of extraordinary hats that never saw the light of day except for christenings, weddings and funerals.

She waited for Gregory to change out of his vestments, looking around the grand old church, glancing at the altar and wondering if she would ever get to stand there repeating the words that would bind her to Gregory forever. Grace Leinster-Parry had said those same words when she'd married her husband, but now it was all over. The fairy tale had turned to dust.

Gregory was standing next to her shoulder before she knew it.

'Are you ready, darling?'

'Yes.'

He took hold of her arm. 'Then let us proceed.'

His words could have been an analogy, not just for proceeding to the wedding reception but for them. She knew he was aching for her to make it an acceptance of a proposal, no matter how vague. But she needed time, not just to get over her mother's death but also to weigh up what she really wanted from life. That of a wife in the little Somerset town of Norton Dene or that of a doctor in a prestigious position. It was a hard choice and thus deserved serious consideration.

33

Wedding service and reception now behind them, Lucy and Devlin travelled in silence, hands tightly clasped and both feeling sublime satisfaction.

The guest list had contracted from that envisaged for June. So had the cake. None of it mattered because they had each other.

Alfred had been booked to take them away in the Compton-Dixon Bentley. All seemed well until he discovered he hadn't quite enough petrol. At first, there was shock and amazement, which was swiftly replaced by great bursts of laughter when petrol was syphoned from the hearse and into the Bentley.

'Thank goodness for that,' said a smiling Devlin. 'Arriving in a hearse would not be a good omen, I think.'

'But it has made us laugh,' Lucy countered.

Their honeymoon retreat was in a friend's house overlooking the sea in North Devon. It was single storey, built to the owner's specifications as per the bungalow he had once lived in above the heat of the Indian lowlands. There were no hot plains but the cool expanse of the sea, some miles south of the place where the muddied waters of the Bristol Channel gave way to the expanse of Atlantic Ocean.

The friend, whose name was Geraldine and was Gaston's sister, had thoughtfully left wide expanses between the furniture so that Devlin would not bump into things. Lucy had noted that the more delicate decorative objects had been placed on higher shelves or behind glass. Devlin's old friend had been thoughtful, as much for himself as for Devlin navigating his way around the house with his stick, tapping away at his surroundings and independently insisting that he did not need her shepherding his every move.

But still she had done so.

Lucy gasped at the view before switching her attention to the gold ring Devlin had gently placed on her finger. She was a wife. Could this really be true?

This wonderful feeling made it seem as though she was hovering six inches above the floor.

She'd laid their nightwear out on the bed. Devlin's fingers felt their way across the eiderdown to the navy-blue silk pyjamas.

'I'll put them on in the bathroom.'

She didn't ask him why, because even though she had seen him naked, they shared an inclination to savour every minute of this special night.

Outer clothes removed, she began taking off her underwear. Once naked, she let her nightgown slip over her head and then her body.

Lucy giggled when he returned from the bathroom as she looked him up and down. 'Are you really going to wear those ridiculous garments.'

'For the sake of decorum on our wedding night. A façade of elegance. Tell me I don't look like a lounge lizard.'

Lucy laughed. 'Lounge lizards wear lounge suits, not pyjamas when they're hanging around hotels.'

'I believe you're right. Now, let's get down to the nitty-gritty. Describe to me what you're wearing.'

'Well,' she said slowly, enjoying the game, a kind of foreplay of words. 'White satin. It's hardly a nightdress, certainly not designed to keep me warm. The straps are too fine for that. It leaves my shoulders exposed and the rest of it is like a sheath, very fine. It skims my body and shows all my curves,' she whispered, as she ran her hand down over her breasts, then the curve of her hip.

'You don't sound particularly shy.'

She laughed. 'Of course not.'

'This is our wedding night. The blushing bride and all that. Are you blushing?'

'Darling,' she said, amused by his jokiness. 'May I remind you that we jointly crossed a conjugal threshold some time back. Long before we were married.'

'You're right. And there's no going back.'

She watched him cross the room and smiled at his confidence circumnavigating the chairs, the sofa, the small side tables, bureau and bed.

Three days to themselves and then it was back to Orchard Manor and her new life living there, still practising nursing, though everyone knew it wouldn't be for much longer.

Their lovemaking continued with as much joy at home as it had on their honeymoon. Playing the 'what are you wearing' game continued, adding as it did a certain piquancy.

'Are you wearing the blue silk or the pale green?'

'Blue.'

'Good. I think the blue one is my favourite.'

She stood before him, the backs of her thighs and legs braced against the bed.

'Ah,' he said, his hands circling waist before sliding down her curved hips and then down the tops of her thighs. 'Yes. It is the blue one. I know the feel of it. The silk is just that bit more slippery to the touch than the green one.'

'You have an amazing sense of touch, my love.'

It was true. That was how he knew which colour nightdress she was wearing. Both had ribboned shoulder straps, but one had a bit more lace and was less slinky than the other. The blue was wispy and not gilded with lace fitting her slender form.

She smiled up at him, her fingertips gently stroking his face whilst his fingers traced her smile from one turned up corner to another. Regret moved her to sadness when she looked at his poor, dead eyes. But she kept her tone of voice upbeat, enjoying the game they played, one she hoped would last for a great many years to come.

'I like this nightdress best too. It fits me like a second skin.'

His hand cupped the back of her head as his naked body pressed against her. Devlin declined pyjamas to bed since that night on their honeymoon.

Her lips parted as his mouth grazed hers, slightly open, the tip of his tongue slipping from between his teeth.

'Yes. I love the silkiness of this nightdress. This *blue* nightdress.' He kissed her once more before his mouth moved, breath and fingers threading into her hair. 'But I have to say, truthfully, honestly, and beyond a shadow of doubt...' His breath was warm through her hair and onto her ear. 'I much prefer your silky soft skin.'

She threw back her head, throat exposed to his mouth and laughed.

Slowly and with the deliberation of a man who knows what he wants and enjoys a certain artistic aesthetic to life, which included sex, he slid a finger under one shoulder strap and let it fall down her arm. He did the same with the other.

Accompanied with more breathless kisses, protestations of love and a hardness in his groin that could not be ignored, he used both hands to slide the blue nightdress down her body, his face following it. Each area thus exposed was kissed and licked until she could stand no more, but grasped his head, cupping his face and bringing him back up to face her.

Falling into bed, both naked, took her to another world. She gasped when his bare leg moved between her thighs, and she opened hers willingly. This was her husband, the man she loved. A brave man, one who had been sorely injured in one of the terrible battles that had bloodied the fields of northern France. She was immensely grateful that he had survived and that he loved her. She hoped such a sharing of love would last forever.

They smoked afterwards, replete of passion and both harbouring a feeling of calm satisfaction, brimming with happiness.

'I'll have Giles drop you off at the hospital tomorrow.'

'If you don't mind.'

'Of course I don't mind. Why should I? You're dedicated to nursing. I admire that.'

He could have added that thanks to the nurses of the battlefields, he had been one of the lucky ones to survive. Being blind did not prevent him from carrying on life; being dead did. He'd often said so.

Holding her cigarette aloft, she kissed his shoulder. 'Thank you. I appreciate your tolerance. Some men refuse to let their wives continue a career.'

'I'm not one of them.'

She smiled. 'No. You're not. I consider myself very lucky.'

'Good. I will continually remind you of my generous disposition.' He said it laughingly.

'I can't think of anyone else like you. So many men want to own their wives, but not you.'

'You're a human being. Your mind and body belong to you.'

Lucy frowned thoughtfully. 'I wonder how long it might be until most men think like you. I can't think of anyone in Norton Dene who encourages his wife to carve out her own career.'

Devlin drew on his cigarette, the thin blue wisp of smoke curling above him towards the crystals of the overhead light fitting.

'The Reverend Gregory Sampson shares my attitude.'

'He's not married.'

'I thought that he and our good doctor were engaged?'

'Doctor Frances is so wrapped up in her latest project and leaves too little time for herself.'

'Is that the reason?'

Lucy put out the cigarette and rolled onto her side. 'Are you thinking there's something else? What else could there be?'

Devlin pouted at the next spiral of smoke curling upwards from between his fingers. 'Doesn't she confide in you? I thought you girls natter amongst yourselves when there's no man around. Even about personal things.'

Lucy frowned. She wanted to remind Devlin that Frances had lost her fiancé in the Great War and perhaps the wound was still raw or at least kept coming back to haunt her.

'It's her choice,' Devlin finally said. 'But I'd like to see the vicar made a happy man.'

Lucy agreed with him. Rolling onto her side, she pressed herself against him, her arm languidly reaching across his chest.

'We're lucky,' she said. 'The two of us are really very lucky. And soon we'll be three.'

He rolled over to face her and for the second time that night they were like one person, conjoined forever – or at least until their passion was spent and they fell asleep in each other's arms.

34

An evening in late March and Frances was in the coach house alone. Supper was a robust lamb stew liberally seasoned with sage, coriander and rosemary. Dessert was a slice of wedding cake, resisted on the wedding day itself and kept moist in a biscuit tin procured by Ma Skittings. The glow of the range tinted the pale walls with a rosy hue.

Hands in warm dishwater, the dishes were washed in a robotic fashion, each item placed on the draining board to dry.

It was about nine o'clock at night. Outside, the darkness of early spring held sway and would do for a while yet. The inky black sky was sequined with twinkling stars. A full moon threw a blanket of silver over the back garden and from somewhere out there, an owl screeched.

'Too whit, too whoo,' Frances said with a hint of melancholy, then smiled. At one time, she could never have contemplated leaving London, where noise abounded at any hour of the day or night. Here, in Norton Dene, the noises were smaller, sometimes indistinct; the rustling sound when the wind stirred the trees and the grass. Birds singing by day or, like the owl echoing, in a strange way, the sound of silence.

The old house creaked and groaned around her as it settled into night. It had been a long while since she'd been in the coach house alone. The period between her mother dying and Lucy's wedding had been punctuated with a measles outbreak. Both she and her team had been busy calling in on those affected. None of them had been serious enough to be hospitalised. She'd also allowed Doctor Reeves to stay for a few nights until other arrangements could be made. He was now staying at a boarding house in town whilst looking for a place he could buy.

'Nothing too large. Just enough for a worthy bachelor.'

What he meant by worthy, she didn't know.

Earlier that evening, Gregory had asked her to dinner. 'Mrs Cross has made a cheese and bacon pie. Not her best dish, but wholesome and filling.'

Frances had declined his offer. 'My mother's room needs clearing. I think I've left it for long enough.'

'Do you need any help?'

She'd shaken her head. 'No. This is something I need to do alone.'

He'd accepted her excuse without comment, although she'd detected concern in his eyes. He knew her well enough to know that she'd been putting off this moment for a while. She dreaded the thought of going through her mother's things, but the task needed to be tackled. *Tonight's the night*, she thought to herself.

Reluctance to do so was pushed aside. She set her jaw determinedly and, with an air of resignation, headed for the room beneath the eaves at the top of the stairs.

Even though the bedroom was small, the bedside light was smaller, its single bulb barely chasing the shadows to the corners.

The rosebuds on the creamy coloured wallpaper matched the pink eiderdown. A bunch of snowdrops wilted in a small glass. They were the latest of several bunches she'd placed in the room since her mother's death – as if she was still there to see and smell them. There would be no more. The season for snowdrops was over.

'I know you loved them,' she said aloud as if someone was listening. A ghost, some semblance of her mother's living presence.

It was wishful thinking, but sometimes – just sometimes – she convinced herself that the wrinkle in the bedside mat hadn't been there before. The towel lying on the floor looked as though thrown there by a petulant hand owned by a person who wanted to be noticed.

And what about the sprigged curtains hanging at the window; surely, she'd left them closed this morning?

Shaking superstition aside, Frances took down the clothes hanging neatly from six coat hooks set into the wall. They were clean and tidy, the material was of good quality and the cuffs of some were fastened with shiny buttons.

Her mother had only had one suitcase. When she'd first arrived, it might have been enough to hold all her belongings, but Araminta, Lady Compton-Dixon, had pressed a few more items on her: dresses, costumes and hats.

Frances smiled when she remembered her mother's look of astonishment and the accompanying exclamation.

'Well just look at me. I'm looking like a lady, and me who used to be a lady's maid.'

She smoothed the skirt of one dress and noted with sadness that even when in relatively good health, her mother had been slight of build.

'They certainly won't fit me,' she whispered.

Carefully, and one by one, she folded the dresses up and

placed them in her own suitcase. Someone would make use of them; she thought to herself. Someone...

Up until now, her eyes had been dry, but a moment of sorrow did wash over her. She ran her hand over her closed eyes, gritting her teeth to control the threatening sobs. They'd had only a short time together. If things had been different, as mother and child they would have had years. Fate again. Fate had lent a hand.

Everything fitted in the larger suitcase that was usually stored on top of the wardrobe in her own room. She now turned to her mother's smaller suitcase, tugging it from beneath the bed. Whilst transferring it from floor to bed, she had the impression of something sliding around inside.

It was likely to be just old papers, things stored in there and forgotten.

The contents turned out to be a single package wrapped in brown paper and secured with string. Nothing else.

Once the string was untied, Frances could see that her assumption had been correct. Old papers abounded. She took them all out and placed them on the bed. Beneath the papers was a small notebook and a wooden box of the sort that children take to school. Inside were three pencils, a rubber and a pencil sharpener.

Such simple things, she thought, and was overwhelmed by a profound sadness. Her mother had left this country with nothing. It seemed she had returned to the country of her birth just as light of belongings.

Old papers, creased with age, the pale blue writing faded by the years, were unfolded and laid to one side to be read at her leisure once she'd gone through the rest.

Inside a leather cover, she found photographs; her much younger mother smiling out from a sepia photograph. A boy of about ten years old stood stiffly at her side. Like all boys of a certain age, he didn't look keen on being thrust into his Sunday best and forced to face a camera.

Frances frowned at the photograph. There was nothing on the back likely to tell her his identity. Perhaps mention would be made of him elsewhere.

She reached for one of the crumpled letters, unfolded and patted it so it was less creased. It was dated over six months ago. She began to read.

Dear Mum,

Hope you found all you wanted in England. Just thought I'd tell you that I've had a bit of luck. Got a job at a mine. The money's good and I'm doing well. In time I might have enough put aside to come to England. Understand there's plenty of mines there to...

Her eyes smarted and her jaw dropped.

Mum! It said it all. This boy who'd grown up on the other side of the world was her brother. Half-brother. They shared the same mother. Had he known about her? She'd certainly not known about him.

Losing Izzy and her natural mother had left a gap in Frances' life. She had no other family except for Beatrice. Like Izzy, they shared the same father. Beatrice was an unapproachable woman, who despised the circumstances around Frances's birth. There was no love lost between them.

But this boy. Was there any possibility of tracing him? Her heart leaped at the thought of it.

35

Spring had tentatively showed its true colours with yellow daffodils, colour-tipped tulip buds and catkins fluttering in the breeze.

Frances welcomed the freshness of the month and the season. Happiness had arrived along with it.

Devlin and Lucy were married and looking forward to the birth of their new baby. At Devlin's insistence, Lucy had given up work. A new nurse would take on her duties in early April.

As for the patients, Mrs Thomas had been delivered of a baby girl and was proud of her achievement. She'd certainly been determined.

The last vestiges of winter were slowly trickling into spring. Plants were budding and birds were singing at dawn, a welcome to the better weather to come.

Wally had placed a jar of early daffodils on her desk. Yellow. The colour of sunlight.

Outside in the waiting room, patients awaited her attention. Most were panel patients in that they contributed a portion of their income into a weekly or monthly insurance. These patients were in the majority. Occasionally, there were private patients, though not too often.

Grace Leinster-Parry was staying at Orchard Manor again and asked if she could come in to see her.

'Nothing serious, I just wanted to pick your brains. You have such a better brain than I.'

What that meant, Frances hadn't a clue but gave her an appointment for later that morning.

After what she thought was the last panel patient, Sister Harrison came in to tell her someone was waiting who had not made an appointment.

'A gentleman wants to see you on a private matter.'

'Did he give you a name?'

'Fairfax.' Sister Harrison pulled a face. 'Foreign by the sound of him.'

Foreigners rarely appeared in Norton Dene and that included residents of the big cities. If you weren't born and bred in Norton Dene, you counted as foreign.

'A Mister Fairfax.'

Frances did not recognise the name but asked Sister Harrison to show him in, her pen hovering over a letter prior to signature, her reply to a last-ditch attempt by the London hospital to woo her into their employ. She'd taken some time to make up her mind. The reminders had kept coming. This, they intimated, would be the final one and the one in which she would turn them down.

The man who entered her office was close to six feet tall. His face was rugged and of a colour that reminded her of summer. He was wearing a tweed jacket. A luminescent stone set into a gold tiepin looked like a chip of silvery moon. A camel-coloured coat that could only have come from the most expensive store engulfed his shoulders. Gold wasn't confined to the tiepin or another he wore on his finger. His clothes, the mix of russet tweed and camel also gave a golden impression.

'Mr Fairfax. Please take a seat.'

'Doctor Brakespeare.' He offered his hand to shake, and she did so. His grip was firm, his large hand engulfed hers and a sardonic smile broke the serious expression he'd had on coming in.

Without comment he folded himself into the seat. His big frame reminded her of one or two of her patients who were miners. He looked to be too wealthy to be a miner.

'My name isn't Mr Fairfax.' There was amusement in his eyes. One side of his mouth curled upwards to extend that sardonic smile. As though he knew something that she didn't.

Hearing his accent and the proclamation that his name was not Mr Fairfax opened a door in her mind. She knew. Without him saying anything more, she just knew.

'You've come from Australia.'

He nodded. The smile lifted both sides of his mouth. 'And my name isn't Mr Fairfax. It's Fairfax Devonshire.' When he swiped his hat from his head, his appearance took her breath away. It was like seeing a reflection of herself – though a male one. Grey eyes. Ash blonde hair. 'You were expecting me? I didn't realise.'

'I wasn't expecting you. How did you find me?'

'Ma sent me a telegram before Christmas. Said it wouldn't be long before she was with the angels. Not that she mentioned angels. I don't remember her ever being prone to religious fantasies.' His grin was infectious, and she knew instinctively that his mother would have approved of his amusement.

Frances let her pen fall onto the desk. This man was her half-brother. 'She wrote to you! I didn't know.'

'That's how come I found you. I bought a car in London to get here and filled up with petrol at the garage in town. Made enquiries whilst I was there. They told me Ma died and where to find you at this time of day.'

'Have you somewhere to stay?'

'No. I anticipated driving back today.'

'You can stay. Perhaps we can talk.' It all came out in a rush. She was that excited.

'That's very kind of you. And you knew I existed?'

'I've been going through her papers. I found a photograph of you as a boy.' She gave an exasperated wave of her hands as though weighing up the pros and cons of what she'd discovered. 'I didn't know you existed before she died and I went through her things. Even then, after reading a letter from you from some time back, I expected...'

His eyebrows rose. He grinned. 'A miner?'

She nodded. 'Well. Yes.'

He smiled as he settled his hat on the desk. 'I am a miner. Of sorts. Won a piece of land in a poker game from a bloke who thought he was a miner, but didn't have the smell for it. Nor the guts to put his life on hold whilst he went grubbing for opals.' He flipped at his tie to better display the tiepin he sported. 'That's what this is.'

Spellbound, Frances stared at the gleaming tiepin that flashed light like a star.

Questions began to surface in her mind. 'Why did she never mention you to me?'

He shrugged. 'For all that, we were treated equal. She didn't mention you to me either until just before Christmas.'

'When she knew she was dying,' Frances added softly, her lashes fluttering over a moistness in her eyes that could easily become tears. Her brow creased in a frown. 'But why didn't she mention our existence to either of us? What was the point?'

His eyes locked with hers. 'Shame?'

'Oh. So, she told you the circumstances of my birth. All the same, why didn't she tell me about you?'

He locked his hands in his lap and raised his eyes to the ceiling. 'Because she was waiting for the right time?'

It came to her that this handsome, wealthy man had known her mother for longer and therefore better than she had.

'I wish I'd known her longer than I did,' she said softly.

'I suppose so.'

'Are you married? Do you have children?'

He shook his head. 'No. I've lived the rough life and ended up married to my business. The opal mine's done well, but I've been advised to invest what I've got. Just in case the opals run out.' Chin held high, he silently nodded before saying, 'I've got some business in London before I go back to Sydney. But before I go, I would like to visit her grave. Do you want to go with me?'

Frances checked the time on her watch. 'I have one more patient to see after you, so if you don't mind waiting.'

'I've come all this way. I'm willing to wait a little longer.'

* * *

Grace glided into the waiting room, feeling a little embarrassed. During her marriage, she'd known little about contraception and although she enjoyed male company, she had an abhorrent fear of remarrying – especially having to remarry.

The man sitting there looked up as she entered and lifted his hat.

She gave a little nod. He looked like a gentleman.

'This way, your ladyship.'

Grace followed Sister Harrison. Doctor Brakespeare was sitting behind her desk. From the very first, Grace had thought her approachable, the sort of person with whom you could discuss the most intimate of subjects.

This was what she did now.

'I want to know about contraception. Even if I never again have recourse to use such things, I think it's my duty as a woman to be informed. I want to be a *new* woman, one in charge of her own destiny.'

'I only have time to give you a brief summary.'

'Brief will be enough.'

Once the conversation was over, Frances escorted Grace out of her office.

'I'm sorry I couldn't give you more time. My brother and I are planning to visit our mother's grave.'

Just as it had seemed strange using the word 'mother' because she'd never thought she'd had one, so it was using the word 'brother'.

'Your brother?'

Grace's eyes fluttered between Frances and Fairfax, who got up from his chair and raised his hat again.

'Delighted,' he said. 'Sorry family matters getting in the way, but I'm off back to London on business, then down to Southampton – if I can get a ticket on a boat back to Australia. Should have booked one earlier,' he said with a laugh.

'I'm going back to London too,' said Grace. 'On the train, though, like you, I haven't booked a ticket. On the train that is. Not a boat.'

Frances was aware of a sudden happening. Here they were exchanging their travel plans as though they'd known each other for ages.

'Perhaps I can give you a lift to London. If it helps,' said Fairfax.

Grace's face lit up. 'Oh, what a darling you are.'

Her lips took on a gushing fruitfulness, as though she was close to throwing him a kiss.

'I'll pick you up tomorrow from wherever it is you're staying.'

'Orchard Manor. Doctor Frances will tell you how to get there.'

'I'll be there. First, there's a family matter I must attend to.'

Grace nodded in understanding and said she would look forward to seeing him.

* * *

Fairfax stayed that night in the spare room in the coach house where his mother – their mother – had spent her last days.

Gregory came to introduce himself, bringing food and wine. They hit it off immediately, but understanding they had some catching up to do, he left early, citing a sermon that wouldn't write itself.

When it was just the two of them, Fairfax filled in the gaps in their mother's life, the hardships, the struggling to survive, the waiting until his father, her husband, had passed before she had the money to find her missing daughter.

'I take it you helped with that,' Frances said.

'What's the use of money if you can't spend it? Money facilitates things. It ain't for piling high in a bank vault. Use it. Live with it.'

The visit to her mother's grave the next day in the company of her brother would stay imprinted on her memory. They both stared down at the headstone, each harbouring their own thoughts.

'I only wish I'd known about you sooner,' Frances said at last.

Fairfax nodded, his big shoulders hunched over, coat collar brushing his chin.

'I wish you could stay longer.'

'Right,' he said thoughtfully as though thinking that through. 'Tell you what, if I can't get a ticket on *Himalaya*, I'll put it off for a month or so.'

'That would be wonderful.' Frances was almost breathless with joy.

'Well. Let's got off this wet grass. If you could direct me to Orchard Manor and I'll pick up the lady – Grace, was it? London here we come.'

* * *

The hug Fairfax gave her was enough to break the bones of a weaker woman. Its intensity stayed with Frances and would do for some time. She sincerely hoped he couldn't get a ticket home. Another month would make all the difference.

The day had been a good one and finished just as well. Gregory waved a wine bottle from the front window of the vicarage. Frances waved back and shouted that she would be there at seven.

The wind rustled the catkins and the heads of the daffodils. The freshness of spring was in the air, a sign of new beginnings. Back in her office, she'd finally signed the letter to the London hospital saying once and for all that she would not be accepting the position they'd offered. Her mother was buried here. Ralph's name was on the war memorial. Gregory was here and who better to exchange her feelings and excitement about having found a long-lost relative.

Gregory looked at her pensively when she shared her news that evening. 'London no longer attracts you? No matter how high you might climb the ladder?'

She smiled as she shook her head. 'My place is here. Everyone I love is here.'

There was a warm glow on his face and his eyes sparkled.

'I take it that includes me.' He looked hopeful.

She nodded. 'One of those I love – most sincerely.'

This was the honest truth. It was as though all that had been precious in her life was gravitating here. So, this is where she would stay. This is where she belonged.

* * *

MORE FROM LIZZIE LANE

Another book from Lizzie Lane, *Escape From Kowloon,* is available to order now here:

https://mybook.to/EscapeKowloonBackAd

ABOUT THE AUTHOR

Lizzie Lane is the author of over 50 books, including the bestselling Tobacco Girls series. She was born and bred in Bristol where many of her family worked in the cigarette and cigar factories.

Sign up to Lizzie Lane's mailing list here for news, competitions and updates on future books.

Follow Lizzie on social media here:

- facebook.com/jean.goodhind
- x.com/baywriterallatı
- instagram.com/baywriterallatsea
- bookbub.com/authors/lizzie-lane
- goodreads.com/lizzielane

ALSO BY LIZZIE LANE

The Tobacco Girls

The Tobacco Girls

Dark Days for the Tobacco Girls

Fire and Fury for the Tobacco Girls

Heaven and Hell for the Tobacco Girls

Marriage and Mayhem for the Tobacco Girls

A Fond Farewell for the Tobacco Girls

Coronation Close

New Neighbours for Coronation Close

Shameful Secrets on Coronation Close

Dark Shadows Over Coronation Close

Tough Times on Coronation Close

The Strong Trilogy

The Sugar Merchant's Wife

Secrets of the Past

Daughter of Destiny

The Sweet Sisters Trilogy

Wartime Sweethearts

War Baby

Home Sweet Home

Wives and Lovers

Wartime Brides

Coronation Wives

Mary Anne Randall

A Wartime Wife

A Wartime Family

Orchard Cottage Hospital

A New Doctor at Orchard Cottage Hospital

Family Affairs at Orchard Cottage Hospital

Bleak Times at Orchard Cottage Hospital

The Kowloon Series

Doctor of Kowloon

Escape from Kowloon

Standalone Novels

War Orphans

A Wartime Friend

Secrets and Sins

A Christmas Wish

Women in War

Her Father's Daughter

Trouble for the Boat Girl

Sixpence Stories

Introducing Sixpence Stories!

Discover page-turning historical novels from your favourite authors, meet new friends and be transported back in time.

Join our book club
Facebook group

https://bit.ly/SixpenceGroup

Sign up to our
newsletter

https://bit.ly/SixpenceNews

Boldwood

Boldwood Books is an award-winning fiction publishing company seeking out the best stories from around the world.

Find out more at www.boldwoodbooks.com

Join our reader community for brilliant books, competitions and offers!

Follow us
@BoldwoodBooks
@TheBoldBookClub

Sign up to our weekly deals newsletter

https://bit.ly/BoldwoodBNewsletter

Printed in Dunstable, United Kingdom